I0692979

His Team

BLUE SAFFIRE

Perceptive Illusions Publishing, Inc.
Bayshore, New York

Blue Saffire/Perceptive Illusions Publishing, Inc.
PO Box 5253
Bayshore, New York/11706
www.BlueSaffire.com

Publisher's Note: This is a work of fiction. Names, characters, places, and incidents are a product of the author's imagination. Locales and public names are sometimes used for atmospheric purposes. Any resemblance to actual people, living or dead, or to businesses, companies, events, institutions, or locales is completely coincidental.

Ordering Information:
Quantity sales. Special discounts are available on quantity purchases by corporations, associations, and others. For details, contact the "Special Sales Department" at the address above.

Ballers 3: His Game/ Blue Saffire. -- 1st ed.
ISBN 978-1-941924-32-7

With love comes sacrifice. It is up to us to know when we're making the right ones.

—BLUE SAFFIRE

CHAPTER ONE

Drowning

Cameron

I'm wide awake. Too much on my mind to fall asleep. Sitting up against my headboard, I reach for my phone and open my text messages.

I stare at the name of the person I want to text but hesitate. This could cause a bigger problem for my marriage. I close my eyes and blow out a breath.

It's not like I can sit and do nothing. After all I've done to get here, I'm not going to allow some bullshit to come along and tear it all apart. I spent too much time second-guessing myself and what I wanted out of life.

Not knowing if friendship was enough to hold love together. Then learning, while it can be, it's also not. Yet again, my character is being challenged.

5

It was so easy to point my twin brother's shit out to him, but here I sit, looking at a big fucking problem and not knowing if this should be my next move.

I shake my head and go to close the app. However, my baby girl whimpers and shifts in the bed beside me. I look down at my little girl and smile.

She looks so much like a mix of her mother and me. Placing my phone down, I then lie back down and reach to brush my finger over my little girl's silky curly locks. Inhaling her sweet baby scent, I allow myself to relax.

Placing a hand over her chest, I listen to the silence of the room while her little heartbeat hums through my palm. I didn't know I wanted a daughter so much until she was placed in my arms for the first time. Rage fills me as I think of how the opportunity to have her was almost taken from me.

"Fuck this," I mutter and sit back up.

I grab the phone and open the app again. This time I tap on the contact I'm looking for. I start the message, but my wife begins to toss and turn beside me and our daughter.

I freeze once again. As a man, I want to believe I'm about to do the right thing. Someone's heart will be broken one way or the other.

However, I'm not responsible for everyone's happiness. It took too long to understand that. I never want to cause that type of pain again, but that means dealing with this bullshit once and for all.

I sigh and toss the phone down. Still undecided on what I want to do. I climb from the bed and lift my daughter to place her in the crib. I'm going for a run to clear my head.

Once my baby girl is in her crib, I tug on a pair of basketball shorts and my sneakers. Next, I grab my arm strap for my phone. I stick my earbuds in my ears and head out of the house.

When I get to the sidewalk, I pull out my phone to find a song that speaks to my mood. I grunt when I come across the perfect song. "Crazy" by 50 Cent fits every feeling I have at the moment.

The song starts as I place my phone back in the strap. I get lost in the beat and take off down the block. We live in a nice community, not far from Caleb and Nicole.

It had been harder than I thought to be separated from my brother. So many times in my life, I've questioned my decisions. The one thing I can say I'm sure of is the support I've always given to Caleb.

I'm happy for him and his family. If only I could say my road has been as easy. Not that anything about Caleb's life has been easy.

He just hasn't made the dumb decisions I have. I've taken a few *Ls*. Our mama can be blamed for a lot, but it's not all her fault. I was a grown-ass man when I started fucking up my own life.

My father's voice floats through my head as I remember the words he spoke the night Caleb got engaged. *You boys make me a proud father. You're both fine young men.*

I can't help wondering if he still believes those words. That makes me doubt this choice even more. Now, if I make the wrong decision, I'll be fucking it all up all over again.

This all could go bad. If things go south, I'll lose it all and there will be no coming back this time. It seems like there is no right thing to do here.

"*Fuck*," I roar.

I stop running and place my hands on my hips. I have kids and a wife to think about. The hothead in me knows what I want to do, but as my children's faces flash in my head, I don't know.

Daddy's words continue to fill my head. *God, I love you. You deserve this happiness; don't let anyone take that from you.*

I'm trying to follow those words and use them as my compass. However, I don't know how to apply them now. This decision will make me someone else.

If I say no, this could come back and bite me in the long run. However, if this works out and no one ever finds out about it, I could be closing this door once and for all.

My wife can be free. I can be the man I want to be for my family, and I can finally live the happy life I've always wanted.

"Just do it, Cam," I growl at myself as I pace back and forth.

I pull my phone from my arm as I continue to grumble to myself. I've done some fucked-up shit in my life, but this will cross the line. I can't believe this is even a debate in my mind right now.

"Fuck it," I murmur as I write the text.

Me: *Let's play ball.*

My thumb hovers over the send button. The last thirteen years play through my mind. Longer than that if I'm honest.

I shouldn't even be here. Anger with myself and what I've allowed to happen fills me. All doubts vanish as my true feelings surface.

"I would have dealt with this a long time ago if I could've been sure I'd get away with it," I breathe.

That's the God's honest truth. The old me, the wild Cam who didn't have children and a wife to think about would have reacted and not given two fucks at all.

"Why give a fuck now?"

I read the text again quickly before I hit send. I have to do this. I have to end this once and for all.

"I'm doing this for us. For you, baby."

How did you really get here, Cam?

CHAPTER TWO

Freshman Year

Cameron

Thirteen years ago …

"We're late," Caleb says in annoyance.

"Relax, we're fine. I told you no one comes to these orientations anyway," I reply.

"You've never been to one before. You can't say that for sure. We shouldn't have been late."

I have tons of shit I could be doing, but my brother insisted he wanted to come to freshman orientation. He's the only reason I'm here. I'm doing this for him, but I drew the line at the courses he's signing up for.

Caleb's ass has signed up for a bunch of nerdy shit I'm not touching. Dakota can handle that shit. I'm here for baseball. I refuse to sit through lectures on physics and don't get me started on the advanced math courses I had to sign up for to shadow him.

It's not that I can't handle the work. I'm just not spending my time here with books tied to my face. Nope, this is going to be four years of coasting. That is if we hang around here for four years. The major leagues are calling our names.

"Look, no one's speaking yet. They haven't started," I say.

"We're late," Caleb repeats.

"I know, but we didn't miss anything."

"It's our first day. We shouldn't have been late. I hate being late," he says, pursing his lips and squinting.

Yeah, I fucked up. We shouldn't have been late. I know that.

This is a new environment for Caleb, and he needs to adjust. Making us late isn't the best way to start off our college life, especially since we're hiding the fact that my brother has autism.

He could totally melt down on me. In my defense, it was Kay's fault. God, that girl can get on my last nerve at the worst times ever. I knew this was going to be a problem.

She couldn't get into college with the rest of us and she's been sulking since we all got our acceptance letters and registered for classes.

This isn't about me, so I couldn't choose a different school she'd gotten into. Caleb is supersmart. When we started to receive offers to play ball, this school was at the top of his list.

The academic program here is top tier. That was as important for Caleb as playing was. Dakota might be shit at math, but with Caleb's help, she made the grades needed to get in.

Kay spent too much time focused on cheerleading and friends. She didn't even focus on competitive cheerleading where she would have had a chance at a scholarship. Her focus was on being popular.

Now she wants to blame me for everything. I didn't fail her classes or choose to leave her behind. None of this is about her or me.

Caleb comes first. He has to be okay before I can figure any of my shit out. I can always find my way. My brother, on the other hand, needs someone in his corner to make sure he does.

That's always been me. It will always be me until he doesn't need me anymore. I don't know if that will ever be the case, but if it never is, I'm good with that.

The world wants to place Caleb in a box I've never thought he belongs in. That's their problem, not ours. I've always accepted Caleb for who he is.

The more I do, the more he grows and does his best. When he gets comfortable in his own skin, he'll shock the hell out of you. I love that about him.

"Come on, let's sit back here," I murmur to Caleb and nod my head at a few rows of empty seats.

"No. If you sit in the back, you don't intend to listen or learn. We need to be closer to the front," he replies like only he can.

I roll my eyes but don't argue. I can tell this will be a trigger. Good thing I see Dakota closer to the front waving to get our attention as she has two empty seats next to her.

"Kota saved us seats up there," I whisper and nod.

Caleb follows my gaze then purses his lips and squints. Then he starts to blink rapidly. I reach for his bicep to give it a gentle squeeze.

We've been working on this one. He flinches just a bit but stops blinking and nods to let me know he's back in control. I release my hold immediately.

"You've got this," I whisper.

And even if he doesn't, I'm here. We'll do this together. My little brother wants to go to college and then make it to the league.

I'm not going to allow Mama, Kayleen, or anyone else to get in the way of that. The next four years are ours to command. Let the pieces fall where they may.

Kayleen

I sit nervously at the kitchen island in the Perry household. I didn't know what else to do, so I called Mrs. Perry to have a talk. I need someone to tell me I'm not crazy.

I feel like Cameron and I are growing apart, and if I don't do something, I might lose him. The problem is, I don't know what to do. The more I try to address things with Cam, the worse it gets.

"You want some breakfast, sugar?" Mrs. Jemma asks as she floats into the kitchen.

Mr. Perry has been sitting with his paper and breakfast while I've been sitting here waiting. Sometimes I question whether or not he likes me. He and my daddy are good friends, but I can't say I always feel like he's a fan of mine or my relationship with Cam.

It wasn't always this way. He used to treat me like family. Things changed about a year and a half ago.

"No, thank you. I don't think I can stomach anything this morning," I say and wipe at the sweat on my brow.

I'm nervous as heck. Mrs. Jemma could call me crazy and kick me right on out of here. I hope she doesn't. I don't know what I would do next.

"Nonsense. Have some toast and juice," she says and gestures for the chef to bring me both.

My family has money, but the Perrys are next-level wealthy. The Perrys have a full staff and live like royalty. At least Mrs. Jemma does, and everyone else lives in her bubble.

The staff members have been around more than Mr. and Mrs. Perry themselves. I smile at Martha as she places a glass of apple juice and a plate of toast and strawberries in front of me. She knows what I like from all the time I spend here with Cam.

"Thank you," I say.

"Now, talk to me, honey. What's going on?" Mrs. Jemma says as she takes the seat beside me.

I peek over at Mr. Perry. I didn't know he would be a part of this conversation. I almost change my mind and ask to return some other time.

Taking a deep breath, I let it all spill out. "I don't know what happened. I tried to get into college with everyone else. I didn't think they would leave me behind. I just feel like things are falling apart.

"Mama says I can go to a community college and then apply again next year, but that's a whole year that Cam will find new friends and create an all-new life without me," I explain.

"I'm so sorry things didn't work out. We tried to pull strings to get you in. Right, Kyle, honey?"

I chew on my lip and my palms become sweaty. Mr. Perry looks up from his paper. His eyes lock with mine before he looks back down.

"Your father and I did all we could. I think I exhausted my favors trying to accommodate my son's needs. I wasn't able to push the subject when it came to your acceptance," he says.

I know right away some of that is a lie. My father doesn't want me running behind Cameron like some lost puppy, so I know he didn't do all he could to help me.

I can understand that Mr. Perry has done a lot for Caleb. Which leaves me with nothing to say. I can't argue that Caleb's needs are more important than mine.

"All senior year we worked on me being a part of Caleb's support team. I just thought ..."

"I think Caleb has enough support. Too many people trying to be helpful could expose him in the end. I spoke with your father.

"He brought to my attention that you're not really sure you even want to go to college. Why not focus on your future and where you're going to end up? If things are meant to be between you and Cam, you two will be together," Mr. Perry says before he downs his glass of juice and stands to walk out.

I sit with my mouth hanging open. I don't know what changed. Everyone used to talk about me and Cam getting married someday. Then my daddy and Mr. Perry started to act as if that were the worst thing that could happen.

"Don't mind him," Mrs. Jemma whispers and reaches to pat my hand. "He's a little grumpy because he's worried about the boys and their first day. It's going to take some time for everyone to get used to all the change."

"Yeah, I guess so. I sure have a lot to get used to," I murmur.

"Now you listen to me. You and my son were meant to be together. You may not be going to school with Cam and Cal, but they won't be in class twenty-four seven.

"What you need to do, honey, is make yourself a permanent fixture on that campus. When Cam isn't in class, you need to be there. You go to any and all the games you can.

"Don't forget you're a woman and you have assets. You use everything you have to make sure you get what you want at the end of the next four years. If he has a little fun in between—" She shrugs and looks at me pointedly.

Then she holds her hands up. "All of this is what you have to look forward to if you can hold on. Your mama and I are in your corner. We'll do all we can to make sure things work out like we always dreamed.

"In fact, we don't leave for Spain until next week. How about I throw a little get-together this weekend and you can make sure to remind Cam of what he has right here at home. It's not like he left the state, darlin'. We have this under control."

I swipe the tears from under my eyes and give a wobbly smile. She does make some valid points. They could have picked that school in Michigan.

"Yeah, that will be perfect," I say and nod.

"Great, that's a plan."

Maribel

I look around at all these people surrounding me as I sit slouched down in my seat. None of them are like me. I already know I'm out of place.

I picked this school intentionally. Someplace to get far away from my real world. I fucked up. I jumped out of the pan into the fire and now I need time to work out a plan.

For fourteen years, I didn't see my father. I knew nothing about him. Just his name and that he and my mother broke up when I was one year old.

Mom never told me more than that about him. Not even when I tried to ask, and I did ask a lot. I wanted to know my dad.

However, she wouldn't say a word about him. It was like he didn't exist. I dealt with it until I was about to turn fifteen. Mom and I had talked about my *quince* for so long.

It was supposed to be the biggest party ever. I had notebooks filled with plans and ideas. I spent months searching for the perfect dress.

Then suddenly, my mother started to change everything. I was so mad at her for taking my dream away. Then I found a box in her room with letters from my dad. One for every single birthday from the time I turned two.

Birthday cards, letters to check up on me and see if mom would allow me to see him—all addressed to my grandmother's place in the Bronx. My anger with my mom only grew and I decided to set out to find my dad, hoping he would step in and be a dad.

He stepped in all right. My quinceañera was one for the books. My father never had another child, so he spoiled me with everything I wanted.

Not only did he spoil me with a huge birthday party and more attention than a girl could ask for, he demanded custody from my mom and took me to live with him.

I spent two years with my dad, getting to know him and the other side of my family. My father and mother are both mixed Black and Latino. However, I was raised more in the Afro-Latino community with my mom. My dad's family opened my eyes up more to my black heritage as well as submerging me into a life of luxury.

If I could explain my life with my father and his family, it would be black excellence meets soul food. At least, that's what I got on the surface. I was too enamored to see the truth of what was going on.

Things were going fine until I turned seventeen. At seventeen, I was introduced to the Demarco family. Everything changed as they entered the picture.

Especially the second oldest son, Dez Demarco. I thought nothing of it in the beginning. Then my father told me I would be marrying him.

Don't get me wrong, Dez is handsome and all that, but I would like to find my own husband. Thank you very much. I also don't plan to marry for my father's business interests.

Then there is this look in Dez's eyes that always unsettles me. Something might be off with that man. In fact, I'm sure there is something dark about him.

So here I am in Texas, doing my best to avoid my fiancé and impending marriage. I have four years to figure out how to get out of this situation because I'm not marrying Dez. I don't care who he is or what my father wants.

Trust fund or not, this isn't going to happen. I'm not sure what planet they woke up on with that dumbass idea, but I'm not having it. I mean, who threatens to cut their daughter off if she doesn't marry some random—to her—guy?

My mom hasn't said I told you so, but I feel like she should. The look in her eyes when I told her I would be coming here to attend college said it all. She knows I'm running from something.

I didn't tell her about what my father wants or about the Demarcos but I didn't have to. She knew something had gone wrong with my dad when I moved back a month before leaving for college.

"Is this seat taken?" A girl with red hair and freckles sprinkled across her light-brown face says with a bright smile on her face.

"Nope, not at all," I reply.

Without standing up, I know I would tower over this girl. She's petite with a lithe but shapely figure. I'd take her for a dancer if not for the camera bag slung over her shoulder instead of a pair of ballet shoes.

I quickly note she seems like another transplant from her long red locks and sweeping bangs, not to mention her outfit and the East Coast skater vibe.

I return her bright smile as she sits down next to me because it's infectious and because she's giving off cool energy. I can't spend four years staying to myself. I guess she's as good as anyone else to start making friends with.

"I'm Taylor. It's nice to meet you," she says and holds out her hand.

"Maribel. Nice to meet you too."

I take her hand and shake it. The way her eyes light up makes me think I've just made my first new friend. We settle in our seats and look ahead, waiting for the orientation to start.

Taylor looks around us, then pulls out the packet they gave us. I haven't even looked at the thing yet. I'm only here because I didn't want to go back to my room.

I don't think things are going to work out between me and my roommate. Something I'm going to need to figure out. I'm not about to live with that for a year.

"Is it me, or do you feel like such a nerd being here? I knew I should have skipped this," Taylor leans over to whisper.

"Are you calling me a nerd?" I say with a straight face.

I hold her gaze and place a little scowl on my face as I narrow my eyes. Taylor's face turns near purple, causing me to burst into laughter. That one was priceless.

"Oh my God, I totally thought you were serious," Taylor breathes in relief.

My sarcasm has to be one of my greatest features. It's the delivery. I nail it every time.

"You haven't told a lie. I wouldn't be here if my roommate wasn't irritating," I say.

Taylor rolls her eyes. "You too? My roommate is just weird. She embodies everything I feared about a college roommate."

"I hear you."

I don't tell her I might already have a plan for that. As an out-of-state student, it's a requirement to stay in the dorms as a freshman. I already know that's about a money grab.

Lucky for me, I have a cousin who has an apartment here. She's a flight attendant and never uses the place. I'll be using her apartment as much as possible.

That stink-face chick can have that shoebox dorm room to herself. I don't know Taylor yet, so I don't want to tell her this. I don't want to get busted.

We sit, getting to know each other as we giggle about the nervous look on the faces of some of the others who enter the auditorium. Taylor was right. Not many of the people here look like the cool kids.

This is why a blonde a few rows ahead of us draws my attention when she starts to wave her arms in the air. She looks like a supermodel. When I turn to see who she's waving at, my mouth falls open. Two blond guys who are equally as gorgeous as the girl are heading down the stairs.

They are huge. Both look close to around six-six or six-seven. The one who grabs my attention most is slightly shorter than the other, with shorter blond hair. I feel like I'm watching a movie as they move in what now feels like slow motion.

The same one who I've been staring at locks eyes with me and gives a cocky grin when he notices I'm staring with my mouth gaping. The other guy with him looks exactly like him with a bearded face. They have to be identical twins.

I bite my lip to hold back a smile. Then realize I have my hair in a fucking messy bun and I'm in sweats. Not the first impression I want to make. I turn forward and slump down in my seat, wanting it to swallow me.

"Wow, the guys here are hot," Taylor whispers beside me.

"Yeah, they're cool." I shrug.

Guys are the last thing I need to think about. I need to keep my focus on getting a degree I can use to avoid being married off. I'm not about to allow my dad to use money, or lack thereof, to lord over me.

"This is going to be an awesome four years," Taylor says excitedly.

"We'll see about that."

CHAPTER THREE

Pressure

Cameron

Caleb and I should be settling into our apartment or hanging with our team and building chemistry, not heading back home for one of Mama's parties. I'm so annoyed with this shit. We haven't been gone an entire week and here she goes with the bull.

If we don't go, she's going to lean on us with the guilt trips. I'll get it the worse, but Caleb will take it the hardest. He doesn't have time to shake Mama and her mess off.

He needs this time to adjust to school and the new environment. We still have so much to figure out on top of entering hell week. Hell week will kick off fall training for the baseball team. The last thing we need is for our mama to become a distraction.

Although the woman is a master at it. I'll be happy when she and Daddy are back on the road, traveling to God knows where while staying out of our hair. Cal and I will have Aunt Judy and Uncle Rusty here for moral support as always.

"I wanted to read the text for class and study my pitching film," Caleb says as we ride in my car, heading home from our apartment.

Daddy purchased us a place right off campus to allow Caleb to have a safe place away from the student body when he needs it. I agreed with the decision. Living on campus might be too much for our goals.

Yet we want him to feel like he's a part of the college experience as much as possible. Certain things come with a thin line—now at least. We're hoping that by the end of college, Caleb will be able to adapt to everything more smoothly.

I know my brother. He just needs a chance. Placing him in the action will give him time to acclimate. He needs to be able to observe, process, and adjust. Every now and then, he'll need to back away, and our apartment will give him that.

"I hear you, man. We'll leave as soon as we can. I have some shit I wanted to do at the apartment too."

"What is this party even for? I don't want to talk to people. I'm not in the mood today."

I snort. It's not like Mama is going to give him a chance to speak, even if he were in the mood. It's one of the things that infuriates me about our mama.

"Don't worry about it. I don't know what the heck this party is for, but you head on up to your room. I'll deal with the party and Mama," I say to my brother.

"Thanks, Cam."

"You know I've always got you. I'll bring you something to eat too."

Caleb sits, flexing and unflexing his hands. He might know he has an escape when we get to the house, but it's still worrying him. Unnecessary stress.

My mama is the queen of creating it. For as long as I can remember, she's made everything about what she wants. The rest of us just have to grin and bear it.

"Will Kay be there?" Caleb asks.

I think he needs a distraction. I glance over and find him squinting and pursing his lips. Fuck, I could strangle Mama for this.

"Yeah, she'll be there. Dakota will too, and Thomas. If you want, we'll come up and hang in your room," I offer.

"No, Mama will get mad I took y'all away from the party. I'll find something to do."

"You excited for the season? I think it's going to be a good one," I ask to change the subject and distract him.

"Yeah, I'm excited, but I don't think Coach Robinson likes us very much," he replies.

"Fuck him. If he gives you shit, tell me or Coach Snider. You hear me?"

"Yeah."

"I mean it, Cal. I'm not going to let him fuck with you as long as I'm around, but if something happens where I can't be there, you let me know right away.

"That dude is an asshole. I picked up on that our first week of meetings."

"I think he's mad because I made him look stupid."

"I'm sure that's what it is."

Caleb is nothing but honest and straightforward. Coach Robinson tried to embarrass him and got embarrassed instead. My brother is far from stupid and if you're wrong, he's going to correct you.

We pull up to the house and Cal releases a groan as all the cars come into view. Mama said it would only be a few people. This is far from a few people. I bite out a curse under my breath.

"You can go in through the side door and head straight upstairs," I say.

"I did good this week, didn't I?"

"Yeah, you did fucking awesome, bro."

"We have four more years. That's a lot of time and people. I'll walk in with you. Baby steps, right?"

He turns and gives me a smile. My chest swells with pride. I'm so proud of this kid.

I nod and try not to get choked up. This is big for Caleb. I've been watching him try to find his own way more and more.

We climb out of the car and head into the house. Music and chatter greet us as soon as we walk into the door. Caleb looks around at all the people then makes a beeline for the stairs to head up to his old room.

I smile and shake my head. I'm not about to force him out of his comfort zone. Just walking in here knowing he could be bombarded by all these guests was a lot.

"Cameron," my mama sings as she floats toward me, her gaze locking on a retreating Caleb.

I step up and tug her into a hug before she starts in on him. She has this thing where she doesn't want Caleb to talk but she wants to show off her handsome twin boys at the same time. Not tonight—at least not with my little brother.

"Is everything all right? Where's your brother going?"

"He had to use the bathroom. He's fine."

"Oh. Well, I just saw Kayleen. She looks lovely tonight. I'm sure you're already missing her," Mama says.

I narrow my eyes. Is this what this shit is about? I haven't seen Kay since our fight the day of freshman orientation.

I've had a lot on my plate. I haven't had time. It's not like I haven't called her or told her she can come by the apartment as long as she didn't harp on the same bullshit while there.

She can't let it go and I don't know what the fuck she wants me to do about the situation. It's not going to change. Caleb and I ain't changing schools and I don't think there is a way for Kay to join us this year, so it is what it is.

I don't want to keep talking about it. It's not like she was accepted to many of the schools throwing offers at me and Cal. If this was going to be such a problem for her, she should have worked harder in high school. She knew the plan.

"Here she is," Mama says, pulling me from my thoughts.

Kay walks over to us in this tight dress that's showing off her breasts. Her mom and mine have been best friends since they were little girls. It has always been their dream for the two of us to get together.

Neither has been shy about it. I think I've heard it all my life. However, Kay was the one to initiate making their dreams come true.

When we turned fourteen, Kay started to look like a smoke show with her green eyes and long, dark hair. It didn't hurt that her boobs got ridiculously big.

The first time she kissed me, I was taken by surprise. I had a girlfriend at the time. It was new, but Kayleen knew about her.

Within a week, Amanda broke up with me and Kay was my girlfriend. We became a thing because it was what our mamas wanted. It's not that I haven't grown to care for Kay.

She's been a friend since I was a little boy. We grew up together and the relationship used to make sense. All the arguing and fighting is just who we are—we've been at each other's throats since she used to want to play with us all the time and I thought she was an annoying girl.

Now, I can't help wondering if this is what we want or what our mamas are telling us we want. This shit with school is only highlighting everything else for me.

"Hey, babe," Kay says as she moves to me and wraps her arms around my neck.

I wrap my arms around her waist. I'm taken by surprise as she lifts on her toes and kisses me. It's not the kind of kiss for this setting. Kay is never this aggressive either.

I tighten my hold on her as she moans into my mouth. I guess she's ready to make up. If she's ready to let the bullshit go, I'm not going to protest.

"Look at you two. Perfect, I always knew you two would make the perfect match," Mama coos.

Kay pulls away and looks back at me lustfully. I lift a brow as I grin back at her. Maybe she'll come back to the apartment later.

"Listen, you two enjoy yourselves tonight. It can be like old times. Cam, I invited some of your friends from high school," Mama says before she takes off.

Her words cause my hackles to go up and I narrow my eyes at Kay. She looks away from me and begins to fidget.

Instead of saying a word, I turn and walk off. There is no way Kay can be this selfish. None of this is about us.

Kayleen

Standing out in the backyard of the Perry home by the pool, I wrap my arms around my middle. There are tons of people here. Some from high school and others who are friends of the Perrys.

All these people and I still feel so alone. This is bringing home how I've been feeling since everyone started school without me. I lock gazes with Cam and he's scowling at me from near the back door of the house.

Oh no. He's pissed at me. This isn't going how I wanted it to. Cameron has done his best not to be anywhere near me.

Not that I haven't tried to be by his side all night. He and Dakota disappeared for a bit. I get that they went to take Caleb something to eat and probably hung out with him while up there.

"That was my mistake," I mumble to myself.

Caleb doesn't do well at these things. I hadn't considered that when Mrs. Jemma suggested this party. I think I might have made things worse than they already were.

I've been giving Cam space to cool off over the last week. I had intended to smooth things over tonight. This has gone wrong so fast.

Maybe Cam is right. I've been so focused on making this work because it's what we've been told it should be. What if this is only what our mamas want?

Cam is a great guy and sex with him is all the things a girl dreams of. I know if we get married, I'm going to live a pampered life but is that all I want?

Cameron will always have this sense of duty when it comes to his brother. I'm not saying he shouldn't. We all look out for Caleb, but is that something I want to spend my life doing?

It was fine when we were younger. I've always protected him like my own brother, just as Cam, Thomas, and Kota have. However, what is that going to look like now that we're all becoming adults?

"Hey, Kayleen."

I jump as I come out of my thoughts—I hadn't heard anyone walking over by me. Turning, I find it was Jareil Reese who called my name. We know him from high school and his daddy knows mine. He was the captain of the football and basketball teams. Well, up until junior year, when his daddy pulled him out and sent him to some expensive school where he had a better chance at going to a great college for sports.

We were friends before he left. Well, he and Cam were friends, but I was always around. I cheered for many of Jareil's games.

"Hey, JR," I say.

"It feels like it's been forever. You look great, Kay. What have you been up to?"

I try not to blush and fail. Jareil is a handsome guy. He's tall with flawless deep-brown skin and dark hair and brows that seem to pop against his complexion. His hair has always been thick, curly, and silky looking.

Any woman's dream. It looks great when he cuts it low in waves and it's gorgeous when he grows it out like now. The lush curls fall around his face, framing his handsome features.

I remember all the girls in school used to crush on him. I had already been with Cam by the time we got to high school, so I never told anyone how attractive I thought Jareil was.

"I haven't been up to much. Trying to figure out what to do now after senior year," I say and smile.

"Cool, so you and Cam still a thing? You two were joined at the hip back in the day. I haven't seen you with him all night."

I give a nervous laugh. I think Cam and I are still a thing. He's mad at me, but we haven't broken up.

"We're still together. Things are just … complicated. He's going off to college with Caleb and I'm … here. It feels weird, like I'm being left behind, you know?"

"I guess I get it. I missed all of you guys when I left for school. I can't say I'm not grateful for the opportunity, but being homesick was a real thing."

"I'm sure you made a ton of friends superfast. You were always one of the cool guys. Always a girl on your arm," I say.

He shrugs. "I made friends. It was all right, but while I was here, the girl I was interested in was always taken. So I never had the right girl on my arm."

I clear my throat and look around for Cam. There is no way Jareil is talking about me. I've never even thought of dating anyone other than Cam.

"That's a really nice dress you have on. If you were mine, nothing would be complicated about us at all. I'd be right by your side."

This time, I feel the blush creep all the way up from my neck to my face. I bite my lip and look him in the eyes. His eyes are so kind and pretty.

A light brown, almost like honey, but not quite that light. They are more of a red honey brown. His lashes are extra thick and long as well.

"Um … I … uh … When did you get back home? Where are you planning to go to college?"

Jareil chuckles. "I've been home since yesterday. I had to come check in with Mama and Daddy. I head back to school in a few days. I'm in Louisiana. It seemed like the right thing to do. You know, remain as close to home as I could while still getting into a good program for basketball and football."

"You're still playing both?"

"Yup. Louisiana is one of the schools that offered me both. It was a no-brainer. Close to home and I could play two sports I love."

"That's great for you."

"Yeah, it's cool."

"You've always been so nonchalant about everything. Too cool for anything to matter," I say.

"Nah, there are things that matter and get a response from me. They just have to be important, you know?"

"Um … I'm going to head inside for something to eat."

"Cool, I'll come with you. I want to keep catching up. You're one of the friends I remember most."

I bite down on my lip. I was trying to get away, but if I'm honest, I don't want this conversation to end. I nod and start back for the house.

As we walk, I note Cam is inside with Thomas and Dakota. They look to be laughing and having a good time. Once again, I'm starting to feel like an outsider. Thomas will be attending college with them next semester, so he's not on the outside like I am.

"How's Caleb? I've yet to see him since I arrived. I miss that guy," JR says, pulling me from my thoughts.

I remember him having so much patience for Cal. Now that I think about it, Jareil was one of us. He supported Caleb whenever he could. This guy has a big heart and he's as protective as Cam is.

"He's in his room. This isn't his thing. I think he's having a bad day."

"That sucks. I wonder if he wants some company. I heard about his big scholarship. I'm so proud of him," Jareil says with a huge smile.

"We all are."

"But … I heard a but in there. What's up, Kay?"

"It's—"

My words are cut off as a loud thudding sound comes from upstairs. Cameron freezes in his conversation with Kota and Thomas. He snaps his head toward upstairs.

The sound continues, it's like a rhythmic banging. Cam takes off without a word. The rest of us are on his heels as we can only imagine what that sound is.

My heart is in my throat and my stomach has turned sour. I'm only aware that Jareil has followed as I hear him behind me telling some others not to follow us. Kota and Thomas are ahead of me, but we all glance back to see some partygoers who were following to be nosy.

Jareil blocks the way with his big body until Uncle Rusty comes and redirects everyone to the main living room, where Aunt Judy starts up a game.

I give Jareil a smile of thanks and turn to follow after the others. When I get to Caleb's room, I think I'm going to be sick. Cam is trying to get inside, but something is blocking the door. He can't open it enough to fit his big body inside.

Dakota tugs at his shoulder so she can try. Cam steps back, looking distraught, as he runs his hand through his hair. Dakota is able to wiggle into the room after a few tries.

"I saw this shit coming," Cam growls.

Everyone remains silent. The banging stops and soon Dakota is able to unblock the doorway so Thomas can swing the door open.

Cam rushes inside and we all pile in after. Caleb is lying on the floor as Kota rubs his hair while murmuring to him soothingly.

She looks up at Cameron. "I think he hit his head. We need to call EMS for this one. His legs were blocking the door."

"I just called 9-1-1," Jareil says from behind me.

"Thanks, man," Cam says as he squats on the other side of his brother. "Someone get Daddy. He'll need to head to the hospital with us."

"I'll get him," Jareil says. "I can drive the rest of you guys to the hospital too. I'll pull up out front."

We all just nod. I think everyone is in shock right now. It's not the first time we've been around for one of Caleb's seizures, but that was pretty scary. I know my heart is pounding.

"This party was unnecessary and in poor timing. We already have enough on our shoulders. To add this party was fucking moronic and selfish.

"Mama only thinks about herself. I swear, if something happens to my brother, I'll never forgive her or anyone else involved with this dumbass party," Cam growls as he looks directly at me.

I want to throw up. I would never do anything to hurt Caleb, but I can't say I wasn't involved in this party happening. I look away from Cam and tuck my hair behind my ear.

This was selfish and stupid. Everything Cam has been saying over the last two weeks rings loudly in my ears. This isn't about me. It's not about what I want.

If I care about Cam, I have to care about Caleb. Caleb only wants what comes easy to everyone else. Who am I to get in the way of that?

I look down at Caleb lying there with sweat soaking his hair and skin. Is that blood? Oh my God.

I vow in this moment never to place Caleb in a position like this again. I need to talk to Cam. He has to know I didn't mean for this to happen.

"Shit, I told that woman this party was a dumbass idea," Mr. Perry growls as he rushes into the room.

I stand, wringing my hands in front of me as I bounce from foot to foot. I feel like complete shit. I did this, and for what?

"Can you folks give us some space?" Mr. Perry says.

I turn and leave the room. The EMS workers rush into the room as I—and the others—file out. Cam and his dad are the only ones left in the room.

CHAPTER FOUR

Can We Talk?

Maribel

It's been a week since I've been staying at my cousin's place. I stop by the dorm every day to at least be seen there. I'm so glad I had options because that dorm room stinks and my roommate's side of the room is filthy.

No way would I have been able to put up with that shit and keep my mouth shut. I'm having a hard time not telling her off as it is. I have no doubt that others are going to begin to complain about the smell coming from that room.

"I'm starving, want to get some Chinese food?" Taylor asks from the couch.

She has actually turned out to be really cool. We have a few classes together and I run into her a lot on campus. One thing led to another and we've become friends.

She's keeping my secret out of pity. She's been to the dorm room. Not to mention her roommate is a bitch to her all the time. She's been camping out here the last few days to have some peace and to keep from throat punching her roomie.

I pull a face and side-eye her. "Chinese in Texas. I'll pass."

"What's that supposed to mean?"

"No offense, finding good Chinese food out of state is a task. The rice be greasy, the chicken flavorless, or the egg rolls are trash."

"I've been to this one place. I promise you it's a good one. Come on, just try it," she says.

I laugh as the microwave dings and the scent of butter and popcorn fills the air. It's the second bag she's popped in the last thirty minutes. My mouth waters and I realize I might be hungry too.

"Okay, fine. We can go before you eat all my cousin's popcorn."

"I'll pick up some more."

"Don't worry about it. I'm going to hit the store tomorrow to stock up on some things."

"I'll give you some cash. I don't want to freeload."

I shrug and go to throw my sneakers on. The weather is fickle here. Yesterday was chilly, but today was hot as fuck. I have on a sports bra and running shorts.

I swipe on some lip gloss and I'm ready to go. It was too hot earlier to think about doing more with my hair than a messy ponytail. I blew it out earlier this week, but the ponytail has been a saving grace for getting up and going.

"Okay, I'm ready. Lead the way."

"You won't regret this. I'm telling you, this place is clutch. You know, we should try to see if they will switch us up and trade our roomies."

"I wouldn't toss that situation on anyone." I shake my head and pull a face.

"I guess you have a point, but that bitch would deserve it."

"It will work out. Besides, this area is cool. Not too far from campus and still has a cool vibe. My cousin doesn't mind at all. She doesn't get to use the place."

"Which is insane. Who pays for a three-bedroom condo they never see?"

"I think she used to have a roommate or something. Then she had all these plans for a business she was going to run on the side out of the other room. Things picked up at work and she doesn't have time, but it all worked out in our favor.

"As long as we don't get ratted out, it's perfect. I'm not moving back to that dorm. They can't make me." I pout.

Taylor laughs. "Unfortunately, my parents would have a fit. Boarding is expensive and they would freak over the lack of campus security."

I roll my eyes. "Not once they get a look at those guys. They are either out of shape or creepy. I swear that one dude be following me."

"The one with the shifty eyes?" she gasps.

"Yup, you know exactly who I'm talking about. I can't stand his ass. I keep my pepper spray on me."

"You and me both."

My phone rings as we get to the entrance of the restaurant. I look to find it's Dez. I want to ignore him, but I've avoided his last few calls.

"Hey, I need to take this," I say to Taylor.

"Want me to order for you? My treat."

"Sure, I'll have whatever you have and an egg roll."

"Got you."

She bounces into the restaurant with that infectious smile of hers on her face. I like Taylor a lot. She's made this all easier.

"Hello," I say into the phone.

"I thought you forgot about me. What's all this about you going to college out of state? I thought we were going to spend time getting to know each other more."

"I've always wanted to get my degree. I got accepted and was offered a scholarship. I don't see why that or my dreams had to go to waste."

"Pretty and smart. I might have lucked out after all. You're coming to stay with me on your next break. Our fathers agree it will be a good thing."

That's nice for them. I'm so happy they are enjoying planning my life. I roll my eyes but hold all that in.

I'm fuming by the second. They are forcing this on me, and no one has asked what I want. Not to mention the fact that I never gave Dez my number; my father did.

"Keep in touch, *my girl*. Don't do anything you shouldn't out there. I don't like sharing what's mine." He hangs up before I can reply.

However, I didn't miss the hint of a threat in his words. I'm not his and he can kick rocks. His words make me want to find the next guy who smiles my way and pounce on him.

I turn to head into the restaurant and plow right into something hard. I stumble back a little and look up to see what the heck I just ran into.

My eyes lock with intense blue-gray ones. The guy stares back at me until recognition fills his gaze. A grin comes to his lips, causing his dimples to pop as he begins to look me over from head to toe.

"Sorry about that," I murmur.

I feel so gross now that he's appraising me. Not because he is but because of what I look like. This is the second time I'm seeing this guy while looking a hot mess.

"You were at freshman orientation," he says with that sexy smile turned up a notch, deepening his cute-ass dimples.

"Yeah, I was."

He shifts his bag of food to his other hand and sticks the now free one out. I look at his hand, then look back up at his eyes. This guy is drop-dead gorgeous. I take his hand and smile.

"I'm Cameron, but you can call me Cam," he says—with a Texas accent that's so attractive with his deep voice—as he shakes my hand and runs his thumb back and forth across my skin.

"Amina," I lie.

I have enough on my plate with Dez. This one here is a red flag for sure. I don't plan on interacting with him ever again, so I think nothing of the lie that slips from my lips.

Although it's not a complete lie. I am Maribel Amina Jones. Mami calls me Mina, Amina when she's pissed off.

"Nice to meet you, Amina. I'll see you around." He winks and releases my hand to walk off.

I turn to watch him go. Damn he's fine. He's crazy tall, so I don't have to worry about wearing heels around him and he's built. Tight ass, broad shoulders, and corded arms.

His blond hair is thick and shiny. He could definitely pull off a few shampoo ads. I'd watch them on repeat.

I shake my thoughts off and turn to head inside. All thoughts of Dez float out the window. In four years, I'm going to figure out how to avoid marrying that man.

He's five years older than me. He needs to keep it pushing and find someone who wants to be married to him. I have nothing I want to offer him.

I enter the restaurant and find Taylor sitting texting on her phone in the little waiting area for takeout. I go to sit next to her, causing her to lift her head. She looks at me with excited, wide eyes.

"You won't believe who was just here," she exclaims, nearly bouncing in her seat. "I had to text Joelle. I totally thought I was going to faint or something."

I only met Joelle once, yesterday. She's cool, but she's obsessed with the jocks and all the school sports. I tuned out after a while.

I look around, trying to figure out what I missed. She's acting like Michael Jackson just walked through the place. I'll be so pissed if I missed someone good.

"Who?"

"Cameron Perry from our baseball team. He and his twin brother are set to take over this place. He looks like an angel dropped from heaven. Oh my God, he smelled good too," she gushes.

I fight to keep myself from rolling my eyes. It is not that serious. Just my luck that guy is going to be a highlight around here—that much harder to avoid.

He is fine as fuck, but she's acting like he's a walking god. I get it. A lot of the girls around here have dreams of snagging a jock freshman year in hopes of riding on through with them to the pros.

Not my thing. I'm here to get a degree that might open up my options. I'm willing to walk away from my trust as long as I have something to fall back on—heck, three years ago, I didn't even know I had one. Although I can totally get why some girls might get all goofy over Cameron.

"Girl, you and Joelle need to take a cold shower. I thought you saw some celebrity or something."

"Are you freaking kidding me? He is a celebrity. I'm getting season tickets to whatever team calls them up. Even if I have to get a second job once we graduate to do so."

I burst out laughing at her. She's dead-ass serious. I'm a Yankees fan and I'm not that dedicated.

"So you're telling me you'd get season tickets for the Rockies just to see this dude? You don't live anywhere near Colorado."

"I never said I was committed to moving back to Connecticut."

"You're crazy."

She shrugs and gets up as our number is called for our order. I'm taken aback by how many bags of food she has, but I rush to help her.

She didn't lie. Once we get back to the apartment, we kill all the food. It was definitely top tier.

I finally have a place I can go to. They could give my favorite spot back home a run for their money. Full and with the weekend to myself, I fall out on the living room floor in a food-induced coma.

Cameron

Caleb had to stay at the hospital last night after getting stitches. They kept him another night for observation. I've been up there all day and was starving once I left after visiting hours were over.

Not in the mood to cook for myself, I decided on Chinese. I had no idea I was going to run into the pretty chick from orientation. She has a pretty face, and I can tell she doesn't wear makeup. It's natural.

When she shook my hand, a spark ran up my arm. I wasn't expecting that. Things are fucked up with Kay, but we haven't officially broken up.

Kayleen was my childhood friend. I don't want to end things badly. I need to figure that shit out before I explore something else. I smile as those pretty brown eyes fill my head.

"Hey, Cam, can we talk?"

I come out of my thoughts and find Kay standing nervously in front of my building. I frown but I already know we need to deal with this sometime. I gesture with my head for her to follow me.

"How is he?" she asks as we walk together.

"He'll be home tomorrow. They just wanted to keep him for observation for one more night."

We're silent until we get up to the apartment and I unlock the door. We push inside and I take my food to the island to sit and eat. I spread the containers out.

Kay usually eats off whatever I have, so I grab two forks so she can tuck in with me. I bought enough as if Caleb were home to share with me, so there's plenty. Kay tucks her hair behind her ear then grabs the shrimp fried rice.

"Thanks."

"No problem," I reply as I tear into my own food.

"Cam, you know I didn't mean for anything to happen to Caleb. Your mama wanted to throw the party and asked me for a list of our friends. I didn't know she was going to make it such a big deal."

I stop eating and glare at her. That's bullshit and she knows it. As much as she knows me, sometimes I wonder if she knows me at all.

"I'm having a hard time believing that. You and my mama are joined at the hip when it comes to me. I explained to you how I felt. This wasn't and still isn't about us.

"He was already overwhelmed with starting college. This should have been his time to focus on that and adjust. You went behind my back, trying to get her on your side and now look."

My voice is rising as I become angrier with each word. I'm not a dummy. I've been stewing on this since last night.

"I'm sorry. I didn't mean for this to happen. I just talked to your mama and told her about how I felt—"

"How *you* felt?" I bite out, cutting her off. "Do you hear yourself? Dakota, Thomas, and I are all doing this for my brother. You say you're upset because you can't help him because you don't feel like a part of his team, but you're not acting like you give a fuck about him.

"You totally made this about you. I call you as much as I can. Before you started this, we were together all the time. The craziest part is that this isn't my fucking fault.

"I warned you to study. I told you to listen to your guidance counselor. You blew us all off, thinking my daddy and yours were just going to drop some cash and get you into any college you wanted.

"This is on you. No one else, *you*," I bellow.

Her lower lip wobbles as her eyes fill with tears. I'm not falling for that. I see my mama do it too often for it to work on me now.

"I'm here because I want to fix what I've done. I get it. I see what I was doing was wrong. I don't want to lose you, and I freaked out.

"I fucked up. I know that. I can still help out and be a part of his team. I'll just have to be there for him in another way."

"This is what I was trying to tell you from the start."

"I know. Can we fix us? Do you forgive me?"

"I don't know what I want to do. Is this really what you want? Maybe we're not good for each other."

She stands from her seat and places her hand on my arm. I turn on my stool to face her and she steps between my legs. Lifting her hand to my cheek, she searches my gaze with her green eyes.

"I have always wanted you. Yeah, we fight, but we always make up in the end. I love you, Cam.

"The next four years are going to be hard on us. I know we'll probably fight a lot, but I'll be fighting for us. If you need some time ... let's take a break for a bit.

"Focus on what Caleb needs and then we can get back to us. I'm here. I want us."

I pause to think her words over. We do make up after arguing. We always end up together.

The thing is, I'm not sure that's healthy for either of us. I'm not sure that's what I want. I want the friendship we have, but I also want some fucking peace.

Everything I do is for my brother. Kay is the one thing I do for me. This shouldn't be so hard—not when she's supposed to be the easy part of my life.

I need something to be easy.

CHAPTER FIVE

Run-Ins

Maribel

"Are you making friends?" my mother asks on the other end of the phone.

"A few," I reply as I check both ways before crossing the street.

She continues to happily chew my ear off. She sounds so excited to hear from me. I didn't realize how much I needed this call.

This morning, I needed to go for a run after all that food we ate last night. I woke up still feeling stuffed. I also had a lot on my mind I wanted to get rid of.

This neighborhood is so nice for jogging. The air was crisp this morning, doing the job I needed. Once I finished my run,

I decided to make my way to the grocery store to stock the apartment up.

My cousin doesn't care about the things I eat or use as it all goes to waste while she's gone anyway, but I don't want to become a leech. I'm going to replace everything we've eaten and get food of our own. Taylor gave me some cash before I left out.

I had asked her if she wanted to come along, but she was too busy texting with Joelle about some party next weekend and trying to find one to get into tonight. I don't take her for much of a runner, but I thought maybe she would be open to shopping with me. I would have gone shopping first if she had come along.

However, I was happy to have the time to myself. I got to clear my mind and called my mom to talk to her for a bit. She's been chewing my ear off for the last twenty minutes.

"Okay, Mami. I'm going to go. I'm at the store now," I say into the phone.

She sighs on the other end. The disappointment clear through the phone. In my mind, I can see the sadness in her eyes. We've been trying to work on our relationship.

It's something I wish I would have done before I left. I know I hurt her when I went looking for my father. In hindsight, I get that I didn't understand everything about their relationship and why she felt she needed to keep me from him.

I'm trying my hardest to see past that. My mother has always been there for me. I had been a fifteen-year-old brat and I'm regretting that now.

If I could rewind time, I would smack my younger self and give my mother the biggest apology I could. I hope I have all boys because if not, I'm in for some shit. I had such a hard head.

"I love you, Mina. Be safe. Call me any time you need me. You know I'm here for you," she says, pulling me from my thoughts.

"I know, Mami. I love you too. I'll call you soon."

I hang up and tuck my phone away. Then I grab a cart to get this shopping done so I can go home and shower. I run through my list in my head as I try to figure out the lay of the store, being it's my first visit here.

Turning into the frozen food aisle, I pause when I see none other than Cam standing there just glaring forward. I think to turn and find anyplace else to be, but there's something in his posture that makes me want to at least see if he's okay.

I stroll closer slowly. He's so deep in thought he doesn't turn to acknowledge me. I take him in from head to toe, wondering what's on his mind.

"Cam?"

He turns to me eerily slow with a hard look on his face, his blue-gray eyes clouded over. The look causes me to take a step back at first. The moment he recognizes me, a smile comes to his face and his eyes soften.

"Amina, right?"

"Yeah, hey. Everything okay?"

"Yeah, just doing a little shopping before my brother gets home."

He says the words but immediately looks as if he said too much. He clamps his mouth shut and runs a hand through his full hair.

"Your twin, right?"

"Yeah, you checking up on me?"

His smile changes to that cocky one I know him for. It says he knows he's gorgeous and could charm his way out of a paper bag. I don't miss the way his gaze takes me in.

My belly drops and starts doing all sorts of weird things. It dawns on me how gross I must look. I begin to shift from foot to foot.

For the third time, I'm standing in front of this guy looking like a hot mess. He probably thinks I'm so slob. I've got to start coming out of the house looking better. This is insane.

"Dude, I didn't know who you were until last night. My friend told me about you and your brother."

"What about my brother?" he bites out.

I shrug. "You guys play baseball. Supposedly you're both a big deal. Look, I should go. You have a good one, okay?"

"Wait, I'm sorry. That came out wrong. You have time for coffee or a quick bite?"

I war with whether coffee would be a good idea. He seems like he could use someone to talk to. I've been there, needed that.

However, my situation is complicated, and I don't think hanging out with this guy is going to help with that any. Cam is ... yeah, I'm not going there. This guy is a problem waiting to happen.

"Sorry, I need to get this shopping done and head home. I need to get cleaned up from my run."

He stares at me for a moment. It's like he's looking through me. His blue-gray eyes are so intense. I don't realize I'm holding my breath until he speaks.

"Some other time then," he says. He then goes to walk by me and leans into my ear. "You know it's meant to be. We keep running into each other. The next time, I'm not taking no for an answer."

With that, he walks off, leaving me standing with my cheeks warm and my mouth hanging open. All kinds of butterflies are swarming in my belly. My skin tingles where his breath fanned.

I noticed last night that a tingle ran up my arm when I shook his hand. I tried to ignore it. But there is no ignoring him today. I turn to look after him and find him staring at me with a smile on his lips.

He shakes his head and turns to disappear. I stand, not having a clue why I came up this aisle in the first place. This guy has fried my brain.

"What the entire fuck?" I breathe.

I need to stay away from him. Another guy isn't my solution to my Dez problem. I don't want to drag anyone into my mess.

Shaking my head clear, I get back to my shopping. Cameron Perry is the last thing I need on my mind. What I need is to keep my focus.

I snort at that thought as I have to move on to start my shopping in another aisle until I can remember what I need from this one. My phone rings, startling me from my thoughts. I pull it out to see it's my dad.

Rolling my eyes, I ignore the call and continue with my shopping. I'm not in the mood for any of the drama back home. Once the phone stops ringing, it begins to buzz.

This time, when I glance at the screen, I see it's a text from Taylor. She's inviting me out to a party tonight with Joelle and her brother Joey.

Joey is her twin, which makes me think of Cam. I wonder why he became so defensive when I mentioned his brother. I probably could have found out if I had taken him up on his offer for coffee.

I sigh at my wayward thoughts before texting Taylor that I'm in. A few hours of dancing and forgetting about everything else might be fun. Lord knows I need to unwind.

I have some reading to do for class next week, but a few hours to let my hair down isn't going to hurt. Heck, if I don't figure something out, I'm going to be a wife in four years. I might as well have some fun now.

But you're not getting married. Don't even entertain the thought.

Cameron

How does a girl I've never seen in more than workout gear or loungewear have my mind in such a chokehold? I haven't been able to get her off my mind since seeing her this morning.

"God knows I've tried," I mumble to myself under my breath.

My thoughts of her are so strong I have to speak out loud before my brain explodes. I could tell she was uncomfortable as she fidgeted, but why? She was adorable in her running gear.

That messy bun is cute on her and shows off her face and neck. I've never seen a girl look so enticing with no makeup and running clothes. She smelled amazing even through the light scent of sweat.

Had she accepted my offer to coffee, I would have made it my business to make sure we kissed before parting. Her lips are mesmerizing. I bet they would feel amazing against mine.

"What's that?" Dakota asks, looking up from her seat on the floor. She's been down there with notes, textbooks, and her syllabus surrounding her for the last hour.

"Nothing, I'm talking to myself."

We have always been close with our cousin Dakota. We're only a few months apart and since Uncle Rusty and Aunt Judy have been such a big part of our lives, so has she. If you find us somewhere, Dakota is usually right there with us.

We never asked her to come to college with us. She sort of told us she was coming. I thought she would move in with us, but she opted to go into the dorms.

It's her college experience too, so I can't be mad at that. She's been here helping us to make the place a home as much as she can. My brother has a great support system outside of my mama. Daddy has gotten better over the years, running interference with Mama like I do with everyone else.

My phone pings with another text from my teammates. They've been group texting about going to a party tonight. Caleb has already begged off, but he wants me to go.

I don't want to leave him here alone. Yeah, I need to lay the groundwork with our team members, but I want to make sure Caleb is fine on his first night home.

My mind wanders back to Amina. I wonder if she has friends on campus. Will she be at some party tonight?

I clench my fists at the thought. I'm sure all the guys will be tripping over themselves to talk to her. She's superhot.

Those long, toned legs, her cute, full ass, those plump, full breasts, and her gorgeous face—a total ten. I had asked her out before I gave myself time to think about it. Something about her keeps drawing me in.

Last night, when Kay said we should take a break, I was hesitant. I thought that would only complicate things more. When I didn't agree right away, she took that as a no and initiated sex.

I knew I should have stopped things, but I wanted to forget the drowning feeling that came over me. I also love sex. Kay knows just what I like.

However, this morning, she was gone, and there was a note. She said she thought it best to give it a few weeks. That our friendship was the most important thing.

I have mixed feelings about that. Seeing Amina stirred something within me. I've started to wonder all the more if Kay and I even belong together.

If our friendship is the most important thing, shouldn't we protect that by remaining friends? Amina made me think about the options I could have. The concern in her eyes spoke to me. For once, someone cared about how I felt.

"Cam, you should go to the party with the guys. I'll be okay," Caleb says from his spot wrapped up in a blanket on the couch.

He's been there all day since Daddy bought him home. I made him a sandwich and his favorite snack. We're eighteen. It doesn't take much to please us.

I know my brother is happy sitting here watching movies all night. He won't miss going out to some party. Although, I can go to feel the guys out and figure out who Caleb will be able to vibe with—if anyone.

It will allow me to know who I can bridge relationships with for him. I can always weed out the assholes. To pull this off for the next four years, I need to be strategic.

"You sure?" I ask, still not convinced.

"Yeah, I'll be fine."

"I'll be here with him," Dakota says.

I drag a hand down my face, still not persuaded that I should go. To be honest, I wouldn't mind staying in to get some much-needed sleep.

Thomas comes out of the bathroom and sits down next to me. This guy has been my best friend for as long as I can remember. He's more like a brother than a friend.

I never have to ask him for anything because before I open my mouth, it's already done. I can always count on Thomas. That's never been a question.

He looks around, seeming to read the room. I'm sure he heard some of the conversation through these thin-ass walls. Either way, I'm sure he'll be down to do whatever I decide.

"So we're going?"

I snort. "I guess so."

CHAPTER SIX

Going On a Date

Kayleen

"Stand strong, Kay. Don't you go calling that boy," I chide myself as I sit in my bedroom in my parents' house.

I've been sitting in the middle of my bed, warring with my thoughts and decisions since this morning when I came home. I did what I thought was the right thing. Cameron needs some space. Time to miss me and remember what he has. My mama was right.

"She better be right," I grumble to myself.

When Mama found out how poorly Mrs. Jemma's plan went, she gave me some advice of her own. She thinks I need to give Cam room to breathe, some space to miss what's been by his side all along.

I'm not going to lose Cameron. Not without a fight. This is me fighting—at least, I think it is. That's what it's supposed to be.

I followed Mama's advice and left Cam with something on his mind. Me. I made sure to sleep with him before giving him this break.

I do feel bad about Caleb. I get that I fucked up, but in the end, not going to college with my star athlete boyfriend will be a problem. Girls see Cam and they swoon. When they find out he's a talented baseball player; they pounce.

I'm only setting up my insurance plan. No one knows Cam like I do when it comes to sex. That's where I'll always win.

"Look, he's calling already," I sing and smile to myself.

I knew I took a gamble this morning. When I left and left that note behind, I took the risk he would call. Cam can be stubborn and petty when he wants to be.

However, I knew things would go my way. They have to. We're going to get married someday.

This call had to come … I freeze and frown when it's a number I don't recognize. It's not Cam. Crap, he still hasn't called.

"Hello," I answer, confused and wondering what Cam is doing that he hasn't called yet.

Caleb was released from the hospital. He has to be with him. That's it.

"What's up, Kayleen?" A deep voice comes from the other line. I knit my brows. "JR?"

He chuckles. "Yeah, my cousin gave me your number."

"Your cousin?"

"Yeah, Simone. That's who invited me the other night."

I palm my forehead. How could I have forgotten that they're cousins? Simone was on the cheer squad with me. I think she had a crush on Caleb, but he wasn't ready for something like that.

I pout as I think of how easy high school had been. I knew my role and played it. I was a part of the team and always thought I would be.

"What's up? What can I do for you?" I say as I shake myself from my thoughts.

"I'm heading out first thing in the morning. I wanted to see if you'd have dinner with me. Maybe catch a movie."

I bite my lip and try to think of a way out of this. I'm attracted to Jareil, but I don't know if I want to date anyone else. It's always been Cam.

"Come on. I read the energy. There's trouble in paradise.

"At least see what else is out there. If it doesn't work out, you can say you tried. You won't have any what-ifs," he coaxes smoothly.

I start to blush and I'm happy he's not in front of me. Not once have I ever thought he was interested in me. Although, I doubt I ever would have noticed because Cam has always been my world.

I still remember the day Mrs. Jemma and my mama talked me into breaking Cam and his girlfriend up. I didn't think twice about it. Cam was my boyfriend a week later.

"If I say yes, it's just as friends, right?"

He gives a deep, rich chuckle. "If that's how you want to start. Sure. What time should I pick you up?"

I blow out a breath and run my hand through my hair. It's not like I'm cheating on Cam. We're on a break.

I've given him a hall pass. Why shouldn't I take mine? We will be together in the end.

"I'll be ready by seven. Is that okay?"

"See you at seven," he says with a smile in his voice.

I hang up with a huge smile on my face. I'm going on a date. A date with someone other than Cameron Perry.

I never in my life thought I would ever say those words. I know nothing other than Cameron. I've been told all my life he's who I'm meant to be with, but here I am going on a date with someone else.

Now ain't that something?

Cameron

I look in the mirror and give myself a wink. I'll admit I put a little more effort into getting ready tonight. The guy looking back at me is single after all.

I haven't been single since junior high school. I was fourteen the last time I could say I wasn't in a relationship. Kay may have done me a favor.

However, I'm not going to give much thought to that tonight. Tonight, I'll enjoy myself. I'm going to have a few beers, hang with some new friends, and maybe I'll find someone worth hooking up with at the end of it all, but that's a big maybe.

"Live your life, Cam," I say to my reflection.

Before I head out, I straighten my white button-up and tuck the front in, leaving the back hanging out of my blue jeans. Then I fix my belt buckle.

One more look over my outfit and I nod at my brown flat lace-up boots. Not sure about my shirt, I try rolling up the sleeves. I get one rolled up and sort of like the look of one rolled and the other down.

I push a hand through my hair, and it falls right back into my face. I'll go for a cut soon. I tend to keep mine shorter than my brother's.

"Time to go," I huff and turn to head out of the bathroom.

Thomas is sitting on the couch scoffing down a burger, already dressed and ready to go. Caleb still hasn't moved from his spot on the couch. I walk over to him and kiss the top of his head.

He flinches away at first but looks up at me and smiles. I don't take offense; my brother has his aversions. But since we were little, he has come to me for hugs and affection when he needs them. The flinching is almost reflexive at this point when it comes to me.

He always smiles it off to let me know he's okay with my displays of affection. I respect when he lets me know it's too much. Caleb is very vocal when he's having a bad day or he's overwhelmed.

"Have a good time. I'll try to come along next time. I want to go to my first college party. I just need more time to prepare.

"Tonight is too soon. I'm not ready for that," he says while searching my face as if to read my reaction.

In fact, I know that's what he's doing. I give him a smile. "I'm not going to rush you to do anything. Rest up. Next week will be the first full week of baseball and classes. The rest can wait."

"Thanks, Cam."

"I love you, bro. Let Kota know if you start to feel sick."

"I'm cool. Don't worry about me. Be you, Cam. Tonight, just be you. Not Cam and Cal, just Cam."

I can't help smiling at my brother. He's the only one who gets it. He has lived it with me. It is rare that we get to be just one person.

Not that I regret anything I do for Caleb. I wouldn't change a thing. It's just hard sometimes always having to be on because everyone expects me to answer for Caleb like he can't answer for himself.

It gets exhausting for the both of us. The brother who is always seen and the one who only wants to be seen. I work twice as hard for my brother to get to be treated the same as me—he knows and understands that.

I nod and head for the door before I get in my emotions. Thomas pounds his chest and releases a loud burp before he hops up to follow me. Kota meets me at the door to pull me into a hug and kisses my cheek.

"You're the best. Have fun, I've got him."

"Thanks, darlin'. Love you."

"Love you more."

I kiss her forehead and head out. I inhale deeply as I step out of the door. For once, I shut my brain off. Tonight, I'm going to go with the flow.

CHAPTER SEVEN

We Meet Again

Cameron

"Man, are you ready for hell week? That shit is going to shred you to your soul," Garrett, one of my new teammates says.

He's a sophomore batter. So far, he's a cool dude. We've been knocking back beers and shooting the shit since I arrived.

I finish the beer in my hand and nod. I heard hell week will have you feeling like your stomach has dropped out of your ass. This is why Caleb needs to get his rest. He needs to be mentally and physically ready for this.

"I'm ready. Drinking this shit might come back to bite me in the ass, but I'm ready. I've never been afraid of hard work."

"Good to hear. Last year, I watched a few guys quit the first day. Couldn't have been me. I worked my ass off to be here. I'm in this until I can't take another breath."

"I hear you. I'm ready to get to work."

"I hope you didn't schedule any classes for afternoon or evenings. I swear those dickheads in the registration office will fuck your schedule up if you don't know better."

"Wait, what?"

"They fuck with freshman athletes. They're supposed to schedule morning or early afternoon classes for us, but they don't and then take weeks to fix it or shove you in some bullshit classes you were trying to avoid," Garrett says.

"You're shitting me, right? I have two afternoon classes. My brother has like one. What the fuck, man?"

I'm fuming. Caleb was getting into his new routine. It's only been a week, but with hell week, that might send him into a spiral.

What kind of fucked-up shit is this? They know we're athletes. Caleb and I were already annoyed with the basic classes they wanted to offer us.

I might want to coast, but that shit was freshman jocks for dummies. We both opted out for our own choice of classes. Now this.

Just fucking great. I won't have a problem changing classes, but that shit will suck if I can't get the classes I wanted. I groan and purse my lips.

I'll have to handle this first thing Monday. Kota might have to change a class too. No wonder Coach wanted to oversee our class scheduling.

It was one of the things Cal really wanted to do on his own. I was proud of him as he studied the course catalog and chose his personal interests and basic classes needed for his degree.

This is some bullshit though. I grab another beer as my annoyance rises. I can't seem to catch a break.

"Don't sweat it, man. Coach has been cracking down on them in the last two years. Someone in the office has a hard-on against the team. They've been trying to nail them to stop the shit.

"I'm sure you'll be able to straighten it out faster this semester."

"Yeah, I hope so."

Garrett belches. "Excuse me, bro. Damn." He shakes his head. "I'm heading for the beer pong table. You coming? My cannabis guy is over there."

I pause and stare at him. He just said he's all in when it comes to baseball. If he is caught with that shit in his system, he could be suspended for an entire year of eligibility.

"Don't look so surprised, dude. Half the team gets high. You just have to know how not to get caught.

"They overlook that shit even when you do if you're one of the boys. You and your brother have been talked about like you're for sure one of them boys. A few hits won't hurt. It just might get you through," he says as he takes in my expression.

"I'll pass."

"Fine, suit yourself, but if you ever change your mind and need the hookup, let me know. I'll make sure you never come up on the radar and I'll get you the good shit."

He slaps me on the shoulder, and we head for the room where I saw the beer pong table set up earlier. We pass by a few other team members and bump fists with them as we go. I don't plan to smoke with Garrett, but this side of the party is rocking.

I smile and bob my head to the music. I lose Garrett as I move deeper into the game room. Not thinking much of it, I find a corner and sip my beer as I people watch.

Whoever is spinning this music is cool in my book. I love Jodeci and they have had a few of my faves in rotation. There has been a great mix of R&B, hip-hop, and alternative music.

More R&B now that the girls are tipsy and willing to grind with the guys. I'm four more beers in when every male in the room seems to straighten and check his breath.

I grin in amusement, searching for the cause of the shift. That's when she comes into view. I know it's her because I'm drawn to her at first sight.

Amina looks like a fucking knockout. Her dark hair is down and curled into big, wavy curls that fall down around her shoulders. It's the first time I've seen it down.

The first time I saw her, it was curly and up in a messy ponytail. The two times after that, it was straighter but still up in a messy bun.

The dark locks only work to enhance the richness of her brown skin. She has this gorgeous bronze tone to her skin that makes it look like it's glowing. The dress she has on hugs her curves to perfection. The heels on her feet accent her long brown legs.

I'm hard enough to bust through my jeans from just one glance across the room. We lock eyes and she gives me a little smile. While every other guy in here drools over her, I fall back and lift my hand to beckon her to me with my finger.

She tilts her head as her smile grows, then she laughs and shakes her head. I lift a brow in challenge and that seems to get her feet moving over to me.

I wait for her to get to me, then place my hand on her hip. I lean into her ear and just inhale her at first. Then I whisper in her ear, earning a shiver that tells me she's not as unaffected as she's trying to seem.

Maribel

"So we meet again. You know what that means, don't you?"

I shiver and squeeze my thighs together. What the fuck. His voice alone has me weak in the knees.

Up until now, this party has been all right. It's a bit crowded, so me and the girls have been in the backyard. I came inside to find the bathroom and then I saw the beer pong session going down and decided to peek my head in.

I wasn't expecting to find Cam in here looking like a whole snack. My brain is telling me to stay away, but my feet brought my ass right over to him. His hand on my hip feels like it belongs there.

The possessiveness of his grasp feels appropriate. Like I already belong to him. I look up into his eyes and I'm speechless.

"No, Cam, I don't," I say and smile back at him.

"Either you're stalking me, or you belong to me and the universe is hellbent on letting us both know this," he says as he searches my gaze.

"Trust me, I'm not stalking you. As for the universe, I'm not sure I can get with that one either. You got anything else?"

"Universe, fate, divine design, whatever you want to name it. You definitely play a part in my life. Whether it's for a night, a few weeks, or a lifetime. We were meant to be something to each other."

"Did you have too much to drink?" I deadpan.

"Maybe, but that doesn't change the facts."

"Yes, it does. I'm sure in the morning, you'll be singing a different song."

"Speaking of songs. This is one of my jams. Come dance with me."

I tune into the song and lift a brow. It's Jodeci's "Ride & Slide." Not what I would expect to be one of this big Texan's favorite songs.

"What do you know about Jodeci?" I tease.

"More than you know. I have all their shit. I've worn out a few albums and had to replace them. This is from the *Diary of a Mad Band* album. Track five."

I pull a face and nod. "Okay, Cam. You're from here, right? Texas?"

"Born and raised. Why?"

I bite my lip and look him over. He's so much bigger up this close. It's so hard to dwarf me, but he towers over me effortlessly.

"Nothing, just trying to learn more about you," I reply.

He drops his hand from my waist and grabs mine, then places his beer bottle down. In the next motion, he's leading me into the next room where people are dancing. Well, grinding is a better description.

Cam lifts my arm above my head and spins me before he pulls my back to his front. He holds me close with a hand splayed on my belly as he moves from side to side with a little bounce to his step.

I smile but keep in step with him. He buries his face in my neck and begins to sing the words just beneath my ear. I feel him beginning to grow hard against my ass.

"You're beautiful, you know that, right?" he breathes in my ear, the scent of beer filling my nostrils.

I should be turned off, but I'm not. Instead, I'm growing a pulse between my legs. He runs his nose against my neck when I don't answer.

I'm taken by surprise as he spins me again and pulls me closer. This time, he dips his head until we're nose to nose. I can't even remember his question. He slips his leg between mine and moves us to the beat of the music.

I wrap my arms around his neck as he wraps his around my waist tightly. When I lick my lips, my tongue brushes his lower lip because he's that close. He tightens his hold and moves his lips to my ear.

"I want you, Amina. I want you so fucking bad."

I jerk my head back as my middle name comes out like a bucket of ice water. I can't do this with Cam. As much as I feel this attraction and want him too, this isn't going to happen.

As if reading my mind, he dances me into a corner where I'm blocked from the view of everyone else. I look up into his eyes and they're filled with lust. Before I can stop him, he lifts his fingertips to my chin and tilts my head back.

The next thing I know, my toes are curling in my heels. Cam slides his free hand down my back to my ass and squeezes. I lift onto my toes and return the kiss.

He's an amazing kisser. It feels like he's fucking my mouth with his tongue. I whimper and he groans, deepening the kiss.

He palms the side of my face as he eats my mouth, his hand on my ass tightens. Sucking at my lips and swirling his tongue in my mouth, he scrambles my thoughts.

He breaks the kiss and presses his forehead to mine. He's breathing heavily and his growing erection is still stabbing into me. I feel like I might faint.

"Wow," he breathes. "We would be so good together. Just one night.

"Give me one night to prove it to you. I won't disappoint. Please, Amina.

"Come home with me. I want you, baby. I need you."

There's that ice bucket again. This time, I shake my head clear and push at his chest. He tries to kiss me again, but I turn my face away.

"Cam, I can't," I say.

"Shit, I'm sorry. You just ... ever since I first saw you, you've had this pull on me.

"Listen, I want to get to know you. Can we get some air and talk? I should probably start to sober up."

I stare down at my feet and shrug. I should say no, but I feel this pull too. I want to know what it is about him that I can't seem to shake.

"Just talking, right?"

He nods. "You have my word. We'll just talk."

"Okay, there's this cool spot out back. We can sit out there if no one is occupying it."

He laces his fingers with mine. I look up into his eyes and smile. His gaze drops to my lips and then back to my eyes.

He gives my hand a gentle squeeze and winks at me. I relax and allow him to lead me through the crowd to get out back. I'm bummed out as we find the area fully occupied.

"Do you live in the area around the Chinese place and supermarket?"

"Yeah, well, I stay over there. I'm supposed to be living in the dorms."

"Cool, my place is nearby there too. Let me walk you home. We can talk on the way," he offers.

"I didn't come alone. My friends are still partying. Besides, how do I know I can trust you with where I live?"

He snorts. "I'm the guy you call to take out the trash, baby. Never the trash that needs taking out."

"Okay, Cam. I felt that. I have to warn you though. I'm no stranger to street fighting. These hands are nice."

He laughs. "I'll keep that in mind. I'm going to text my friend to let him know I'm leaving. You should do the same. You can tell them I'm walking you home."

I think his words over. I don't think I want to tell Taylor or Joelle that Camron Perry is walking me home. Thoughts of how they were tripping on the way here about the potential of baseball and swim team guys attending the party comes to mind and I know I'm not going to tell them.

Instead, I take my phone out and text them that I need to go home because I'm not feeling well. Taylor replies immediately telling me to wait so she can leave with me. I tell her not to worry about it; I'll see her when she gets in.

"All set," I say and look up at Cam.

He takes my hand, and we start in the direction of our neighborhood. I regret the decision to walk home about two blocks in. I pull to a stop and do a little foot-to-foot dance, trying to relieve the pain.

"Those shoes killing your feet?"

"Yeah, just give me a sec. You were saying you've been playing baseball all your life."

"Pretty much," he says as he bends down and starts to unlace his boots.

I look at him curiously. He straightens as he toes them off. He then turns them to face me.

I yelp as he lifts me from my feet. My heels fall off and he lowers me into his boots. With a smile on his lips, he kneels to tie the boots to my ankles. Picking up my heels, he laces our fingers together again.

"What are you supposed to wear?" I ask.

"I have on socks. I'll throw them out when I get home."

"Cam, you could hurt yourself. You have to start practice next week. Please take your shoes back."

He leans to kiss my forehead. "I'm good. So, where were we? No siblings?" he asks and winks at me.

"No, I'm an only child."

"Where are you from? I still haven't placed the accent. I know it's from up North, but not sure where," he says.

"New Jersey by way of New York. You're hearing the New Yorker in me. I haven't lived in New Jersey as long. Is your brother your only sibling?"

"Yup. Just me and Cal, but my cousin Dakota is pretty much like a sister."

"That must have been fun, growing up with a twin."

Something shifts in the air as he stiffens a bit. He doesn't like talking about his brother. Got it. I think of something else to talk about.

However, I stumble in his big boots and almost fall on my face. He catches me and tugs me into his chest. I look up into his eyes as my heart races.

His gaze drops to my lips. He begins to lean in, but I clear my throat and step out of his hold. He releases an awkward laugh and turns, then waves me forward.

"Hop on. I'll carry you the rest of the way."

"Dude, I have your shoes on. I'm not about to make you carry me while I have them on my feet."

"Hop on, Amina."

I frown and do as he says. I need to place distance between us. I've told this lie that's hanging between us for a good reason.

He carries me the rest of the way as we continue our conversation. By the time we get to my building, I feel like I'm hanging with an old friend.

Once outside the doors to my building, he puts me down on my feet. I take my heels from his hands and drop them on the ground. Then I go to take his shoes off and step into mine.

He shoves his feet into his boots and stands staring down at me. It's like he's holding me in a trance. I can't look away. He lifts a hand to tuck my hair behind my ear.

"I want to hang out again. When can I see you?"

"Cam … I can't. I like you, but—"

My phone rings, cutting me off. I pull it out and find Dez's name screaming back at me. This is why nothing can happen between us. I need to be rid of Dez first.

I go to look up to finish my words, but Cam crushes my lips with his, cutting my words off. I grasp the front of his shirt with my hands as he wraps his arms around me. This kiss is better than the last one.

He inhales me like a much-needed breath. I'm left breathless when he breaks the kiss. His intense blue grays seem to only be blue now.

"You feel this connection like I do. Don't shut me out. Let's explore it.

"I was in a rush earlier because of the alcohol. Now that I've sobered up, I see that was some dick shit. I've dated the same girl since I was fourteen.

"I might not be great at this shit, so I'm going to slow down because I want to get to know you more. Let me have your number. We can talk or text or whatever."

"Cam—"

"Take my number."

"Why me? You're about to be a star on campus. If you've been with one girl since you were fourteen this is the time to explore, not hook up with the first girl you're attracted to."

"I'm more than attracted to you. And you just proved my point. I'm headed for the major leagues and you're still shutting me down. None of that matters to you.

"I just spilled all that to you on the walk here and you're not giving me that look. You're trying to run," he says.

"What look?"

"That 'Here's the ticket. This one is going to be a bag. If I fuck him, he'll be my meal ticket.'"

I laugh. "You're serious?"

"As fuck. You would be surprised how often I get that look. My own girlfriend had it more times than I'd like to admit. You see me, Cam. I like that about you."

"Cam, my life is so complicated. I don't think I can give you more than friendship."

"I understand complicated, believe me. My life is more than complicated. If that's all you can give me, I'm willing to take that. I want that."

"Even if no one can know?"

He looks at me, puzzled. For a moment, I don't think he's going to answer. However, he takes in a sharp breath.

"Yeah, there's something between us. I'll take a secret friendship. Something tells me it will be worth it in the end. I could use a friend more than you know. Someone outside my world."

"Okay, Cam. I'll give you my number."

"Good," he says with the brightest smile, those dimples popping like little cheek craters.

I know the moment I give him my number I've just changed my life forever.

CHAPTER EIGHT

Guilty Conscience

Kayleen

As I look in the bathroom mirror, I keep wiping at my mouth as if I can wipe what I've done away. I keep wiping and wiping and nothing has changed. I feel so guilty and wrong.

"Kay, you all right in there?" JR calls from the other side of the door.

I cover my face and start to sob. He has done nothing wrong. He's been sweet to me all night.

I don't know why I thought this was a good idea. Everything was fine until I turned and dropped to my knees for him to pull the condom off and come in my mouth. It's like the moment his cum hit my tongue and lips, it all became real.

I fucked someone else.

Panic set in and my mind began to race. Will Cam be able to tell? Will my mama find out and kill me?

The worst part is that I liked it. JR was gentle but firm. He's gifted like Cam in size and skill. However, I wouldn't say they are the same.

Cam was my first, and at one point, I thought he would be the only. Knowing what I've chosen to do makes me feel so dirty. Like I betrayed Cam.

"Kayleen?"

I sniffle and run my forearm under my nose. I know I should answer him, but I'm embarrassed. I don't want him to think I'm a slut.

"Kay, baby, talk to me. What just happened? Did I do something wrong?"

Feeling bad, I turn to leave out of the bathroom. JR stands outside the door, looking concerned and confused. I drop my gaze to the floor, unable to look at him.

Covering my breasts and lady parts, I then try to find my clothes. Our things are thrown around his bedroom floor from our frantic rush to get each other in bed earlier.

"Kay, slow down and talk to me," JR snaps, bringing me to a halt.

I turn and flop down on the foot of the bed. He comes to sit beside me. I still can't look at him.

"I'm assuming we moved too fast and now you're freaking out."

I nod, still not able to talk. He places his hand on my back and starts to rub circles. I peek up at him.

"I'm sorry."

"No, I'm sorry. I may have gotten carried away. I've had a thing for you for a long time.

"I knew you needed time. I should have thought about that. Listen, I don't want this to ruin things between us. I want to keep in touch and hang out when I come home," he says.

"I don't know. Everything is happening so fast."

"No disrespect to Cam. He's always been a good guy. I'm not saying that he doesn't treat you well.

"It's just … You said you guys broke up and I took an opportunity. You and Cam have this relationship that's always felt more like two siblings to me. The way you guys argue all the time.

"It always comes off like two friends or brother and sister. I mean, I fight with my sister all the time the same way. I thought maybe I could show you what it's like to have a boyfriend you're not—"

"JR," I cut him off. "This was really nice. I had fun on the date and all of this."

I look back at the bed and around the room. The room we just went several rounds in. Several long hot rounds.

I bite my lip, then continue. "You were amazing. I just don't know that I'm ready to let Cam go. I don't want to lead you on."

He sighs and purses his lips but nods his understanding. I don't know how to feel right now. I want to go home and place distance between what I've done.

"We're good. I'll give you the time you need. You have my number. If you want to explore us, call me. Let's get dressed. I'll take you home," he says.

"Thanks, JR."

"No need to thank me. I'll always be here when you need me. I mean that, Kay. This was about more than sex for me."

I reach to hug him tight. He's being so cool about this. A real gentleman.

I feel even worse because he's being so nice. I can't help wondering if this is a sign that I need to think more about what I want and not what others want for me. Jareil might not be my mama's choice, but I don't think I would be upset if he were mine.

Cameron

I walk into the apartment expecting to find Caleb still on the couch. I look around, but he's nowhere in sight. My brother must be feeling better.

The mess I made over the few days I was here alone has been cleaned up. There isn't a thing out of place. I smile.

It's good to see he's done something that proves he's feeling like himself. Aunt Judy always calls me the messy twin. I've never seen it like that.

With so much pressure from our mama to be perfect, I've always felt it was my job to fuck that up. We were kids, so we should have been able to do kid shit.

My brother's episodes were never as bad as Mama made them seem. He would adjust once he figured out how to handle situations. The older we got, the more he could adjust.

Isn't that how it works with kids? It always felt to me like we were acting more like adults than she was. Even Daddy would look annoyed with her shit.

I knew how to rock the boat to get attention off my brother, so I did. A messy room was only one of the things that drove Mama crazy, so I made sure to have one. Caleb, on the other hand, has to have things in order. I bring the chaos for us both.

"We're going to be okay. We'll show them all we can make this happen. You and me, bro. We'll do it our way," I murmur and head for my room.

CHAPTER NINE

Smile

Maribel

Two weeks later …

Cam and I have been texting back and forth since the night I gave him my number. I spent most of that first Sunday smiling at my phone while answering his texts. I've felt like my face is going to crack from smiling so much.

Not only have the texts continued, but he calls me in the evenings as well, even though he had to deal with hell week and his conflicting schedule. They still haven't fixed one of his classes.

He won't tell me which course it is, stating he doesn't want me to see him for the true nerd he is. Cam, a nerd? Never that. I can call him a lot of things, but a nerd isn't one of them.

If nothing else, I can always count on him for a good laugh. Our sarcasm makes for fun conversations. He's been helping me keep my mind off the drama going on back home.

My father keeps calling, trying to get me to come home for an engagement party. An engagement party I never plan to have. As far as I'm concerned, no one ever needs to know about what they're trying to force on me.

When my father isn't calling, Dez is. It seems I haven't run away far enough. I should've gone to school overseas or something.

"You still have that goofy smile on your face," Taylor teases, pulling me from the fog I'm in as we walk the campus, heading to class.

The sun is beaming down on us, but there's a chill in the air. I'm glad I put a hoodie on this morning. This beanie has been working miracles as well.

"Whatever, I'll see you after class." I laugh her off and shake my head.

She's been teasing me since the texts between me and Cam started. I'm glad she hasn't pried or tried to get me to tell her who they're coming from. Although I can tell she wants to.

"Are we still heading to see a movie?"

I chew on my lip. Cam asked me to hang out tonight. I haven't committed to anything yet, but I'm so tempted. It might be fun.

The only reason I haven't agreed is because that kiss from the party has been living rent-free in my mind. My toes curl in my shoes from just thinking about it.

With Dez breathing down my neck, insisting I come home for the holidays, I can't bring myself to give in to my feelings for Cam. I shouldn't even be allowing them to grow. Thankfully, Cam has respected our friendship over the phone.

"I'm not sure yet. Can I think about it and let you know after class?"

"Sure. I'll see you." She waves as I turn off for the science building.

I'm lost in thought as I make my way to class. My morning chemistry class is the only one I have on Fridays. It's actually one of my favorites so far. The professor has a great personality and makes the lectures fun.

I'm startled as someone wraps an arm around my head and I'm tugged into a strong side. I look up at Cameron in shock. When I look around me, I see his brother and cousin a few feet away.

I look back up at Cam as my chest heaves. He smiles back at me as he grabs my face and turns my head from side to side, pushing my hoodie back slightly. I stare back at him curiously.

"I thought you had headphones on or earbuds in or something. I was shouting your name, but you kept walking and ignoring me," he says as he knits his brows.

"Oh, I was running through my notes for class in my head. I didn't hear you. I wasn't paying attention."

"Cool, got you. You on your way to class now?"

"Yeah, you guys on a run?" I ask as I nod toward his brother and cousin.

"We were. I'm starving now, so we're heading to get something to eat. Too bad you're a good girl. I'd try to talk you into skipping class to join us."

I smile back at him. "I would like to meet them both. Maybe this once I could make the exception."

The smile drops from his face as I look over at the two waiting for him. I'm not sure what just changed, but it's clear something has. I tug my hoodie back in place.

"You know what, on second thought. I already had breakfast, and we're secret friends, so that's a bad idea."

Seeming to relax, he reaches for my hand. "Are we on for tonight? It will be fun, I promise."

"I don't know."

"Come on, Amina. You said we could be friends. Friends hang out all the time. We're just going for a bite to eat and bowling or something."

"I don't know. Taylor wants to go to the movies."

"What time is the movie over? We can meet up after. It's Friday. You don't have class tomorrow morning."

I think about it and almost tell him no. However, he gives me that smile and those dimples pop and I can't deny him. When he wraps his arms around my head and pulls me into him as he rocks my body from side to side and buries his face in the top of my head, my restraint breaks.

His arms feel so comforting. Cam has this way of making me feel safe so effortlessly. I wrap my arms around him and inhale deeply.

He's sweaty, but his cologne still clings to him. It should be illegal for a guy to be this manly in every way. I nearly cream my panties when he begins to speak.

"You know you want to hang with me. Stop overthinking things. If we're friends, spending time together isn't a big deal. Come on, darlin'. Hang with me tonight," he says.

"Okay," I murmur into his chest.

He releases me and has a huge smile on his face. I'm in so much trouble when it comes to Cam. That smile alone is a problem.

"I have to get to class. I'll text you later," I say as I look at the time.

"Cool. Have a good morning, friend." He winks and turns to jog away.

I feel guilty as I watch him go. I need to tell him my first name and soon. There is something that keeps pulling us together and I don't want something like a lie to get in the way of whatever is happening.

Maybe I'll figure out a way out of my situation and Cam can be an option. That's a big maybe, but I'm holding onto it for now. Cameron Perry is going to cause me to risk it all.

Cameron

It's so easy for me to forget when it comes to Amina. I wasn't thinking when I asked her to skip class to come with me, Kota, and Cal for breakfast. Seeing that smile only made me want to be near her.

Today wouldn't be the best day to introduce her to Caleb. He's still adjusting, and the last two weeks have been hard. We were out running so he could settle some of the extra he had going on today.

Her reminder that we're secret friends brought me back down to earth. I have my own secrets I can't share. I'm accepting this distance between us because of those secrets.

"Who was that?" Caleb asks as we make our way to go grab a bite.

"A friend."

"Does Kay know about your friend?"

"Kay and I are taking a break. She doesn't need to know anything about her. Besides, she's a friend."

"So that was a girl," Caleb says, sounding more curious than anything else.

"Gah, do frogs hop?" I grumble, frustrated with myself for chasing her down in front of him.

Caleb is silent for a moment. I foolishly believe that's the end of it from his silence. I should know better.

"Actually, no, not all do. Some walk instead of hopping. There are four species with modified hind legs that allow them to reach places by walking. If I'm annoying you, just say so."

I sigh and pinch the bridge of my nose. That's such a Caleb response. I'm still working on sarcasm with him.

Sometimes, he can filter through my sarcasm. Sometimes, he can't. Especially when he's not looking me right in the face. He's not annoying me, but I don't want to talk about this.

"So we're in the business of running *friends* down? Sure looked like more than a friend to me," Dakota sings, saving me from having to explain to Caleb that I'm not annoyed with him.

"I said she's a friend and it's my business."

"What happened with Kayleen?" Caleb asks, changing the subject. "She hasn't been around since the party. Did I do something to make her go away?"

I clench my fists. I don't want him thinking he's the reason we broke up. All of that is on Kay.

She started calling me a few days ago, but I'm not ready to talk to her. It's dawned on me that I've been with the same girl since I was fourteen. I mean, that shit has set in heavy.

Talking to Amina has allowed me to see there's more out there. I haven't had a single fight with her. In two weeks, Kay and I would have had at least a dozen by now.

That shit is toxic. It's exhausting. I've been able to think clearly since we've broken up.

Being single isn't so bad. I miss having sex, but that's even something that's made a difference in my life. I don't think I would have made it through hell week if I had been fucking all the time like I do when Kay and I are together.

"No, it had nothing to do with you. Things are changing and we needed to give each other some room to breathe," I say.

My brother will never be made to feel guilty about my relationships. My mind goes back to Amina. I don't know if I can trust her with our secret.

I need to do better about keeping her from finding out. Anyone I bring into my life has to be a part of the team. If I can't trust them, they can't come in close.

God, I hope I can trust her.

CHAPTER TEN

Life Is Happening

Maribel

"I will book a first-class flight for you. We should plan the engagement party while you are here. I'm thinking of hiring a planner to get things squared away," Dez says on the phone while I roll my eyes.

"It will be the holidays. Who's planning anything?" I grumble.

"You'd be surprised what a little bonus can do."

"Well, I'm not coming home for Thanksgiving. My friends and I have plans here on campus."

"My patience is growing thin. You didn't discuss going to school with me. We didn't discuss you moving to Texas either. You've been treating me like an option when I'm anything but, Maribel," he snaps.

"An option I didn't ask for. No one discussed with me if I wanted to be married or to who. I'm going to school for me. This is what I want," I snap back.

"You have been mine since before you were born. Your father made promises to my family he will keep."

"What?"

"Oh, so you don't know why your mother left? She thought she would take you away and hide you from me and my family. Little does she know.

"I always get what I want. Ask my brother. Oh, sorry. You can't. He's no longer with us," he says darkly.

Dez had an older brother who was going to take over the family. About a year ago, he died mysteriously and Dez stepped into the grooming for the promotion his brother was supposed to get.

A shiver runs through me as I catch onto what he's implying. I'm still getting to know my father and learning about his world. If this is true, there's no telling the danger I placed myself in by finding my dad.

Tears begin to well in my eyes as I feel so stupid. This is all my fault. I walked right into this.

"Have your fun with your friends. I will see you before the year ends."

With that, he hangs up. I sit staring off into space as the truth sets in. I can't for the life of me think of what my father got in exchange for me. How do you promise off your baby for anything?

"If we want to make the four o'clock show we need to head out," Taylor says as she pokes her head into my bedroom.

Quickly, I swipe at the tears that have fallen. I need to pull it together. I don't want anyone here to know about the craziness happening back home.

"I'll be right there."

"Are you all right? We don't have to go if you're not feeling well."

"I'm fine. Just give me a second."

"No worries. I'll be in the living room if you need me," she says with worry in her voice.

I get up from my bed and look in the mirror at my outfit. I should change into sweats and tell Cam I'm not going to be able to meet him later. I had dressed in blue jeans and a cream sweater with thigh-high boots for our hang-out session.

Now, I feel silly. How do I get out of an engagement I don't even want? Dez was cool when I first met him. I thought nothing of it when he kept coming by my dad's house to see me.

I felt like there was something dark about him, but he was always nice to me. Taking me out and showing me attention. I was seventeen and a handsome older guy was showing me attention.

I thought I was hot shit at first. Then my father announced that Dez was to be my fiancé. I thought I was going to be sick that day.

It felt like my life was over. All my choices were taken away from me. It was like I was nothing more than a pawn or some form of currency.

I was trapped in a nightmare with no way out. Then my acceptance letters started to come in. I had been so bummed out as I went through letter after letter. Hopelessness settled in with each one until I got to this one with the offer to come here with a full scholarship attached.

It was a godsend. I didn't tell anyone but my mom what I had planned to do until I arrived here in Texas. My mom was the one to remind me my cousin lived right here in the city.

I knew it was God when I learned how close she lived to campus and that was before I met my roommate. I take a deep breath as I look down at my phone in my shaking hand.

"God, if this is all you, I'm going to trust you to fix this," I murmur as I delete the text I was about to send Cam.

I blow out a breath and turn to head out. I can use a good laugh with a friend. Cam is just what the doctor ordered.

I'll see this movie with Taylor and then I will meet up with my friend. This will be a good night. Dez isn't here now. He can't dictate my every move.

"Assholes."

My father is going to hear from me. I also owe my mother a huge apology. I hope she can forgive me.

"Stupid girl," I breathe as I walk out of my room.

Man, I feel so dumb.

Cameron

I lift my big toe and turn my foot on its side like that's going to help me decide on which pair of shoes to wear. I can't make up my mind. I pucker my lips and start to pop them as if that will miraculously give me some answers other than what I would look like as a fish.

Glancing at the mirror, I wonder if I'm going too casual. We're just hanging out and getting something to eat. The light-blue distressed jeans with the tears in the knee and thighs seemed safe when I first put them on. So did the plain white T-shirt.

Now I'm second-guessing everything. I haven't even put my socks on yet. I think to start all over but roll my eyes as my phone rings, breaking through my musings.

Ignoring it, I grab my cowboy boots and hold them up. A frown comes to my face. These are cool, but not for a date with Amina.

"This is not a date," I chide myself.

It's not, but I don't want to come off as some big country-ass dude when she probably has guys back home who have tons of swag. I drop the cowboy boots. It's now between my sneakers and my flat lace-up boots. The boots do give the rest of the outfit a vibe.

"Go with the boots," I mutter.

They will dress up the outfit a little and make it a little less casual looking. I snap my fingers as I think about the fact that we're going bowling. Remembering that I have a similar pair of black boots with faux laces and a side zipper, I head to the closet to dig them out.

Once I get my socks and boots on, I have time to check my messages. My mama has called, demanding I call her back. I snort and chuck the phone.

She only wants one of two things, to get me to talk to Kay or to annoy me about something else. I'm not in the mood for either. Kay wanted to take a break, so we're taking a break.

Right now, I just want to be left alone. I don't have anyone nagging me and I haven't been stressed out. I smile and laugh more than I have in a long time.

"Cam, you want something to eat?" Caleb calls through the apartment.

I walk out of my room to find him in the kitchen at the stove. This guy can cook his ass off. If he ever decided ball wasn't for him, he could cook for a living.

"Nah, but you can make me some for later," I say as I sit at the island.

He turns to look at me. "You're going out?"

"Yeah, not for long, just a few hours. You cool with that?"

"Yeah, not like I need a babysitter."

I lift a brow and chuckle when he gives me a smile. I nod and toss a napkin from the countertop at him. He's getting better at joking around more.

"Don't get your ass kicked."

"Are we going to that kickback? The one the team invited us to?"

"Do you think you're ready for that? I mean, I'm down if you want to go, but are you ready to try?"

He purses his lips and squints. I give him time to gather his thoughts and feelings. I never like to assume I know what he's feeling or to rush him through his thought process.

Patience is key with Caleb. You get more from him when you allow him to take his time. Parties are harder. However, my mama won't be involved with this one and I think that's a positive thing for my brother to be able to relax and cope.

"I want to try. The guys invited me. It's not like I'm trying to tag along with you. That felt good. To be seen and invited.

"I might not like it once we get there, but at least I can know my limits early on and say I've had the experience," he says, shaking his hands out at his sides.

"Well, we have two weeks to work on things like that," I say, pointing to the handshaking.

Over the years we've worked on his different tics and stims. Not because I thought he needed to change for anyone, but because our mama would get so mad when he couldn't stop whatever it was she deemed as weird or inappropriate.

My mama is a trigger for my brother and she's too selfish to realize when she would get angry with him it only made things worse. So I helped lessen the behaviors for him, not her or to hide who my brother is. Although all that work has gone a long way in helping us now.

Caleb clenches his fists and grinds his teeth. "I can do this, Cam. I want to do this."

Determination fills his eyes and my heart swells with pride. This guy is going to shock the shit out of the world one day. I can't wait to see him prove our parents wrong, our mama more so than our daddy.

Daddy only wants the best for Caleb and to protect him from the world. Sometimes, in her own twisted way, I believe my mama wants the same.

"Then we will go. If you hate it once we're there, we'll leave."

"Thanks."

"You got it, bro."

CHAPTER ELEVEN

Hanging Out

Maribel

My chest warms as I see Cam up ahead. He looks great even from this distance. He's wearing a pair of light blue jeans that are hugging his thighs. His head is down, and his hands are in his pockets. The jean jacket he has on over his white tee fits his broader shoulders nicely.

As I get closer, he lifts his head, and a smile comes to his face that blows me away. His eyes sparkle with it and his face lights up. I'm pulled into his smile as we close the small distance between us.

I'm so caught up; I lean in to kiss him but catch myself at the last minute and turn to kiss his cheek. Cam wraps his arms around me and pulls me into a hug. His cologne wraps around me as well, hugging me just as tight.

"How was the movie?"

"It was good. I needed the laugh," I reply.

"Oh yeah? Want to talk about it?"

"Not at all. I came to hang out with a friend and forget all of that drama."

"Then let's go. I plan to have a ton of fun kicking your ass in bowling," he says and frowns.

"What? What's that look about?"

"If I knew you were going to wear boots like that, I would have planned something else. It's going to be a shame for you to trade those out for them ugly-ass shoes."

I burst into laughter and shake my head. "Whatever, Cam."

"See. I already made you laugh."

I smile wide. "That you have. Now, about you kicking my ass. Not going to happen."

"We'll see."

He wraps his arm around my shoulders and leads me into the bowling alley. Cam keeps me laughing the entire time we're renting our shoes and setting up our game. We're having so much fun as we play neck and neck.

I think I take him by surprise when he sees how well I play. Both of our competitive sides come out. Cam throws another strike and turns to taunt me.

He looks so hot as he does a little celebration. I bite my lip as I watch him and the way his muscles flex beneath his T-shirt. Cam has this effortless way of drawing you in.

"Your turn, twinkle toes," he croons.

"You're celebrating like you've won or something. You do know I'm one strike away from tying this up for good."

"No way you're going to get another strike."

"Sounds like you want to place a wager."

He shrugs and pulls a face. "If you get another strike to tie the game, I'll buy you lunch for a week."

"If I didn't know better, I'd say you're just trying to get me to hang out with you during the week," I tease.

He winks at me and shrugs. "If you don't mind waiting around for me to finish practice, we can have lunch all week. Friends have lunch together."

"You know what, you're on. If I win, you're treating me to Chinese at least twice next week. Not for lunch, I want dinner," I say.

"You're on."

"At your place?"

He takes a pause to think for a second. I'm testing him. I feel like Cam has been trying to hide something from me.

I have a lot of nerve since I haven't told him my real name, but I'm still curious. He runs his hand through his hair and turns on that smile of his. I start feeling like a mouse caught in a trap.

"Yeah, sure. We can have dinner at my place. That's cool," he finally says.

"Deal."

I stand and grab my bowling ball. I go to take my turn, but Cam comes to stand behind me and wraps his arms around me. He leans to whisper into my ear.

"When you come to my place, make sure you don't dress like this. I don't know if I'll be able to keep my hands to myself. Especially if you smell this good."

I roll my eyes in my head and try not to moan. Butterflies fill my belly and that pulse between my legs that's starting to become a constant when I'm around him begins to throb viciously.

He begins to sway me in his arms as if we're dancing to our own music. I'm lost in the trance he's creating and almost forget I'm supposed to be taking my turn.

"Amina, you know you feel right in my arms, don't you?"

I open my eyes and gasp, coming back to my senses. Tears prick the backs of my eyes. I should be able to fall for someone like Cam. I'm being robbed of falling for someone of my choosing.

I tug free of his hold and make sure to miss a few pins. Being in Cam's space is the last thing I need. I don't want to get either of our hopes up for more than the friendship we have.

"Now you don't have to worry about any of that," I chirp as I turn to face him.

He narrows his eyes at me. "Best two out of three. Let's go again."

"I thought we were going to grab a bite. I'm starving. I'll even let you count this as one of my lunches." I smile sweetly with my words, but he keeps his gaze narrowed on me.

"My brother cooked, so we could go to my place," he says with a cocky grin.

"He'll be home? So it won't be just the two of us?"

"Yeah, he'll be there. He goes to bed early, but we can eat then hang in my room."

The pulse between my legs tells me this is not a great idea. I chew on my lip, thinking about accepting the offer, but my phone rings before I can answer. I pull it from my back pocket and groan, rolling my eyes as I scowl.

I guess Dez didn't get enough of telling me how much my life sucks because I'm going to marry him whether I like it or not. His timing couldn't suck more. I send the call to voicemail, not wanting to deal with him again tonight.

"Can I take a rain check? I think I should head home."

"Is that the drama you were talking about?" he asks and gestures his head toward my phone.

"Yeah, something like that."

"Cool. I won lunch with you for a week. I won't be greedy. Can I take you home? I can get in a few more laughs before I get you to your door."

"Sure, I would like that. I had fun, Cam. Thanks."

"No, darlin'. Thank you. This was the most normal date I've ever been on."

I hear a note of a story in those words, but I don't pry because I get the feeling that will make things too intimate between us. We are already skating a thin line. Instead of asking questions, I keep my mouth shut and go to change my shoes.

Cameron

I probably shouldn't have pushed things at the bowling alley, but I couldn't help myself. When she asked to come to my place, I couldn't help wanting to let my guard down with her. For a moment, I dared to dream about her being safe—being able to join the team.

If not as a support for Caleb, then a support for me. Sometimes I just need a space for me. I need time not only to be an individual but to decompress from being a shield and role model.

I wouldn't want my brother to have to count on anyone else to model after, but sometimes it's exhausting to have to remember I can't go with my first reaction. Especially when I've been doing so almost all my life. Caleb looks to me first for what's an appropriate response to situations and I can't fail him.

I think he would love Amina. I know her sarcasm would challenge him as much as mine does, but that would be good for him. He learns from immersion—fully being involved.

I hate to lose, even though I would have won either way. I only meant to distract her from making a strike. However, she threw her turn to lose.

I don't know how to feel about that. I might be coming on too strong. I've never felt this self-conscious in my life. Amina has made me think more and more about how much I haven't experienced because of my long-standing relationship with Kay.

"Cam?"

I come out of my thoughts as Amina calls my name. I glance at her in the passenger seat. She's looking back at me with her brows knitted.

"I'm sorry, what was that?"

I didn't mean to space out. I just haven't been able to stop thinking about the change in her face and body when her phone rang at the bowling alley. I've been wondering what's keeping her from giving me a real shot.

"You mentioned skating and hanging out again. I think skating would be fun."

"Want to go next weekend? I'm going to the team kickback the following weekend," I reply.

"Sounds cool. We can do that."

"Cool. I'm down."

"Tell me more about this kickback?"

"No big deal. Just the baseball team getting together for a bonfire or some shit."

I get ready to invite her but pause. Cal will need me to be there for him. I don't think it would be a good idea to introduce her for the first time that night.

Then there's the fact that I wouldn't know how to introduce her. I sort of don't want to be rejected either. If she tells me no because of our secret friendship, that's going to sting.

"Sounds fun. That's good for the team, right? Time to bond and get to know each other."

"Yup, that's what we're aiming for. I think it's going to be cool."

I find a spot to park so I can walk her to her door. Once I'm in the space, I get out of the car and round it to open her door. She steps out and I can't keep myself from allowing my gaze to roam over her.

She's so gorgeous no matter what she wears, but tonight, this outfit she has on makes me want to hold her close and keep her in my arms. My mind goes back to holding her in the bowling alley. That thought keeps me from tugging her into my embrace.

Again, I think my actions might have been too much. Several times during the night, I had to keep myself from kissing her. Those lips of hers are so sexy and inviting.

I clear my throat and take a step back. She looks up into my eyes, searching with her own. I have no doubt she feels this connection between us, but something is holding her back.

I'm trying not to pry or push. I want to respect her boundaries. It's my hope that, with time, she will tell me what's holding her back and then I can work around it.

I want Amina and I'm not going to walk away easily. The peace I have when I'm with her is worth fighting for. It's something I've never had.

"I'll text later," I say as we get to the front door of her apartment building.

"Thanks again for tonight. You make a great friend."

"You know, someday you're going to look back on how hard you tried to keep me in the friend zone, and you're going to regret the time we lost pretending this isn't already happening."

I lean in and peck the tip of her nose. "You make a great friend too. I know you're going to make an even better baseball wife." I wink and turn to leave.

With a glance over my shoulder, I find her staring after me with a dazed expression. I had to learn patience as a young boy. Amina has no idea how long I'm capable of waiting for what I want.

CHAPTER TWELVE

Burning Down

Kayleen

A month later …

"May I be excused?" I ask as I push my food around my plate.

"Of course, honey. I'm here if you need me," Mama says.

I push my seat back and stand. I think I'm going to be sick. Quickly, I rush from the dining room before I hurl.

"This can't be real, this can't be real," I repeat to myself with each step I take.

I'm trying not to hyperventilate as I stumble upstairs to my bedroom. It's like my entire world is falling apart. I never thought this day would happen to me and I still don't understand why it's happening.

My life used to be picture-perfect. Things like this aren't supposed to be happening. I'm so confused about how this is happening to me.

My parents are getting a divorce. They just told me over dinner. I had to get up and leave. There was no way I could sit there and choke down the rest of my food with a straight face and pretend like my entire world wasn't falling apart.

"This isn't happening. It can't be real. What the heck is going on?" I mumble.

In a daze, I stumble blindly into my room and flop down on the side of my bed. My thoughts are all over the place. I can't seem to get them to flow in a straight line.

Is this my fault? Would this be happening if I got into college and attended school like the rest of my friends? Why have my friends ditched me?

Did they see this coming, that I'm going to be a tragic case? Is it too late for me to do anything about this? Did Daddy cheat?

How didn't I see this coming? What's Mama going to do now? What's going to happen to my family?

Will my parents want me to move out now that they're separating? How do I stop all of this from happening? There are so many questions without answers.

I glance around my room, trying to find an answer to at least one question. Nothing, I find nothing. Instead, anger fills me, and I jump up to toss the pillows from my bed.

What's the point in everything looking perfect when it's not. Everything is far from perfect. Everything I thought I had is now slipping away, my boyfriend, my friends, my family.

Everyone is too busy to hang out, no one has time to talk on the phone. I feel so stupid for not having a solid plan for after high school.

Once the room is fully wrecked, I drop to my knees and gasp for air. What have I done? When I close my eyes, I can't see anything pass my night with Jareil.

Is this my punishment for sleeping with him? We've spoken a few times on the phone, but I feel guilty every time we do, so I stopped answering his calls.

My phone lights up somewhere underneath all the blankets and tossed pillows and sheets. I scramble to try to get to it, hoping it's someone I can talk to in order to make this all make sense.

When I find it, I frown and sag in my spot on the floor. It's only my alarm for my hair appointment tomorrow. I wonder if Sasha would hire me as an assistant; she's always talking about how she needs one.

My lips tremble as big, fat tears cling to my lashes and spill down my cheeks. I miss my friends. This is something I would go to Cam about or sit down with Kota and come up with ideas.

"I don't want to be alone," I sob.

I open my phone and pull up Cam's number. I really need to talk to him. When is he going to get over all of what happened? It's never been this long before.

My heart breaks when his number goes to voicemail. It's the same thing every time. This has been going on for the last month.

I only meant for us to take a break for a few weeks. The only reason I haven't gone to the apartment is because my mama told me to let Cam come to me. Well, she's getting a divorce, so I don't really think her advice is the best.

"Screw this," I growl.

I jump up to find my shoes and head out. However, as I go to storm from the room, my phone rings. Thinking it's Cam calling me back, I answer without looking at the caller ID.

"Hello," I sniffle.

"Kayleen? Are you all right?"

"JR." I sink to the floor in defeat. I really fucked things up with Cam. "No, I'm not. Can I call you back later?"

"You can, or you could talk to me and let me help," he says.

My heart skips a beat from his voice. I want to accept his offer. I cover my face with my hand as I begin to sob some more.

I want to talk to him and forget everything happening in my life. I open my mouth, but there's a knock on my door. I bite back my sobs and shake my head.

JR's family is perfect. I can't talk to him about this.

"I'll call you back. I promise," I whisper.

Cameron

"It sounds like you boys are settling just fine," Daddy says as we sit around the table having dinner at our parents' house.

They just got back from God knows where. I've lost track of all the places they've been this year. If they're not in one place, they're in another. It all sounds the same to me at this point.

"We are. The team is great, and Coach Snider thinks we'll both start this year," Caleb says.

Daddy gives him a proud smile. If I'm honest, Caleb has been doing great. Better than we expected he would in just a month.

His grades are amazing, as always, and his focus on the team has improved with each day. He has overcome any obstacles quickly. Our teammates love him and go to him for pointers all the time.

An adjustment here and there and it's all been smooth sailing. No one has asked why Kota and I are always around him; it's just become the norm. Doesn't hurt that our cousin is hot, and guys can't keep their eyes off her.

"That's great news. You sound happy. Let me know if there's anything I can do to help," Daddy says.

Caleb and I scoff down our first plates and move for seconds in unison. One thing I can say I miss about being home is the cooking. Mama can't cook for shit, but our chefs do a damn good job.

Caleb and I aren't huge for nothing. We've been eating like two vacuums since we were fifteen. I'm sure we'll both have a third plate before we get up from here.

Daddy watches us both with a huge grin on his face. Mama sits with her bird-portion plate, looking like she's trying to find something to say to us.

I feel the moment she's about to sour my appetite. The hairs on the back of my neck stand up and the air in the room shifts. I drop my fork and look up as I feel her eyes on me.

"Have you spoken to Kayleen?" she asks.

"Not in a while," I reply.

"You should give her a call. She's going to need her friends," she says cryptically.

I work my jaw. I don't know why I thought I would get to come here and not talk about Kay. I haven't forgotten about her. I've just been enjoying life without the drama.

Amina and I have been bowling, skating, and the movies. We've even had study sessions on late nights at a coffee shop not far from our neighborhood where not too many people would recognize us.

I'm getting used to smiling and laughing more in my life. Opening that door to Kay will open the door to all that shit I want to get away from. I want to enjoy this peace for a little while longer before I deal with Kayleen and the final decision on our future.

However, as her friend, I don't want to leave her high and dry if she needs someone to lean on. Kay has tons of friends, but we're her closest friend group. We're her safe place.

"Okay, I'll bite. What are you talking about?"

"Tammy Bell and Jimmy Dean are getting a divorce. I haven't got all the details just yet, but there's some stuff about the firm, a lawyer, and about some missing money. Somehow Jimmy Dean is caught up in the middle of everything and Tammy wants out," Mama says.

I scrub a hand up and down my face. That is fucked up, and knowing Kay like I do, she's probably taking it hard. I'm not ready to deal with us, but I can't allow her to go through this on her own.

"That's fucked up," Caleb says out of nowhere.

I turn to look at him and he's looking between me and my mama. I groan. He's not going to allow me to ignore this, just like my mama ain't.

"I'll give her a call," I grumble.

"That's my boy. Kay is family. We help our family in need," Mama says.

"You can be her support, but don't let that family's mess become your problem," Daddy says.

"How can you say that? Tammy Bell is like a sister to me," Mama gasps.

"And if I lost every dime tonight, would she be there to hold your hand?"

"I … I." Mama gives a nervous laugh.

"I don't think so," Daddy says with a frown. "She'd run away from you faster than a plate of wings trying to get away from a pan of grease. I think you're forgetting we have funds tied up in all this. It might be wise to separate ourselves from it all sooner rather than later."

"Tammy Bell and Kayleen have nothing to do with the mess Jimmy Dean has gotten himself into. I always knew Howell was good for nothing—he's the real one to blame.

"Jimmy Dean allowed him too much access. We're all getting burned because of that scumbag. This is probably why Jimmy couldn't make things happen for Kay to go to school with the boys," Mama huffs.

"I don't want to talk about this at this table. I thought we agreed we weren't going to share the details with the boys. You don't even know what Tammy and Jimmy told Kay. Cam, I'd use caution in what you say to Kay if you do talk to her. This is still a very delicate situation."

From the pointed look on my daddy's face, I get that my mama has shared a bunch of other folk's business that ain't none of mine. I'll keep that in mind.

I frown down at my unfinished food, no longer having an appetite. Pushing my plate away, I grab my glass and wash down the food I didn't get to finish enjoying.

Welcome home, Mama.

CHAPTER THIRTEEN

Chemistry

Cameron

They finally changed my late afternoon chemistry class for a morning one. Thank God for Dakota. She's been sitting in for me, taking notes for the last four weeks. The professor is super cool and understands the situation.

He even allowed me to take the two exams I missed during his office hours. He was actually the one who got me into his morning session. Friday was the only class I could get with him as my professor.

I'm dragging this morning because I was up all night talking to Kay. She's really fucked up over her parents. I still can't get my head around all the shit that's come to light since my mama brought it all up a week ago.

I'm lost in thought as I walk to class with my hands in my hoodie and my head down. I never got around to calling Amina yesterday. I hope I get to see her in the science building this morning.

She has a class here around this time. I remember that from the morning I ran her down. I hope we can hang out this weekend. After all the shit going on with Kay, I could use one of our good talks and a few laughs.

"Maribel, wait."

I lift my head as someone calls out. Looking ahead, I find Amina and the redhead she's always with. The redhead runs up to her and hands her something, then they hug and Amina ducks into the class I'm headed for.

With a smile, I pick up the pace and head to class. I want to surprise her, so I pull my hoodie low as I slip into the room quietly. The small lecture hall is already packed.

This course has one hour for lectures and one for labs. I'll have to make up a few labs in the next few weeks, but I'm not sweating it. Chemistry is one of my strong suits.

A grin comes to my lips as I find a seat a few rows behind Amina. I watch as she talks to another girl while she laughs. It's like people gravitate to her light.

Others flock over and join their conversation. I watch on, observing how gorgeous she is. I don't think she knows how effortlessly she holds everyone's attention.

The professor enters the hall and puts his bag and coffee cup down. He looks up at the little crowd around Amina and shakes his head. A smile comes to his lips.

"Why am I not surprised my star student is the center of everyone's attention. Miss Maribel Jones. Why don't you come to the front of the room? You can hand out the pop quiz I'm sure you're going to ace," the professor calls out.

I knit my brow and freeze as Amina stands and heads to the front of the room. Everyone else groans as they go to settle in their seats. I can't take my eyes off Amina.

"Hey Maribel, spill his coffee on the papers," someone calls.

Amina laughs and shakes her head at the guy who shouts out to her. I narrow my eyes as my chest begins to tighten. I'm confused.

Why would she tell me her name is Amina if it's Maribel? We've been friends for weeks now. I thought I could trust her.

Clearly, she doesn't trust me if she couldn't even tell me her real name. I feel sick. The one person I thought cared, the person I was beginning to trust and thought I could bring into my inner circle, is nothing but a fucking liar.

My eyes are glued to her as she moves up row after row, counting off quizzes and passing the stacks down. When she gets to my row, I push my hood back and stare right at her.

She freezes and drops the remaining quizzes to the ground. I get up and move to the end of the aisle to help her pick them up. She looks up at me nervously.

"Good morning, Amina. Or should I say Maribel?" I bite out.

"Cam, I can explain."

"Don't bother."

I grab a quiz for myself and hand her back the others. For the rest of the class, I act as if she doesn't exist. I turn my focus to my exam and keep it there.

When I'm done, I turn it in and head out of class. I'm fucking fuming. At least with Kay, I know what I'm getting.

How could she lie to my face for weeks? If she could tell one lie how many others has she told. All I wanted was someone to be real with me and who I could be real with.

"Fuck," I roar as I head toward the parking lot to get into my car and head home.

"Cam, wait. Cam."

I don't turn to acknowledge her. I'm too hurt to look at her right now. Trust is everything to me.

I almost risked my brother's future to have this girl in my life. If she could lie to my face like this, there's no telling the harm she could've brought to Caleb and my family.

"Cameron, please."

I round on her and glare. She stops running and walks to me slowly. So many things fall into place as my mind races.

The time I called her name, and she kept walking like she didn't hear me. The way she stiffened every time I called her Amina. I should've questioned it all from the beginning.

"What do you want?" I snarl.

"I want to explain."

"You don't owe me anything. I don't know you, so you don't have to explain anything to me. You have a good one, Maribel."

"Cam," she chokes out.

I shake my head at her. I have nothing else to say and I don't want to hear anything else.

I keep walking. I'm so pissed off I can't see straight. Un-fucking-believable.

"Hey, Cam."

I stop and freeze. Before I can pull my thoughts together, everything is turned on its head. This looks bad. This looks really bad.

Maribel

I swallow hard as Cam turns to walk away. From the moment I saw him in class, I could see the hurt in his eyes. This is my fault.

I should have told him the truth. I had planned to. I was getting sick of hearing him call me Amina. I just couldn't figure out how to tell him the truth.

Now, as he's walking away from me, I know I should have just come out and said it. He said he doesn't know me, that's a lie. Cam knows me better than most.

"Cam," I whisper once more.

He doesn't hear me, and he doesn't turn. My heart feels like it's spilling out from my body. That's when everything changes.

"Hey, Cam," the dark-haired girl walking toward him calls out.

She's pretty and tall like me. The way she rushes into Cam's arms speaks of a familiarity some random girl wouldn't have. She cups his face and kisses him.

I've never been punched so hard in my chest in real life, but this feels like I've been punched right in my heart by Tyson in his prime. I stumble back and wrap my arms around my middle.

I only lied about my name. Dez isn't my boyfriend. He's nothing to me, so I can't say I've been cheating on him with Cam. However, it looks like Cam has had a girlfriend all along from the way this chick is kissing him.

Cam looks into my eyes from over her head. I nod as I bite back my hurt feelings and turn to leave. This was never meant to be.

I played myself, getting involved with a guy I knew nothing about. At least I figured it out before I did something stupid like sleep with him. Although, I did fuck up and fall in love with him.

"This is for the best," I mutter as I head back to class for my bag.

CHAPTER FOURTEEN

I Want You Back

Kayleen

I'm not surprised when Cam tugs away from my kiss, but it still hurts. After our talk last night, I thought we could work things out. I didn't think he was going to answer my call, but I was happy when he did.

Getting to hear his voice made everything seem right in my world. He listened and made me feel better. When I woke this morning, I just wanted to see him and have that comfort in person.

That's why I went to his apartment. When I didn't find him there, Caleb told me Cam had a morning class over on this side of campus. It was good to see Caleb.

He seemed genuinely happy to see me as well. I came to campus, hoping I would find Cam. I almost gave up and then I saw him walking toward the parking lot.

I rushed to him, not even thinking. Now he's pushing me away and I feel silly. I tuck my hair behind my ear and take a step back.

"What are you doing here?" he murmurs.

"After talking to you last night, I realized how much I missed you. I miss us. I thought maybe we could talk and work things out," I say.

"Don't you have enough going on?"

"Yeah, Cam, I do. That's why I need some normalcy. I need something to be the way it should be. Something safe that I can count on.

"I know I can always count on you. We're safe. I miss knowing I can climb into your arms and have a safe place that I know," I plea.

Cam looks off in the distance for a moment, then shakes his head. I know he is mad at me, but the hard scowl on his face is throwing me off. After our call last night, I thought he had had enough time to cool off.

He looks back to my eyes and nods. His face softens slightly. I watch as it seems like a million thoughts cross his face and mind.

"Yeah, I know what you mean. Safe and familiar is something I need right now," he says.

I break into a face-splitting smile. My heart leaps for joy. I knew we wouldn't stay broken up. I move into his side, and we walk to his car.

Cameron

Kay is familiar. I can trust her. I was reaching for something I'll never have.

I don't get to choose my happiness. I never have and it seems like I never will be able to. So I might as well stick to what I know and can trust.

I know what I'm getting with Kay. I don't second-guess myself with her because our relationship is second nature. We're friends, we fight, we fuck, those are things I can expect from our relationship.

I could use a good fuck right about now. Something to erase Amina ... wait, Maribel from my mind. I was falling for her. I just don't understand.

"Cam?"

"What's up?"

I glance over at Kay, fidgeting in her seat. She looks back at me and smiles. Wow, has she always worn this much makeup?

I shake the thought off. Kay is pretty and she doesn't deserve to be compared to a fucking liar. I drop my eyes to her shirt, which is barely containing her cleavage.

I wonder if she knows her breasts would be just as sexy if she covered them up. Amina had this way of wearing things that weren't revealing but were still enticing, nonetheless.

Fuck, Cam. Let that shit go.

"I just wanted you to know how much I missed you. I'm sorry about everything. Our time apart showed me how much I love you and I can't see myself without you in my life," she says.

I have to grind my teeth as guilt fills me because I don't feel the same. I missed Kay as a friend. Not having her in my life? Yeah, I wouldn't want that if it meant I'd lose our friendship, but in a romantic sense, I might be all right.

"I missed you too," I reply as I feel her staring at the side of my face.

"Is something wrong?"

"No, just a lot on my mind with school. I just took a pop quiz. I'm not sure I did so well on it," I say.

"I'm sure you aced it. You and Caleb are crazy smart. You used to ace your tests without even studying.

"I guess I shouldn't have thought I could do the same. I flunked every time. Jokes on me, right?"

I sigh. I don't want to touch this one. It feels like a trap to take us back to where this all started. I don't want to start fighting already.

"You know. Community college isn't the worst thing ever. I'll help you with your classes if I can. Give it a year and you could transfer. Kota would help out, I'm sure," I say.

"I'll think about it. I don't know if any of that is an option at the moment. So much is going on at home. I know my parents aren't telling me something.

"They stop hissing at each other every time I enter the room. This divorce ... I can't help feeling like something bigger is happening."

I keep my mouth clamped shut. If only she knew. There is so much more to it. I feel bad for her. She's a daddy's girl and he's about to break her heart.

All I can do is be here for her when the shit hits the fan. Oh, it's going to hit and she's going to be devastated. Her family could lose everything when it's all said and done.

Rumor has it the divorce is an effort to try to at least leave Tammy and Kay with something before all Jimmy's assets are seized and frozen. I don't think Kay is going to take any of this well.

It's definitely time for her to start thinking about what to do with her future. She's not going to have Daddy's money to fall back on like she's always thought she would.

"Ugh, forget all of that. Want to rent a movie and get some takeout?"

"Sure, darlin', whatever you want," I murmur.

"I'm glad we're back together. There's so much I need to make up for," she purrs and reaches for my thigh.

My cock twitches in my sweats, cutting my words off when I go to tell her I never said we were back together. Working things out and being back together are two different things. Kay grabs my growing erection and gives it a squeeze.

Who am I kidding? We always end up back together. It's what we know.

CHAPTER FIFTEEN

Happy Holidays

Kayleen

Three months later …

The last three months have been tough, but Cam has been there for me. However, something about him has changed. It's like he's putting on a show for everyone else—pretending to be happy when he's really not.

We haven't been fighting as much, so I haven't asked him about the change because I don't want to trigger an argument. I give him space for practice and homework, but I do spend a lot of time at the apartment. At first, I thought it was another girl, but I know he doesn't have time for that.

Besides, I've been to a few of the parties on campus with him. He's never shown interest in any of the girls other than to help Caleb hook up for the night. I've never gotten in the way of that.

If Caleb is anything like Cameron in the sex department, I consider those girls lucky. As long as they don't get any ideas to turn back for my man, it doesn't bother me at all. I mean, I can't blame them. The twins are hot.

"You want me to make you something to eat?" Caleb asks as I tiptoe into the kitchen.

Cameron is still knocked out in his room. I haven't wanted to address the change, but it's starting to become an elephant in the room, and I have an idea of how I can breach the subject.

"No, I'm fine. Hey, listen. Your mama said she and your daddy will be downstairs in about twenty minutes. I thought we could let Cam sleep in a bit, and you can ride up with them. I'll ride up with him later. I know you wanted to hit the powder early," I whisper.

While the boys are on vacation, we're all headed up to the ski resort just before Christmas. My mama will be joining us, but my daddy has other plans. I'm still so confused by everything going on with them.

I could use a break from the two of them, to be honest. Cam and Cal will be heading back for Christmas day to go to a game their daddy bought them tickets to. Cam asked me to join them in the box, but basketball isn't my thing. I would just be bored.

I plan to return with them, but I have plans with some friends of my own. However, I thought Cam and I could lag behind to spend some time alone before being thrown into all the holiday fuss with our families. This way, we could talk.

Caleb purses his lips and squints. I know this wasn't the plan, but I'm hoping this doesn't throw him off too much. Caleb loves to snowboard. I'm hoping that will outweigh everything else.

"I don't know. Cam and I had plans to board together. I don't want him to miss out. Are you sure he'll be okay with this?"

"He should be fine. I'm sure your daddy wouldn't mind taking Cam's place. Some time for the two of you alone," I say.

It's no secret Mr. Perry wants a closer relationship with Caleb. I know he would love to have this time with his son. Mr. Perry loves both his boys, but he struggles with showing them how much because Mrs. Jemma is always at something.

I love the woman like my own mama, but at times, she can be hard to deal with. However, she's in on this plan to help me get some time with Cameron, so I can't complain too much.

"All right, if you think Cam won't mind. He better not get mad at me, Kayleen. I'm going to blame you," he says.

He gives me an adorable smile and I can't help but return it. I love this guy. He's so darn sweet. I truly hope he gets all he dreams of.

"I'll take the blame. You have fun up there. I'll take a trip down with you once we arrive, that cool?"

"Cool. I can't wait. We're still on for hot chocolate by the fire, right?"

I smile. "Of course. I've never missed a year."

It's something we've been doing since we were little. Kota, myself, and the guys always have a cup in front of the fire and we exchange one gift. A secret Santa gift. I got Kota this year. I can't wait to see her face.

"Okay, I'll see you later," he says as he cleans up all the food he had out to make breakfast earlier.

I quietly return to Cam's room. As quietly as I can, I grab his phone and turn off the alarm he set for us to wake. Putting the phone back, I slip back into bed.

A sigh leaves my lips as his warm body heats me up instantly. I always feel so cozy lying next to him. As I lie here, I have no doubts that I could do this for the rest of my life.

I want to belong to Cam. We can make this happen. Some alone time is just what we need.

Cameron

I wake with a sharp breath. Something feels wrong right away. I jump up and grab my phone to check the time.

"What the fuck?" I hiss.

Ah no, no, no. Fuck.

Caleb wanted to hit the powder first thing this morning. We needed to be out of the door four hours ago. How the fuck did I oversleep?

This is all he's been talking about for the last three weeks. Why didn't he come in here and wake me up? As that thought floats through my head, my heart begins to race.

I jump up and race out of the room. When I get to Cal's room, he's not there. I knit my brows and turn for the living room and kitchen area. However, I don't find him there either.

"What the fuck is going on?" I mutter.

I race back for my phone and call Cal. I have so many scenarios going through my mind. My alarm was set. It should have woken me up. If not the alarm, then I know Cal, and he would have woken me up.

"Hello," Cal answers his phone.

"Yo, bro. Where the fuck are you?"

"I'm at the resort having lunch with Daddy. Did you and Kay leave yet?"

"You're at the resort?"

"Yeah, I rode with Mama and Daddy like Kay asked me to. Is everything all right?"

"Yeah, everything is fine. I'll see you when I get there."

"Okay. I love you, Cam. Snowboarding with Daddy was fun. We have to get him to join us next time. Be safe; it's been snowing up here."

"I love you too, bro. I'm glad you're having a good time. I'll be there as soon as I can."

I hang up and I'm fuming. I storm back to my room and find Kay sitting up from the spot where she had lain beside me. If looks could kill, she would be finished.

"Have you lost your fucking mind?" I snarl.

"What? What did I do wrong?"

"You sent my brother to the resort with my mama without me? Did you bump your fucking head, Kay? How could you?"

I chew her out while tugging on sweats. I need to get there before my mother causes a disaster. There's no telling what could happen if she triggers him.

"Cam, slow down. I thought we could spend some time together and your mama suggested Cal ride up with her and your daddy. Caleb seemed excited to go. Why are you overreacting?"

"Overreacting? Overreacting? Why are you acting like you didn't grow up around my family?

"That time Cal broke his arm after losing his shit? Who set him off?"

"Your mama, but—"

"That time on the boat when he cracked his fucking head, what happened before he freaked out and I tried to get him below deck?"

"Your mama had—"

"I blinked for a fucking second to take pictures with you for prom. Cal ended up having a seizure right there on the front porch. Who stressed him the fuck out and caused it?"

"Your mama was only trying to—"

"My mama, my mama, my mama. Do you see the problem here? That woman is a trigger whether she knows it or not.

"I'm the buffer. I'm the shield. You took my brother's safety away. Once again, you've placed him in a fucked-up situation."

"Shit, I wasn't thinking. I figured we'd be right behind them. I just wanted to give us a chance to talk," she says.

I ignore her and pull up the app to check the weather. We all had planned to leave early this morning because a storm was supposed to come in.

Rage fills me as I look down at my phone. This can't be happening. I'm fucking sick to my stomach.

"Fuck," I bellow.

"What? What is it?"

"They're closing the roads up there. The storm already hit. We're not going to get through."

"Oh no, I'm so sorry, Cam."

"Why?" I demand.

"Why what?"

"Why do you keep allowing her to manipulate you? My mama uses you to get her way. You're such an easy target for her."

"How did she manipulate me? I didn't think anything was wrong with spending a little extra alone time with my boyfriend. We needed some time to talk."

"Then talk to me. Don't go doing shit behind my back that fucks with my brother's well-being."

"You say that now, but you've been ... ugh. I can't explain it. It feels like we're drifting apart."

"Kay, for once, we haven't been fighting. Things have been good. If you had talked to me, you would have known I worked things out with Kota so we could share a cabin alone. She and Cal were going to take the girls' cabin this year," I bite out.

"Oh."

"Yeah, oh. Now I'm not going to be with my family for Christmas and my brother is trapped with my crazy-ass mama with no me to back her down."

"We can try in the morning. I really am sorry."

I stand and head for the door. I'm done talking to her. I swear, she's turning into my mama and it's getting on my last nerve.

"Where are you going?"

"To take a shower. Don't be here when I get out. I'll pick you up in the morning if they open the roads."

"You'd rather be here alone? I said I'm sorry."

"I might change my mind later, but right now, I need you to go."

"Okay, I'm sorry, Cam."

CHAPTER SIXTEEN

Need a Friend

Maribel

"Why aren't you on your flight?" Dez growls into the phone.

"I missed it. I had to stay to work on an assignment my professor gave me an extension on," I say.

That's total bullshit. I don't want to go home to be around my father or Dez. I'd rather be anywhere but there. I missed that flight intentionally, but he doesn't need to know that.

I would rather spend my Christmas and New Year alone than go back home to be around Dez or my dad. My father isn't listening to me when I tell him I'm over this and it's not what I want. It's like I'm screaming into an empty room with no one to hear me.

"I will book you for a flight in the morning."

"And I won't be on that either. I will be here until the first of the year. I can't leave before then. I promised my mom I'd drop in for a few quick days after the new year."

He sighs heavily on the other end. I roll my eyes. You would think he would get the point by now.

"Maribel, I'm not asking you to come home. I'm telling you. If you're not here by the opening of the year, I will come there, and you won't be finishing the semester.

"You will be barefoot and pregnant within the year. That's a promise. Do you understand me?"

"What the heck is the rush?"

"Not that I need to explain myself, but there are moves being made in my world. I need to establish myself and my role before those things come to fruition. In order to take my brother's place, I need a wife.

"You are that wife, Maribel. You were promised to me. I don't take promises lightly," he says.

My stomach twists. I still don't get how I fit into all of this. I have no idea why my father decided to promise me off to this man. Heck, he wasn't even a man when this promise was made.

"I need to get back to my assignment. I'll talk to you later," I mumble.

"Merry Christmas, Maribel. I will have your gift when you arrive."

I shiver in disgust, not liking the way his words come out. I don't want anything from him but my freedom. I hang up before he can say anything else.

I toss my phone down and bury my face in my knees as I sit on the couch with my legs pulled into my body. I'm still in my PJs. This apartment feels so empty without Taylor here.

She left for Christmas break a few days ago. I waited until the last minute to book a flight I knew I wasn't going to take. I want to scream and tear my hair out.

At this point, I don't even care about the money. My father can keep the fucking trust. It's not like I'm going to miss it.

I don't mind working for my own. However, at this point, I don't think I'm going to get to walk away no matter what I want. I fucking hate my life.

"I should fake my death," I mutter and punch the couch.

I need to get out of here and get some fresh air. It's like everything is suffocating me. The loneliness, the demands, my thoughts.

I'm eighteen. I should be enjoying my life, not dreading my future with each day that passes. I stand and stomp my way into my room. Tearing off my pajamas, I jump into the shower.

The warm spray does wonders, but it's not enough. This feeling of despair won't wash away. I can't believe this is my life.

"Come on, Maribel. You can figure this out. You don't have to do anything you don't want."

I shut the water off as determination fills me. It's time to come up with a plan. I will get the last say on my life.

I return to my room and throw on some clothes to make a trip to the store. I could use some ice cream and cookies to help me think.

Construction boots on my feet and my favorite black jeans on my legs, I'm all set to head out. I toss on my jacket and hat, then grab my small bag and leave. My stomach grumbles on my way out, so I decide to get some Chinese while I'm at it.

I make the trip to grab my food first. I'm grateful when I arrive and I'm able to place my order quickly. Once I have my order in tow, I make my way to the supermarket.

I'm staring at the ice cream when I get this feeling and turn. A gasp leaves my lips as I find Cameron standing with a scowl on his face as he looks into the freezer before him.

He turns to look in my direction and I can see the sadness in his eyes. He also looks like he might have been crying at some point. My feet are moving toward him without my permission.

"Hey, are you all right?"

He shakes his head no as he swallows hard. I note the bag of Chinese in his hand and smile. We think a lot alike.

I lift my bag to show him. "I've got dinner for one. Pretty sorry, right?"

He lifts his bag to show me. "No, I have the same. Just deciding on which flavor will fuck my stomach up once I scarf all this shit down."

"I was going to go with the vanilla bean since they don't have eggnog. That or rum raisin."

"If I buy you one of each, would you hang with me?"

"Your girlfriend isn't going to have an issue with that?"

"Amina," he pauses and clears his throat. "Maribel, Kay and I weren't together when we were hanging out."

"My name is Amina."

"No, I'm serious. We were on a break, and I liked you. Kay and I—"

"No, Cam. Amina really *is* my name. It's my middle name. Maribel Amina Jones is my full name. I never lied. It's just—"

"Complicated," he finishes for me.

"Yeah, complicated."

"I miss my friend. It's been a long fucked-up day. You want to come to my place, and we can clear things up on both our ends?"

I nod. "I think that would be cool."

I've missed him and our talks. I could use a friend right now more than he could ever know. With a smile, he grabs a few pints of ice cream from the brand he was staring at and we head to the register.

This is the lightest I've felt in months. I probably shouldn't open myself up so easily, but this is Cam. This is the safe feeling he brings out of me.

"Maribel is just as pretty," Cam says with a smile as he pays for our ice cream.

"Thank you."

We walk out of the store once our purchase is made. I'm surprised when he turns to head in the direction of my cousin's building. I didn't know we lived so close to each other.

When we get to his place, I note that we're only about two blocks away from each other. We're quiet most of the way. It's once we step into his apartment that he begins to speak.

"It's not much, but it's home," he says as he takes my coat from me.

I kick off my boots as he takes off his, then I follow him to the kitchen, where we put down our food, and he puts away the ice cream.

"Are you kidding? This place is nice. You're really neat for a guy."

"That would be my brother's doing. He's the neat freak," he replies.

"Is he here?"

A frown comes to his face. "No," he bites out. "He's with my parents on a ski trip."

"Why do you sound so angry about that?"

I take my egg roll out and start on it as he grabs glasses and forks. He pours me a glass of punch and grabs himself a sports drink. I smile my thanks as he settles on the stool beside me.

"My brother is prone to having seizures when stressed. I got a call from my dad about an hour or two ago." He shakes his head. "I lost track of time in my anger. He's had one while there. I was supposed to be there, but I'm not," he seethes.

"Cam, you can't blame yourself for something like that. Is he okay?"

He snorts as he stabs at his rice. If I didn't know better, I'd think he was stabbing at someone's face in that container. I get that he's protective of his brother, but I don't see how he believes this is his fault.

"He's in the hospital, but my father says he'll be fine. And you're wrong. If I were there, I could have kept it from happening."

"Why aren't you there? It sounds like something happened."

"Something did. I was supposed to leave out with the rest of my family early yesterday morning so we'd all beat the snow. I got left behind and the roads were snowed out before I could leave."

"Oh, I'm sorry. That sucks."

"Yeah, it does, but why did you lie about your name?"

I tilt my head as I take him in. Clearly, he wants to get the conversation off him and his brother. From the redness in his eyes and the hurt on his face, I take the hint.

"I can't believe I'm about to say this out loud. I haven't told anyone, not even my mom. Would you believe me if I told you I'm engaged?

"Well, I'm supposed to be. I keep dodging the official announcement and the guy I'm supposed to be engaged to. I came here for college to get away from him and my dad, who's trying to arrange this marriage in the first place," I say.

Cam stabs his fork into his food and places the carton on the countertop. He looks back at me in shock. I look down at my fingers and fidget with them.

"Wait, what?"

"I didn't give you my real name because I hadn't planned on getting to know you. With all the drama I have going on, I didn't want to drag anyone into any of it. I gave you a fake name, thinking I'd never see you again.

"Then we kept running into each other and ... Cam, you were a choice I got to make. A friendship I chose and wanted. I knew I couldn't have more, but I didn't want to give up what we had either.

"I was afraid to tell you my real name because it was going to take away ... I don't know. It doesn't make sense to me anymore. I hurt you and that wasn't my intention.

"I'm sorry. God, you have no idea how good it feels to finally say it all out loud," I say and bite my lip.

"That's crazy. Just back this up a bit for me, darlin'. Let me make sure I understand this.

"You're being forced to marry some guy you don't want, so you ran off to Texas. To come here to hide from that engagement? And here I was, trying to force you into a relationship with me.

"I'm the one who's sorry, Maribel. Fuck, so much makes sense now. I'm so sorry."

"You didn't know. You couldn't have known. It's so crazy. I didn't want anyone to know.

"I couldn't even go home for Christmas because he's waiting for me and wants to throw an engagement party. I thought I had more time, you know? The next four years.

"I thought I could figure out a way out by then. I can't marry him. It should be my choice who I fall in love with and marry," I whisper the last part.

"I understand more than you think. Trust me, I do," he says.

I look at him and knit my brows. He reaches for a napkin and then wipes the tears I hadn't noticed I allowed to fall. Grabbing his food and drink, he gestures for me to follow him.

We go into the living room and sit on the couch. Cameron then begins to tell me all about Kay, his childhood friend who became his girlfriend. I feel like I learn about a whole different side of Cam.

***

"You know, I've been wanting to ask you something for a while," I say as I lie on the couch, staring up at the ceiling. Cam is sitting on the floor with his back against the couch while we digest our food.

I've grown more comfortable with each passing second. I think he's been able to get his mind off his own worries as well. We've fallen back into our familiar friendship.

"What's that?" he asks.

"How did the Jodeci thing come about? I mean, I expected you to be a Garth Brooks fan, Shania Twain, Keith Urban maybe. Not Jodeci."

Cam laughs. "Do you remember The Box?"

"Yeah, I remember wanting to call in so bad, but my mom would have whooped my butt."

"Well, my parents were never around to keep us from getting into shit, so I would call in to order videos all the time.

"The fucked-up part was, you had to wait through all the other videos for yours to come up."

"Right, it would take hours. My friends would call in at their houses and I always had to leave before we got to see our video," I snicker.

"One night, I was sitting up waiting for a video. I couldn't even tell which one it was now if you asked. What I do remember is these four cool-ass guys in the desert.

"Wearing leather pants. That shit was so fire. Someone else thought it was too, because it came on, like, a dozen times before my video did.

"By the time my video did come on, I had called in for their video to play again and I had their moves memorized. I went out and got all their shit I could find after that."

"'Cry for you'? You got hooked off the 'Cry For You' video?"

"Baby, I'm begging, baby, I'm begging, begging, begging," he croons.

I burst out laughing. It makes so much sense. Our dance at the party. I can tell he spent time watching and mimicking those videos.

"I do like Garth, Shania, and the others, but Jodeci is my shit. I know every album, every track, every word. If I play one of their songs for you, you know I mean the words from my heart."

"You don't know each album by track. That's bullcrap," I scoff.

"Want to try me? I have all their albums in my playlists. Pick a track, I'll give you the album and title of the song. Here, take my phone," he says after grabbing the remote to turn on the sound system and connecting his device.

I smile as I see the collection of albums on his phone. I go for the earliest album and look through the list. I click on one of the songs and wait for it to play.

Cam looks me in the eyes with a smile on his face. As soon as the intro plays, his eyes light up and his smile grows.

"Track two. "Come & Talk to Me." The *Forever My Lady* album. It's also track three on the *Back to the Future-The Very Best of Jodeci* album," he says confidently.

"Oh, come on, it didn't even start. How could you know that?"

"Hit me with another. Try something you know wasn't one of their popular songs. Make it hard for me."

I go to another album to do as he says. I bite my lip as I choose the next one. I click on the next song and look up into his eyes.

The smile that comes to his face makes my belly flip. He allows his gaze to roll over me before he answers. I sit up and clear my throat.

"Track twelve. 'Let's Do It All.' *The Show, the After-Party, the Hotel* album," he says as heat fills his eyes.

I tune into the lyrics and realize my mistake. I quickly jump from that album and find something else. The song comes on and Cam stands and holds his hand out.

I hesitantly take his hand and stand with him, dropping his phone on the couch. He pulls me into his arms and begins to sway me in his embrace. He looks me right in the eyes.

I'm lost in his gaze. My heart is pounding and that pulsing between my legs is happening.

"'What About Us.' Track four. *Diary of a Mad Band* album. Also track nine on the *Back to the Future-The Very Best of Jodeci* album. This one is perfect," he murmurs.

As Jodeci croons about being in need of love, I know I should back away. It might even be time to go. However, instead of running like I should, I wrap my arms around his neck.

I bite my lip as my mind screams all the reasons we shouldn't do this. He's angry with his girlfriend, but they're not on a break this time. I have a madman waiting for me to return to marry him.

As much as we feel like we should be together, we can't be. Cam reaches beneath my hair and palms the back of my neck. When I look into his eyes, I can see him pleading for something, but I can't give him an answer as my own confusion takes over.

He dips his head to kiss me, but I duck at the last minute and his lips meet my forehead. He allows his lips to linger against my skin as I drop my arms from around his neck and place my hands on his waist.

"Sorry," he says and releases me to back away.

"Cam, I—"

"We're friends. We both have a lot of shit going on. Kay doesn't deserve this.

"This isn't who I am. I'm sorry. Thanks for the company. You really took my mind off things. Let me walk you home."

I nod. "Okay, thanks. I had fun. Maybe we can text or hang out sometime, like we used to."

"I'd like that. I'll definitely stop giving you the cold shoulder in chem class."

I snort. "Yeah, same here."

I go to collect my trash and empty containers while he grabs our coats. I don't really want to leave and go back to my lonely place, but he's right. I'm not that girl. I'm not about to sleep with someone else's boyfriend.

"Maribel, can I call you Amina?"

I turn to look up at him and smile. "My mom calls me Mina. It's been my nickname since I was little."

"I like that. Is it okay for me too?"

"Yeah, Mina or Amina are fine."

"Cool. Mina?"

"Yes, Cam?"

"Don't give up. Things will work out. I believe you'll find a way out."

"Thanks, Cam. I needed to hear that. I think you and Kay will figure things out too. Sounds like you two used to be good friends. Try to keep that in mind.

"We grow up and life changes, but true friendships have a way of lasting. Don't give up on the good things," I reply.

He looks like he's going to say something, but he clamps his mouth shut and shakes his head. So much has changed this evening. I think I have a friend for life.

I look down at the time on my phone. "Cam?"

"Yeah?"

"Merry Christmas."

"Merry Christmas, Mina," he says and kisses my cheek.

CHAPTER SEVENTEEN

Games & Tempers

Cameron

Caleb wasn't going to make it back for the game, for which my father got us a box for Christmas, so I texted Maribel to ask her to come along with me. I was afraid she would say no at first. Kay didn't want to come when I asked her after Daddy first gifted us the box.

It made sense for him to get us a box when the gift was for me and Caleb. I would have felt dumb going all on my own. Maribel was all for it.

I'm glad I asked her. This has been so much fun. I haven't laughed this much in I don't know how long. I'm enjoying myself so much I've been trying not to excuse myself to go to the bathroom.

However, if she makes me laugh one more time, I'm going to pee myself. That would be so fucking embarrassing. Not wanting to totally ruin the night by wetting myself like a toddler, I give in.

"I'll be right back. I need to use the bathroom," I say and stand up.

"Dude, I've had to go for the last twenty minutes," she laughs.

"Thank God there are two in here. You better handle your business."

"Okay, let's go. Break," she says and claps her hands before she takes off for the restroom.

I run for the other one and make it just in time. I find myself smiling as I relieve myself. We have to do something like this again.

I wonder who this guy is she's supposed to marry. I get the feeling he's not some ordinary guy. My dad has connections, but I don't think he has the kind Maribel needs to get free of this guy she's supposed to marry.

"There has to be a way," I muse.

I don't just want to help her because I want her. She's my friend and that shit is terrible. Kay and I will never get married if something doesn't change.

I shiver at the thought. I couldn't stomach being married to a version of my mama. Kay isn't as bad, but was my mama the way she is now when my daddy married her? I doubt it.

I feel bad sometimes because I don't think Daddy would still be with her if she didn't have me and Cal. It's not that he doesn't love her. I've seen when he looks at her and the love is there.

I've also seen when she's pissed him off and he looks like he wants to toss her overboard and tell everyone she slipped and there was nothing he could do. However, the days of wanting to toss her seem to have become more frequent than any.

I don't want to live my life like that. I've been thinking a lot about all the things I do want. I'm starting to realize that while I love playing baseball, I'm not sure if I want to play in the majors.

I'll do it for Cam, but if he doesn't go, I don't think I plan to try. I also don't know if I ever want to get married. Not as soon as my Mama and Kay have planned for me.

I don't know that I've experienced anything that I should have before jumping into all that. I've watched a hell of a lot of porn, but I've only ever been with one girl. Sure, I know what I like, but I don't know if there are things I would like more or things I wouldn't like at all.

At eighteen, I know I haven't lived. I couldn't imagine being married off to some stranger. Maribel is so strong for trying to deal with all of this on her own.

"Kay's not a stranger, but aren't you dealing with the same thing?" I mutter as I go to walk out of the bathroom.

When I step out, I freeze. My blood begins to boil. I don't even think, I react.

My fists are flying before I can check myself. I start knocking motherfuckers out; I might ask questions later. What I'm not expecting is for my friend, who I think I'm protecting, to jump in.

Maribel

I can't stop dancing as I cover the seat to be able to pee. I get it covered just in time. The conversation and laughter had been too good to interrupt to excuse myself to go to the restroom.

I was grateful when Cam said he had to go. I relieve myself and roll my eyes in my head as I do. God, this feels good.

I was going to burst if I didn't go when I did. I smile as I go to finish my business. Cam is such a fun person. At first, I thought it was weird that his father got a box for just him and his brother.

I had reservations when he texted earlier, asking me to come along. However, not wanting to spend Christmas alone overrode all those thoughts. I'm glad it did.

Not thinking about all the other things going on in my life for the night has been good for me. I've laughed and smiled and felt joy just like you're supposed to on the holidays. I wish my life was like this all the time.

When I step out of the bathroom, there are some guys in the box. I think nothing of it at first. Maybe Cam invited some of his other friends. That would make sense after that near kiss last night, or should I say early this morning.

"Hey, sugar. Don't you look sweet," one of the guys says.

I take a closer look at those guys, and I don't think they're friends of Cam's at all. One is helping himself to the wings while another is sucking down beer like he's just stepped out of the desert.

"I'm sorry, but were you invited in here?" I say as I look around at the four guys in our booth.

I've heard of box crashers in New York. I wouldn't put it past folks here in Texas. People will people just about anywhere.

The guy scoffing down the wings looks me over. I glare back at him. However, it's the one who spoke that moves to get right up in my face.

"Sure, we were. The Perrys told us to come right on in and have a bite. Didn't know we were going to get a sweet thing like you too," he purrs while one of the other guys goes to the door and locks it.

I remember Perry being printed outside the room when we arrived so it would be easy for them to know the name of the party renting this box tonight. I take a step back from the guy standing in front of me as I piece together what's going on here. He reaches out and grabs me by the arm.

I go to shove him, but Cam comes out of nowhere and grabs the guy by the shoulder before he knocks him out. The guy falls to the ground, looking stiff.

Then all hell breaks loose. The other three guys try to jump Cam, but Cam keeps swinging. He's doing just fine on his own, but where I'm from, you don't stand there and watch your friend get jumped.

I tap one of the guys on the shoulder and when he turns to swing on me, I duck and come up with a two-piece.

My hits land with precision. A jab to his face and then an uppercut to his jaw. He doesn't drop right away, being a bigger dude, so I go for another combo.

However, before I can land my attack, he pops me with a good one in the face. I could have ducked it, but I was already in motion to throw a punch and stupidly left my face open. I can feel it throbbing, but I ignore it and get to work on his ass.

Two to the body as I duck low, then I come up for another uppercut. This time, he folds like a bag of potato chips. I don't take time to admire my work as the other two are still trying to attack Cam.

However, as I go to help, Cam lays one guy out and puts the other in a naked choke hold. Once he drops the guy to the floor after he puts him to sleep, he rushes to pull me into his arms.

"Are you all right? What happened?"

"I came out of the bathroom and they were in here. I thought maybe you knew them and had invited more friends to join us, but then something didn't seem right. You came out as they locked the door and were about to try something," I say.

"Fuck, I'm sorry. Let me call security and get someone in here."

Cameron rushes to unlock the door and steps halfway out the door to call for help. Tell me why I'm not surprised when I end up in cuffs along with the guys who tried to attack me.

Cam is fuming as he tries to tell them I'm his guest. No one will listen to him, and soon he's in cuffs too. Damn, this guy has a temper.

I probably could have de-escalated the situation without his help if he wasn't losing his shit. Instead, I learned that you don't mess with what's Cam's. Tonight, I belonged to Cam—as he made so very clear.

Yay, Merry Christmas, everyone.

CHAPTER EIGHTEEN

My Daddy

Cameron

This is un-fucking-believable. Those assholes broke into our box and ruined our night. How the fuck did Maribel and I end up in cuffs?

I had no choice but to call my daddy to get us out of this mess. He said he'd be on a plane or helicopter or whatever would get him here fastest to get us out of here. I'm pissed because he should be with Caleb, not coming to rescue me.

He didn't sound happy about this, but he wasn't about to let them cart me and Maribel off to jail. That's what they were trying to do at first. This is all bullshit.

Everything was fine until one of the security guards started acting like an asshole while questioning Maribel. I saw this shit coming and I exploded without thinking. Sometimes I believe having Cal around is a good thing for me. I think first when he's with me.

"Cameron, what the heck is going on?" Daddy growls as he storms into the room they've been holding us in.

I stand with my hands still behind my back. Maribel is sitting with an ice pack against her cheek, but her hands are still cuffed as well. The only reason she has the ice pack is because I threatened to sue once this was all straightened out.

"We did nothing wrong. Those guys crashed our box and then tried to attack my friend. It was self-defense. I mean, look at her fucking face. They locked the door and had planned to assault her, not knowing I was on the other side of the restroom door," I say.

Daddy looks to Maribel with his mouth hanging open. When he gets a look at her holding the ice pack to her face, rage fills his eyes. He moves closer and holds out his hand.

"I'm Cam's daddy. Kyle Perry. Nice to meet you, darlin'. You mind if I take a look?"

She drops her hands to shake his as best she can with the cuffs on. Daddy hisses when her face comes into view. Her cheek has a huge bruise on it.

"The other guy looks much worse. I'm Maribel. It's nice to meet you, sir."

"None of that. You call me Kyle. You're a pretty little thing. Not even that little bruise there can take that away from you."

"I hope not. I would hate to have to sue your son for my failed modeling career."

Daddy narrows his eyes at her, but the wrinkle line around his eyes forms as he realizes she's just pulling his leg. He rumbles with laughter and throws his head back. When he finishes his laugh, he looks at me with a smile.

"She has your smart-ass sense of humor. I like her." He then turns on his heels. "I bought that box for my sons to enjoy with their friends. If you don't get them out of those cuffs in the next five seconds, I'm going to have all your jobs, and you'll never work within the next three states bordering any side of Texas."

The asshole who started all this rushes to uncuff me first. I tug away from him. "Get hers off first. She should've never had them on," I snarl.

He pulls a face but goes to uncuff Maribel as he mutters under his breath. One of the others comes to uncuff me. I rub my wrists as I move over to Maribel.

"Hey, you okay?"

"Yeah, I'm fine," she says.

"This isn't over. I'll deal with the stadium later. Let's go get something to eat.

"You can tell me why you like hanging with this guy instead of spending Christmas with your family," Dad says.

I stiffen. The last thing I want is for her to feel pressured into talking about her situation. However, in true Maribel fashion, she surprises me and makes my dad laugh again.

"I only hang with guys willing to fight for me. Your son is hot and he can throw hands, so I'm giving him my time this year. He was lonely and a little desperate for a friend.

"In the spirit of Christmas, I took pity on him. I mean, look at him," she replies.

"Whatever, Rocky," I chuckle.

She winks at me. "I told you I got hands."

"That you did, darlin'."

Kayleen

I should be having fun with my friends, but I've been sulking in the corner by myself. This party would be more fun if Cam were here. However, he's not speaking to me.

We haven't spoken since the afternoon when he threw me out. I learned from my mama that Caleb did, in fact, have a seizure, so I can't blame Cam for not speaking to me. Once again, I fucked up.

When I saw we weren't going to make it through to the resort the next morning, I knew it was only going to get worse. I texted Cam to see if he wanted to spend Christmas Eve together since our families were out of our reach, but he didn't bother answering me back.

"Why the long face? Santa didn't bring you what you wanted?"

I look up into the pretty honey-brown eyes of JR. He has his curls pulled back off his face, showing off his clean edges. He smiles down at me and his entire face lights up with it.

He has such a beautiful smile. Flashes of him smiling up at me as I rode his dick fill my head. I clear my throat as if that will clear my mind.

"I wouldn't know what Santa brought me. All my gifts are at a resort I never made it to," I reply.

"Wow, that's messed up."

"It's my own fault. I ruined everyone's Christmas this year."

"Really? Come on, you sure you're not being too hard on yourself?" He sits next to me and bumps me with his shoulder.

"Nope, not at all. It was me. I did it. I meant well, but my actions were selfish."

"Is that why you're over here all by yourself? Cam didn't come out with you tonight?"

"He had tickets to a basketball game. I'm sure that's where he is. Or maybe not. I don't know if he still went alone. Caleb couldn't go with him."

"He didn't want to take you instead?"

"I told him I didn't want to go when he first got the tickets. I don't mind cheering at a game, but I'm not big on sitting in a box to watch one."

"Are you going to feel that way about watching me play one day?"

I groan. "Please don't ask me to come. I'm already trying to put on a brave face to go to Cam and Cal's baseball games and they're not even in the majors yet."

"Does Cam know how much you hate going to games?"

I laugh. "God no, are you kidding me. I'm never going to tell him either."

"Well, I guess asking you to come out to Louisiana to see me play is out."

"Why would you want that? I barely answer your calls. Aren't you tired of trying with me?"

He leans into my ear. "Kayleen, I still think about you sucking my dick before you hopped back on it to ride me. That night was amazing. When I think of you, I can still feel you around me.

"No, I'm not tired of trying. One of these days you're going to look up and see you have all you want right here. When that day comes, I'll be waiting."

I bite my lip as I look into his eyes. I won't lie and say I haven't thought about that night. I spent a lot of time thinking about it before Cam and I got back together. The guilt just wouldn't allow my mind to linger.

"This is wrong. You and Cam are friends. We can't hook up again," I breathe.

"Your lips are saying one thing while your eyes are saying another. Cam is a friend. If I didn't feel so strongly about you, I would back off.

"However, I know we're meant to be together more than you and Cam are. You guys have this thing between you because you grew up together. It's a friendship, I respect that, but what you and I have is something more."

"What makes you so sure of that?"

He leans in and takes my lips. Butterflies take off in my belly. I should pull away, but I don't. Instead, I open my mouth for his tongue to enter.

He groans and cups my face. It does feel different, which makes me confused. How can I love someone but want to sleep with someone else?

"Stop thinking so much, Kay. Go with your feelings. What do you want?" he says against my lips.

"Can we go to your place like last time?"

"Did you drive?"

"No, I came with Marsha."

"Let's go."

I bite my lip and think it over for a bit. Cam has the next four years to do whatever he wants. This can be my secret.

"Okay."

Cameron

"I like her, Cam. I really like her," Daddy says once I get back into the car from dropping Maribel home after dinner.

Daddy pulled some strings and got us a table at one of his friend's exclusive restaurants. I wasn't expecting that, with it being

Christmas and all. Sometimes I forget that people find it hard to say no to Kyle Perry.

"I like her too, but we'll never be more than friends. We both have complicated situations."

"Nothing is too complicated for love. I want to see you happy, Cameron. You give so much of yourself for others. I need you to remember to take your turn for you."

"I have time to figure all that out."

"Do you? Time is something we take for granted. Life has a way of snatching the time we think we have from us."

"I hear you."

"I hope so, son. I hope so." He gets silent and I think that's the end of it, but he turns in his seat and looks at me. "If you like that girl, don't let your mama find out about her.

"Kayleen is a beautiful girl. I love her like one of my own. I might not like some of her latest decisions or how she thinks we'll buy her out of her poor decisions, but she's a good girl."

He pauses to point out of the window. "However, that young lady right there will give you love and peace. She'll keep that smile on your face. You mark my words on that one.

"Keep your mama away from that one until she's good and yours. Jemma has this vision for your life that lives in her head. I only want that for you if that's what you want for yourself, but your mama ... You know your mama," he grunts.

"I hear you, Daddy."

CHAPTER NINETEEN

Seniors

Cameron

Three and a half years later …

"I can't believe it. We've made it through four years of this shit," I say as I sip at my beer.

This place is a hidden gem. About a year after Maribel and I became friends, we found this secret rooftop spot on campus. We meet up here at least once a week.

"We've made it through three and a half. We still have five more months. Don't jinx it," Maribel says.

"You have a point. God, these last few months are going to take a bite out of my ass. I can feel it."

"At least you don't have some sleazeball waiting to marry you the moment you graduate."

I grind my teeth and work my jaw. I hate it when she mentions that guy. He doesn't deserve her. If it were up to me, he would never have her.

I take the joint from her fingers and take a puff. After the day I've had with my mama, I need this smoke session. It's my last semester, and more and more, I'm not sure I want to go to the majors, so I don't give a fuck if I lose eligibility at this point.

Besides, Garrett was right. They never test the stars. They always find some way to keep us from having to take those random drug tests.

I've been smoking for the last two years and never have I had to take a random test. Maribel only started smoking after busting me up here once. I guess you can say I've corrupted my sweet northern friend.

"If only I could figure out how to stick around for another year. Heck, I'd take a semester or two."

I chuckle. "You should talk to Dakota then. I still don't know how she fucked her credits up and has to do another semester."

"But she gets to walk with us, right?"

"Luckily."

"I might have to talk to her. I'd do anything to buy myself some more time."

"What would happen if you were already married?" I muse.

"Ha. What are the chances of that happening?"

"You never know. You have a whole five months. Anything could happen."

"Bro, I would love to see the look on his face," she snickers. Then she sobers up. "He'd probably try to kill me and my husband."

I blow smoke out the side of my mouth and nod. "Right, Cuban Mafia and all that."

"The corporation, actually. More cartel than Mafia, to be honest," she replies.

"All the same shit to me. I play baseball, darlin'. I'm not trying to kill anyone or force women to marry me."

"Speaking of which, are you going to enter the draft? Have you talked to Kay about it yet?"

I frown and hand her back the joint. Kay has been acting weird. We didn't really hang out much during the break.

When we did, we didn't talk much. She would initiate sex and then make up some excuse for why she had to take off. With the draft coming up, our daddy didn't feel like we needed the time off. He shelled out a ton of money on trainers for the winter break, so I didn't have time to give any of it much attention.

Instead of telling Maribel all of that, I shrug. "It's my life, my decision. I'll be fine either way. The only difference it makes to her is how big a trophy wife she gets to be."

"I would hope she's with you for more than the money."

I wrap an arm around her neck and hug her to me. I then kiss her temple and inhale her sweet scent. She always smells so fucking good.

"You're the only one who loves me for me. I could throw it all away and you'd still love my bum ass."

"You sure about that?"

"No one knows me like you do. I'm pretty positive."

"I mean, we can't afford for you to be a bum. You're up against a gangster. We'll need money to evade him."

We burst into laughter. "I sure as shit better not enter the draft in that case. I wouldn't want to expose us."

"I wish," she pouts and rolls her pretty eyes.

"We have a few more months. Something will change for us."

"Well, nothing has changed yet. I need to head home and answer the asshole when he calls."

She stands and kisses me on the cheek. I look up into her eyes, eyes I've come to know so well. She smiles and pushes her hand through the front of my hair.

"Love you, Cam."

"I love you too, sweetheart. Same time, same place?"

"I'll be here. That shit was trash. I'm bringing the weed next time."

I roar with laughter. "I miss Garrett and his guy."

"Ugh, I know. Why did they both have to be seniors? I think you're right. This year already bites. The next few months will probably be more of the same."

"As long as we have each other, we'll make it through. Maybe this semester, we won't have to hide our friendship."

"That shit must be kicking in, or the beer has soured your brain."

I scowl and look away. I can't help feeling like she's ashamed to be my friend. I understood in the beginning, but it's been three and a half years.

She cups my chin and turns my face back to her. "Why would I want to let the world in on our perfect bubble? You know I'd fight a bitch over you. Do you know the kind of ass whipping I'll have to do if these girls on campus knew how close we are?

"Besides, you know I have a sneaking suspicion that Dez has me watched while I'm here. It would kill me if something were to happen to you because of me. It's best if we keep things the way they are."

"One of these days, the world will know how much you mean to me and I'm not going to deny it for another second."

"*Cameron Perry,*" she drags out and bites her lip. "Good night. See you around campus."

"See you around campus, Mina. Text me when you get home."

The days of me walking her to her door had to end after freshman year. Cal and I broke out that first season and everyone knew our names and faces. We can't even meet up at our favorite Chinese place anymore.

Maribel usually grabs our order when we want to eat together. She has become my greatest secret. In another life, I would shout from this rooftop that she's one of the most important people in my life.

Maribel

I swipe at my tears as I text Cam that I'm home safely. It's getting harder and harder to spend so much time with him. I'm completely in love with him and yet I'll be leaving to marry someone else soon.

I didn't mean for that to happen, but we've been best friends for the last three and a half years. It's kind of hard not to fall for someone who completely has your back when you don't have anyone else.

Taylor is still a good friend, but I've never shared my deepest, darkest secrets with her. She moved into the dorms full time sophomore year when she got a roommate who was much kinder than her first one.

I hope she gets that lucky again this time. Her roommate from the fall semester dropped out. She's been stressed all break about her replacement.

I'm too attached to my privacy and have continued to live at my cousin's place. Ximena's apartment might as well be mine. She's never home and even allowed me to change some things around.

My cousin has become a friend when she is here. I will forever be grateful to her. She lends a listening ear when she's around, but that's not often.

"Hey," Ximena says as I walk into the apartment.

I jump, startled out of my thoughts. She laughs and shakes her head. I sigh and kick my shoes off.

"Hey, I didn't know you were going to be home. I didn't get your text," I say.

"I forgot to text. My flight was canceled at the last minute. I couldn't find another to work, so I came home to hang with my little cousin.

"You're graduating soon. I'm going to miss having you here. I'm thinking about getting rid of the place," she says.

"I'm going to miss it here. I wish I could stay."

"You're welcome to as long as you want. Just let me know and I'll hold onto the place."

"I wouldn't want to put you out any more than I already have. Thanks for the offer though."

"You haven't put me out one bit. You actually did me a favor. The offer stands. I got pizza and wine. You in?" she says with a smile.

"Yeah, I'm going to hop in the shower first, if you don't mind."

"Take your time. I promise not to polish off the bottle."

I laugh and wave her off as I head for my room to strip and gather my things to take my shower. I'm moving slowly as I think over my conversation with Cam. We tell each other that we love each other all the time, but I don't think he means it like I do or knows how much I mean it.

I've never disrespected his relationship with Kay. Although I've always thought he could do better. She just sounds like everything is about her.

He loves her, but I don't think he's in love with her. If not for the pressure from his mother and hers, I don't think he would still be with her. However, I read something in his face tonight when I asked about her.

It could be my stupid heart wanting something I can't have, but Cam just sounded over it. I do my best to stay out of their relationship. It's not like I can offer him what he needs.

Not that the chemistry between us is gone. We have plenty of that. Cam and I could light a city with the electricity that runs between us.

That's what's been making things so hard lately. I'll be leaving to return home and Dez is there waiting. These feelings I have for Cam are only making my future seem more bleak.

"Why can't you just stay away from him?" I say as I stand under the spray in the shower.

I have a ton of reasons to stay away, Dez being only one. I know Cam better than he knows himself and yet I know he's still keeping secrets from me.

I've never pushed because I have no right to all his thoughts or his life. When it comes to Cam, I'm happy to have a friend I can talk to on those days when I feel alone in all of this.

I step from the shower and wrap myself in a towel. Before I can get my clothes on, my phone rings. I know right away it's Dez. I don't fight him on these mandatory nightly calls because he did back off some after freshman year.

"Hello," I answer the phone.

"Good evening, Maribel. How is my fiancée doing? How was your day?"

I roll my eyes. I don't get what the act is for. I already know who he is.

"It was fine. I'm getting ready for bed."

"Did you receive my email? What do you think about the venues I sent over?"

"I didn't get a chance to look them over. Today was busy. I had to get all my books and things for class."

"Um, I want to hear your thoughts. I thought we could use one for the engagement party and the other for the wedding."

"I'll have a look before I go to bed. Hey, my pizza is getting cold. Can I talk to you tomorrow?"

"You're eating pizza before bed? Careful, Maribel. I remember that tight body from when we met. I hope you haven't ruined it in the last three years. I would hate to have to push the wedding back for you to go on a diet."

Gah. I silently scream into the mirror. He's such a fucking asshole.

I have to bite my tongue to keep from saying something smart. Maybe if I return a hundred pounds heavier, he'll leave me the fuck alone. That's it, I'm going on a beer and pizza diet.

"I'll be fine," I mutter into the phone instead of telling him off.

"Circumstances have afforded you time to get this all out of your system. However, I look forward to claiming all that is mine. I count down the days until you're with me.

"I trust you've remained my good girl. Sleep well, Maribel. We will be together soon."

I hang up and make a gagging sound. There isn't enough pot for me to smoke to make me okay with calling that man my husband. Cam is right; I have at least four more months to figure this out. If I can figure out how Dakota pulled another semester, I might be able to swing at least a summer session.

There has to be a way out.

CHAPTER TWENTY

Conflicted Heart

Kayleen

"You seem distracted. What's going on?" JR murmurs as he walks up behind me and wraps his arms around my waist.

"I just have a lot on my mind," I say.

"Want to talk about it?"

"Look at these pictures. Your family, your parents, everyone looks so happy in them. When I look at photos in my home, something is always off. You know what else is different?"

I turn to look up at him. Everything about him is breathtaking. Even this home we're in.

I say home because his family's house is just that. You can feel the homeyness about it, as if the people who live here are bathed in love and comfort. I can't remember the last time I felt that.

"When you look at the pictures around my house, they're all filled with Cam and his family or me and Cam. The ones with smiles are all the ones with me, Cam, Cal, and Dakota."

"Okay, you're losing me."

"I've lost myself. This wasn't supposed to go on for this long. We've been together for almost four years, and I've been with Cam that entire time.

"I'm hurting someone I've loved all my life. I still feel guilty after we have sex. I feel like the most disgusting person in the world."

"So you want to break things off with me?" he asks, taking a step back.

"That's not what I said." I run my hand through my hair. "I'm confused. I don't know what to do. I love Cam, but I love you too.

"You're what I want, but he's what I'm supposed to want. My mama is already planning the wedding. I don't know what to do," I say, looking down at the ground.

"What's your heart telling you to do, Kayleen? What makes you happy?"

"I don't know. Being with Cam isn't all bad. He's caring and protective, but so are you. I just … I don't know."

"Why bring this up now? You had all break to say something. Why do this right before I have to go back?"

I begin to sob. I know the reason why, but I don't tell him. I think Cam is starting to suspect something is off.

He's been pulling away. Yeah, I've spent less time with him over this holiday break because JR is home, but when I'm with Cam, he's not there with me, especially over the last few weeks.

"I don't know. I just don't want to end up like my parents with their weird relationship," I sob.

"There's nothing weird about their relationship. Your father divorced your mother to protect the both of you. They stayed divorced after the investigation was over just in case," JR says.

I look up at him in shock. "How could you know that?"

"People talk. My mom is an attorney. I went from a criminal justice major to a biological sciences one. I think I can put two and two together. It's not rocket science."

"Don't talk to me like that. I'm not dumb."

"I didn't say you were. Baby, calm down. I'm just trying to talk you through this.

"I know you feel this like I do. We belong together. Once I pick which league I want to enter, we'll be set.

"I can give you all the things Cam can. We can be happy together. You don't always have to do what your mom wants. You have a right to make your own choices," he says while cupping my face in his palms.

I look up at him and search his gaze. My heart aches because I love him, but I don't know if this is the right thing for me. Cam is safe. Cam is what my mama wants for me.

With Cam, I know we always have something to fall back on. Cam has his daddy's business and his trust fund. Jareil's family is really wealthy, but I get the feeling his mama doesn't like me.

If his career goes south, I don't know if his family would want to support us. Then there's the fact that he's Black. Messing around is one thing.

I don't know what our lives would be like if we were to get married. This all feels so overwhelming. I know I love them both, it's just different, but I know I need to make a choice.

"I don't want to keep feeling like this," I sob.

"Like what?"

"Like I'm dirty. Like I'm betraying the one friend I know would come running whenever I need him."

"Friend. You keep calling him a friend. Doesn't that tell you something?"

"Why feel dirty about something that makes you feel good? We make love. I treat you like a princess. We hardly ever fight.

"Baby, I watch you laugh and smile with me. We have more than a friendship. Stop acting like you don't already know what's right. We are right together."

"Don't do that."

"Don't do what?" he huffs.

"Throw in my face that Cam and I fight. It's not fair. You know what? I think we should take a break. I need to clear my head."

JR throws his hands up and turns to walk away. I look after him with tears running down my cheeks. It feels so wrong to watch him walk away.

"Call me when you know what you want," he calls over his shoulder.

CHAPTER TWENTY-ONE

Call a Friend

Cameron

Practice just ended, but Coach wants to talk with me and Cal. There's some calendar shit coming up that the team has to participate in. Caleb has come a long way, so Coach wants to give him options for this.

I come out of the shower and head for my locker. When I open it, my phone is ringing. Seeing it's Maribel, I answer it right away. She never calls this time of day unless there's an emergency.

"Hey, you okay?" I answer.

"I'm sorry, Cam. My car broke down again. I'm going to be late for class."

I tuck the phone between my shoulder and my ear as I start to tug on my clothes. I hate that fucking car. She shouldn't be riding around in that damn thing.

"Where are you? I'm on my way."

"Are you sure? I shouldn't have called you. I'm sorry. Never mind."

"Amina," I growl. "Text me your location. I'm on my way."

I hang up and remember the meeting with Coach and Caleb. I close my eyes and throw my head back. I can't leave her stranded.

"Fuck," I breathe.

Thinking quickly, I come up with a plan. I'm not in Caleb's next class. Coach can handle talking to him on his own. I just need to make sure Caleb gets to his next class without anyone trying to get too close.

"You okay?" Caleb asks from beside me.

"Yeah, listen, I'm supposed to meet up with Kay. I forgot all about it. Are you going to be all right to meet up with Coach?" I ask, dropping my voice.

"Yeah, sure. I'll be fine."

I feel bad for lying, but it would take longer to explain I'm rushing out to help a friend. Caleb still doesn't know about my relationship with Maribel.

"Cool," I murmur as I text Kota to make sure she meets Caleb at the field.

I would normally walk him to class and make sure he meets up with Dakota before I take off. I'm trusting all will go well and there will be no issues. When Kota texts me back to let me know she'll meet him at the field, I grab my bag and rush out for my car.

I glance at the address Amina sent. Knowing exactly where she is I peel out of the parking lot to get to her. She's my friend. I'm always going to make sure she's taken care of.

Maribel

"Hey, are you a part of the photographers working on those calendars?" Cam asks as he works to find the problem with my car this time.

"I got an email about something like that this morning. There's a chance to win a trip to Paris or something," I reply.

"You should shoot mine. I'd go to Paris with you. It would be fun."

I laugh. Theirs no way I'm going to Paris with him. Dez would kill me.

"You, sir, will be in the major leagues. You won't have time for me and trips to Paris."

He looks up from what he's doing to look me in my eyes. I can see the wheels spinning. Something serious crosses his face.

"But what if we did win and we run? Think about it. You wouldn't have to go back home.

"If we win, it would be like a sign, and we could go. I'd cover the costs for the first year as we figure things out. We could hide you away. I would keep you safe," he says.

"That's sweet, Cam, but you have a life and family here. I don't want to take you from all of that. You can't just run off with me and forget your own life."

He frowns and looks away from me. I'm not stupid. Cam wants to run from his own life as much as I need to run from mine. However, he loves his family, especially his brother. He wouldn't be happy running with me.

"You're still shooting my calendar," he grumbles. "My brother and I might do it together."

"That would be cool. I've never really gotten to know him. Are you two much alike?"

He shrugs. "In a lot of ways, we are, and in others, we're not. Twins aren't always the same," he mutters.

"I meant no offense. You're not just twins; you're siblings. The chances of being similar aren't far-fetched."

"Yeah, I know. I'm sorry."

"Don't be. I'm sure people make assumptions about you guys all the time."

"You have no idea."

He continues to fiddle around with the car, and I fall silent in thought. He might be onto something, I don't need him to run away with me, but what if I ran again, farther away this time? I'd have no contact with my dad this time and ditch my cell phone.

"You know, I wish I'd never told you I know how to fix this piece of shit," Cam says as he slams the hood of my car closed, jerking me out of my thoughts.

I'm trying so hard not to ogle him in his sweats and T-shirt. His hair looks like it's still drying from his shower. God, he's an insanely handsome man.

He has only become more attractive over the last three years. Those dimples get me every time. I love to see him smile—too bad he's frowning right now.

"If you didn't want to help me, that's all you had to say," I grumble.

He places his hands on his hips and frowns at me. I know that look. He's annoyed.

I can't blame him. I had to call him while he was at practice. I got lucky to catch him right after.

"I'm not saying I don't want to help you. I'm saying I wish you'd let me buy you a new car. You're lucky I'm never away when it decides to act up," he says as he turns and props his butt against the car.

"Cam, for the millionth time. I'm not allowing you to give me a car. I have this one. I got it with my own money, and it's been doing its job since freshman year."

"I've been doing my job keeping it on the road. It's done nothing but conk out on you every chance it gets. Come on, Mina. It will be my graduation gift to you.

"Let's go to the dealership this weekend. We'll make a trip of it."

"Don't you have a road game you're heading to?"

He shakes his head. "No, that's next weekend. I'm all yours. I'll take you on Saturday."

"No, you won't. I'm not accepting a car from you."

"Why not?"

"For starters, what would your girlfriend think of you buying me a car?"

He shrugs as a scowl comes to his face. "It's none of her business. It's my money. My friend needs a car. I want you safe, so I plan to buy you one."

I lean my head on his shoulder. "Thanks, Cam. I know you mean well, but I'm not taking a car from you."

"Why are you always so stubborn?"

"Am not."

"You are."

"But you love me. Why complain when I'm going to get my way?"

He sighs. "We'll see about that. Come on, I can't fix it this time. I'll give you a ride to campus."

I go to grab my backpack and camera bag out of the car and lock it. Cam is scowling at his phone as he waits for me. I walk over to him. Once I stop in front of him, he looks up with annoyance in his eyes.

"Everything okay?"

"Yeah." He nods. Then he frowns. "Actually, no, it's not."

He clamps his mouth shut and shakes his head. "You know what? Never mind. Come on, so you're not late."

I follow him as he opens the passenger door for me. Climbing in, I buckle up and wait for him to get in behind the wheel. He tosses his phone on the dash when he gets into the car.

"Are you sure you don't want to talk about it?"

"Nah, not this time. Let me get you to class."

I sit chewing my lip, not wanting to pry because I get the feeling it has something to do with Kay. That's none of my business. I'm not going to get in the middle.

CHAPTER TWENTY-TWO

New Girl

Maribel

I smile down at my phone as I rush to class. Cam has been sending me links to cars since he dropped me off, asking which make and model I want and like. I'm not letting him buy me a car.

As I walk to class, I note the line outside of it. When I take a closer look, I realize this is the baseball team. My mind goes back to Cam's words.

I can't believe he said he'd run away with me. What if I did win? Would that really be a sign that we're meant to be together? Would Cam end up hating me for taking him from his life?

I shove those thoughts down as I walk into class. It's silly to get my hopes up. There are some amazing photographers in this school. What are the odds that I would win anyway?

My eyes widen as I see how many players are lined up. I don't know what I had been expecting. I read the email again on the way to campus.

Cameron told me to sign us up and let him know what I need from him. He had something else to do, so he didn't come to interview anyone. Besides, he already knows I'm going to partner with him.

"What the heck? I knew everyone was going to go nuts about this assignment, but there's a line of jocks outside the class," I say as I walk up to the table Joelle and Taylor are sitting at.

"I stand corrected, once again. Nicole, this is Maribel. Now you have officially met everyone you need to know," Taylor says to the pretty girl sitting next to her.

I've never seen her on campus before. I would have remembered her if I had. I give the girl a smile. I shrug my camera bag off and place it on the table as I go to take a seat.

Nicole gives off a shy vibe from the jump, but she isn't giving bitch vibes, so I give her a chance.

"Nice to meet you," she says.

"I would say nice to meet you, too, but I want to go to Paris and you're now one more camera in my way," I deadpan, with a smile on my lips to let her know I'm harmless.

"Oh, you don't have to worry about me. I'm not sure I'll even participate."

Okay, this girl might be weird. Who doesn't want a free trip to Paris? Even if I weren't trying to run away, I would want this free trip.

"Are you kidding?" Taylor and Joelle say in unison, speaking my thoughts.

"No." She shrugs with true indifference.

Curious, I go to ask her what's up with that, but the professor calls class into session. My phone grabs my attention as Cam continues to text.

I lift a brow as he sends a link for a Mercedes and another for a BMW. If I were going to allow him to buy me a car, it wouldn't be either of those brands. That's way too much money for a friend to spend on a friend.

While I scroll through the links, thinking of purchasing myself a graduation gift, the professor explains the assignment and how it will all work. The baseball team needs to interview us to see who will give them the best chance to win the competition.

I half listen as Cam has already made his choice. Glancing up from my phone, I see Caleb and Dakota at the front of the room. I furrow my brows, wondering what she's doing here with him.

I knit them further as it dawns on me that I've never seen Cam's brother without him or their cousin. I shrug it off as Cam sends me another link.

Me: *You're not buying me a car. Stop sending these texts.*

Cam: *Stop being so stubborn. Pick a car and color.*

Me: *Keep it up and I'm going to go with another partner for this assignment.*

Cam: *Your loss. Would have allowed you a few nudes for your personal collection. Something to look at to get in the mood for your husband.*

I frown at my phone. The thought of Dez wanting to touch me in that way makes me sick. He's such a cold man. I can only think of his touch as cold.

Me: *Not funny.*

Cam: *Yeah. Thought about that after I sent it. Sorry, darlin'.*

Suddenly the air seems to shift at the table. I look up to find Caleb hovering over Nicole, looking like he wants to eat her. Up close he's as handsome as his brother. I wonder if he has dimples beneath that beard like Cam does. Then I wonder what Cam would look like with a beard.

I would miss his dimples if he covered them up like I think his brother does. He would still be fine as fuck. That much I know for sure. My phone buzzes, grabbing my attention.

Cam: *You still there?*

Me: *Yeah. You're fine. I'll hit you back later. I have to look like I'm paying attention.*

Cameron

"I need to go to the bathroom before we go," Cal says as I pay the bill for our lunch.

After I dropped Amina off, Kota texted me to let me know she and Caleb were heading here for a bite to eat. I was starving, so I came right over.

I wait until Cal is out of ear shot, then I turn to Dakota. The smile on her face tells me she already knows what I'm about to ask.

"Tell me more about this girl."

"She's gorgeous," she coos. "And she's Black. Nothing like your type. The total opposite. This is all him."

I bite back my response. No one would know my type because I've never really dated anyone other than Kay. This Nicole might be more my type than Kota knows.

I frown at the thought. If things were different, I know I would want Maribel without question. However, neither of us have that option.

"Did you get the vibe from her that he could trust her? I don't want him to get his hopes up only to have his feelings crushed."

Kota bites her lip as she looks at me. This is an honest question. My brother's happiness is important to me. I'm not going to let some girl hurt him because she can't wrap her head around who he is.

"In all honesty, I have a good feeling about her. Give him a chance to figure this one out, Cam. I think it will be worth it."

"I hope you're right. One of us should get to be happy," I mutter the last part to myself.

Caleb returns a few minutes later and we all go to leave. I text Kay to see what she's up to before I head home to the apartment. I step out of the diner with Cal and Kota, my stomach full from devouring half of the menu.

I might knock out before I start on some reading later. Today is a light day. I only had practice, no classes. Caleb and Kota had the one class.

"Hey, you boys kill 'em out there this season," a guy calls as we exit.

"We'll do our best," I say and give a salute.

"Wow, this is going to be our last season here. It feels bittersweet. I still remember freshman year. You guys must be so excited," Kota gushes.

"I don't know how I feel. There will be more change and I'm nervous enough about that, but I think I'm a little excited too," Cal says.

I look to my brother and smile. I'm still curious about this girl he ran into and now has a crush on. Nicole. She must be something.

My mind goes to Amina. I'm still pissed at myself for that dumbass joke I made earlier. I was only teasing, but once I sent it and read it back, I realized it was a dick move.

I'm so fucking frustrated with myself. I would have been thinking clearer if I hadn't been texting with Kay at the same time. She's on one and I'm starting to look at things more closely.

Something has been off for a long time now. Kay won't travel for one of my away games, but she's always traveling somewhere. Which wouldn't spark my attention if Kay actually had a damn job.

She doesn't, so where the fuck is she always going? It's never bugged me in the past because I'm always busy with school or baseball. However, something in her tone lately has caused me to home in on her behavior.

That and the fact that my mama keeps asking me when I'm going to buy her a ring and when I plan to propose. Like that's a part of some list I need to check off for graduation.

"Where to now?" Dakota asks as Cal and I go to climb into my car.

"I want to get my paper done," Cal answers as my phone pulls my attention.

It's Kay replying to my text, asking if I can pick her up. I shoot her a quick text, letting her know I'm on the way. I look up from my phone to give my brother and cousin my attention.

"Kay wants me to pick her up first. You cool with that? If not, I'll take you home then go get her," I say.

"No, it's okay. I'll take the ride. I can arrange my notes on my laptop," Cal replies.

I nod as he and Dakota climb into the back seat. Once we're all settled into the car, I pull off and head to Kay's house.

Kayleen

"I'll see you later, mama," I call out as I go to head out the door to wait for Cam to come pick me up.

"You going to see Cam?"

"Yes, ma'am. I'll probably be over there for a while."

"Good, you two need to spend more time together. I don't know how you think you're going to get a ring when you're always off doing God knows what with God knows who," she chides.

I roll my eyes and ignore her. I'm trying my best to figure things out. The pressure she's been placing me under isn't helping.

I haven't spoken to JR since he left to head back to school. However, he's still sending me money. He's been sending me a weekly allowance for about three years now.

I haven't had to get a job because he spoils me. Cam never tells me no either. My lifestyle hasn't taken a hit since Daddy nearly lost everything.

We were all able to take a sigh of relief when his business partner Howell took the fall for everything. It was all his doing in the first place—at least, that's what Daddy says.

I step outside right as Cam pulls up. I run to the car before my mama can step out of the house and drive us both crazy. Smiling, I wave at Cal and Kota in the backseat. I then slide into the front seat next to Cam.

"Hey," I say and lean in to kiss his cheek.

"Hey," he says and reaches to tuck my hair behind my ear before kissing my forehead.

I take a deep breath to inhale his cologne. His scent is so comforting and familiar to me. So many memories are connected to that scent.

Settling in my seat, I go to click my seat belt into place. As I pull the belt across me, something grabs my attention. I pick up the gold piece of jewelry off the seat and cup it in my hand.

Peeking at Cam out of the side of my eye, I make sure his eyes are focused on the road. Once I confirm he's not paying attention to me, I open my hand and look down at the bracelet in my palm.

It's a pretty gold bracelet that clearly belongs to a female. I close my hand and sit stewing. Jemma told me Cam would explore.

I shouldn't be mad, but maybe this is a sign. He's no different from me. If Cam is seeing someone else, can he be mad at me for JR?

CHAPTER TWENTY-THREE

Turning Tables

Cameron

A week later ...

"Do you want some popcorn?" I ask Kay as we stand in line for the concession stand at the movie theater.

She glances at me and rolls her eyes. I sigh and order an extra popcorn for her and some of those candies she likes. I'm trying.

I don't feel guilty for the reason she's angry with me. In all honesty, it's bullshit. Kay found Amina's bracelet in my car after I gave her that ride to campus.

I picked Kay up after I left the diner with Cal and Kota. On the way to the apartment, she found it. Because Cal and my cousin were in the back seat, she sat stewing until we were alone in my room.

178

That was the beginning of the fight we've been having for the last week. I say fight and not fights because it's been the same fight every time. For the last week, she's brought it up every chance she gets.

She even accused me of forcing Caleb to go to that party because I wanted to see whoever the bracelet belonged to. Granted, Amina was there, but I hadn't known she was going to be there until after we arrived and I saw her. As per usual, we kept our distance from each other.

I don't blame Amina. The clasp was broken, making me believe it got caught on something and snapped. I don't even know if she realizes it's gone. We haven't had much time to meet up lately.

"Can I have a slush drink?" Kay murmurs when I go to finish up my order.

"Yeah, anything else?"

"No, I'm fine."

I nod and ask for the slush. As the guy hurries off to make our order, I place my hand on Kay's back and pull her closer. She stiffens at first, bringing a frown to my face. I'm not going to keep arguing over something I didn't do.

What are we arguing about? She has been accusing me of cheating. I've never cheated on her.

Not that girls aren't always throwing themselves at me. I ignore them all. Kay doesn't even go to my school, but everyone knows she's my girl.

Heck, I have to beat the girls off when we stay overnight for an away game. If I wanted to cheat, I'd have plenty of opportunity. Yet, I'm always faithful.

I would have told her about Amina a long time ago if we weren't keeping our friendship from everyone. To this day my daddy is the only one to know anything about Amina. He asks after her every now and then, but he's never revealed anything about her to another soul.

"The movie is about to start," Caleb says as he holds Nicole possessively to his side.

I really like her for my brother. That morning after the party, when I caught her watching him, I wasn't sure she was going to stick around. I had known right away that she figured him out, but I wasn't sure she was going to be able to handle it.

She's proven me wrong. Seeing her patience with him gives me all kinds of hope for his future. This was the goal.

He's on a date with someone who gets him and he's happy. Kay sighs beside me, reminding me my brother is the only one happy these days.

"I don't know what you want from me. I told you that bracelet belongs to a friend I gave a ride to after her car broke down. We're friends. We're not fucking and I'm not cheating.

"At this point, it feels like you're trying to force a fight. I thought double dating like this with Cal would make you feel like a part of the team. Isn't that what you wanted?" I say tightly, annoyed with her attitude at this point.

She blows out a breath and looks down at her feet. When she looks back up, she has tears in her eyes. I throw my head back and groan. Dear Lord, not this shit.

"I'm sorry. You're right. Let's go see the movie. I'll pull it together. Thanks for the snacks," she says.

I nod and collect our things to follow Cal and Nicole into the theater before she changes her mind. However, I can't shake the feeling that she's been looking for reasons to fight and argue. I've never given her a reason not to trust me.

Kayleen

I feel like complete trash. I've been blaming Cam for cheating when I'm the cheater. I'm the one looking for a way out.

If Cam breaks up with me, I won't have to face our mamas. I'll be able to give things a chance with JR and find out if we truly work better together. If this is on Cam, then I won't be the one who hurts him.

It all makes sense in my brain, but it's making me sick to my stomach. I don't think he's been cheating. I know Cam.

If he says the bracelet belongs to a friend, it belongs to a friend. When you're a friend of his, there's nothing he won't do to help you. I could totally see him giving some girl a ride to campus and her bracelet popping off in his car.

"I like Nicole," Cam says, pulling me from my thoughts.

I'm staying over tonight after feeling bad about being a bitch all this time. Cam has been trying. The more he tries, the more I've been pulling away and that's not fair.

It's not his fault I don't know what I want. He doesn't even know that all this time, I've been sleeping with and seeing someone else. I've made so many trips to Louisiana to spend weekends with JR while Cam was either training or away at a game.

"Yeah, I do too," I say as I swallow down my guilt. "Cal seems to be crazy about her. I can see how hard he's trying."

"Yeah, he's amazing. I can tell he's falling hard for her. I hope she doesn't break his heart," he muses as he strips from his clothes.

I look away from his hard body, feeling unworthy of getting to see him like this. While he's concerned about his brother's heart, I've been doing all the things to break his.

"Do you miss it?" I whisper.

"Miss what?"

"That feeling. You know, the one you have in the very beginning. The excitement of getting to know the person you're falling in love with and all that."

"Kay, I knew you from the time I was in diapers. I don't think we had that. I mean, it was exciting to see you every day at school and all that, so I guess I get what you mean."

My heart sinks because he's right. I don't remember a time like that either, not like I remember it with JR. I, too, remember the excitement of seeing him in school each day, but it's nothing like the feeling of getting to know someone new.

Cam climbs under the covers and I go to climb in beside him. I snuggle into his warmth and sigh. This does feel right to me. It's my place of comfort.

As he wraps his huge arm around me and kisses the top of my head, I try not to burst into tears. I didn't think things would turn out this bad. The four years are coming to an end, and I feel like I've made all the wrong decisions while Cam has stayed true to his word.

"Cam?"

"What's up?"

"I love you."

"I love you too, Kay."

My heart breaks because I know he does. The question is, is he *in* love with me. I know I love him too, but I have the same question. Am I *in* love with him?

CHAPTER TWENTY-FOUR

Stay

Cameron

I have so much on my mind. I haven't been thinking about what I plan to do much. However, dinner with Coach Snider has forced me to think about the future.

I'm down for whatever my brother needs from me, but hearing him say he doesn't want me giving anything else up for him cut deep. Now I'm left wondering what's next. I've been living for what he needs and never even considered my plans for my life.

My daddy has always assumed we'd both go pro, and my mama has been planning my wedding since I was fourteen— sooner if I'm honest with myself. I don't think I want any of that. I would rather travel the world and figure shit out in my own time.

"Hey you," Amina croons as she appears before me on the rooftop. "I came with the good shit."

I take the baggie she holds up from her hand and smile. I get to rolling a joint as she grabs a beer and sits down beside me. I bring the open baggie to my nose and give it a sniff.

"Thank God. Thanks for looking out. I need this," I say.

"My boy can't send me a text saying he needs to talk and me not look out. What's going on? You look like you have the weight of the world on your shoulders. Talk to me."

I silently finish rolling up as I get my thoughts together. So many thoughts hit me at once. I light up and think of how to say what I need without exposing my brother.

"Coach had a talk with me and my brother about the majors today. After Cal and I had a talk," I say as I blow out the smoke from my first pull.

"Okay, this is exciting, no? This is what you've been working for, or have you decided you're not going?"

"That's the thing. You're the only person I've told I don't want to go, but my brother knows. I didn't realize I wasn't hiding my feelings."

"Is he upset with you?"

I smile. "No, Cal isn't upset with me. He wants the best for me, just like I want for him. I've just never thought of what I would do if I didn't follow him."

"You're very intelligent, Cam, and you're talented. Why not do what your heart wants?"

I squint at her through the cloud of smoke we've created. When she says it like that, it all seems so easy. However, my heart feels out of use.

"I've been following what everyone else wants for so long, I don't know what my heart wants. If I'm not watching Cal's back,

I don't know what I'm doing," I say before I can cut the thought off.

"Yeah, I've noticed you're super protective of him. Is that like a sibling or twin thing? As an only child, I wouldn't know."

"Sort of," I say, then I change the subject. "Got something."

She looks at me expectantly as I reach into my bag and pull out the little Bluetooth speaker. I connect my phone while she laughs beside me. Amina has been working to introduce me to new artists since she found out about my love for Jodeci.

"I'll let you pick the first five songs before we get into the good stuff," I say.

"This obsession has to be criminal. You must drive your brother and Kay crazy," she snickers.

"Cal ignores me, and Kay hates my taste in music, so I don't play it around her. Her loss." I shrug.

"So I have to deal with it?"

"Come on, you love it. Some of our best smoke sessions up here have been to their shit."

"Fine, you have a point, but I'm going with some gangster shit tonight. Let's start with M.O.P."

"'Quiet Storm'?"

"No, that's Mobb Deep. M.O.P. is 'Ante Up' and 'Cold as Ice.' Come on, Cam."

"I've got you, darlin'. I was teasing."

"I'm going to miss this. If you do go to the majors, maybe you'll end up in New York and I can sneak away to come to your home games. That would be something, right?"

"That would be something. We'd have to have at least one beer after the game."

"You're on."

Maribel

I have a nice high. Cam has pulled snacks from his backpack and we're laughing our asses off as music plays softly in the background.

It's amazing how we can shut the world out when we're up here. When I first arrived, I could tell his mind was heavy with thoughts. Now, he's laughing as if he doesn't have a care in the world.

I wish things could always be this way. I'm trying my best not to think about why they can't be. On my end at least.

Dez is a problem I still haven't solved, and time is running out. He's becoming more cocky when he calls. I get the feeling things are going his way back home. Soon, I'll be there, and he'll have his one missing piece.

"It's my turn. I get to pick the next song," Cam says.

He gave me more than the first five songs and we've been vibing out to my choice of playlist. I try not to laugh because I know what he's changing the music to.

At this point, I probably know all these songs by heart as well. I'm expecting him to go with one of the more upbeat songs like "Get On Up," but "Stay" begins to play.

I look up as he stands, holding his hand out to me. Those blue-gray eyes suck me right in. I place my hand into his and he tugs me from my seat.

Pulling me into his chest, he begins to sway me to the song. It's not hard to get caught up in the moment as his strong arms wrap around me. I allow myself to think of what it would be like to be his.

He places his chin on the top of my head, causing me to reel it back in. This is my friend. This song isn't meant to tell me anything.

I'm projecting my feelings onto him. My heart becomes heavy, and I have to fight back tears. He doesn't understand how hard this is for me, but he clearly needs me to be his person.

So I stay. I stay and lock my feelings down deep. Cam can never know how I feel. I'll take all these emotions to the grave.

If I don't it could be the end of us both. I will never pull him into my mess. These stolen moments will have to do.

I wish things could be different, Cam. I really do.

CHAPTER TWENTY-FIVE

Who Is She?

Kayleen

My stomach is twisted in knots. I sit deep in my feelings as the game is in full swing. I try to cheer and look like a good girlfriend, but her words have been ringing in my ears.

Oh, so nice to meet you. I'm Maribel, Cameron's future wife.

I don't know if it's jealousy on my part or the ring of confidence she had in her tone. She is beautiful in that exotic way black women have about them. I believed her more when she said she was Cam's future wife than I did when she said she was far from his type. The girl I stole him from looked more like her than me.

"You okay?" Dakota asks as she places a hand on my arm.

"Mm-hm. I'm fine."

"I'm sure she was only teasing. Don't look so upset."

188

"I'm not," I say harsher than I mean to.

"Oh my God, yes, Cam. Let's fucking go," Maribel screams, cutting off my next words to Kota.

I focus on the field. Cameron has hit a home run, and the crowd is going crazy. However, it's Maribel's voice I hear the most, not because she's in my row or because she's louder than everyone else, but because, for once, I'm not confident that what's mine is safe.

Who is the girl?

Cameron

"Oh my God, why do I keep running to the bathroom?" Joelle groans as she jumps up.

"Maybe because you've been drinking up all their damn beer like you don't have any home training," Maribel calls after her. "Or you're doing some weird shit in their bathroom like smelling their towels or some shit."

"I'm going with option number two," Taylor giggles.

I snort a laugh and shake my head. I switched to water a while ago. I may smoke and drink more than I used to, but I never overdo it.

Besides, the tension in this place could be cut with a knife. I could have strangled Kota when she invited Nicole and all her friends over to my place after the game. I'll admit, Amina is on one tonight.

However, I don't think she's joking to be mean—that's not her vibe. I know her well enough to know it's one of her quirks. Not to mention, she's dialing it down when it comes to Kay.

I'm starting to see it as more of a nervous mechanism. This shit is uncomfortable for her and her way of coping is her sarcasm.

I'll be honest, I'm not helping. I've been matching her energy all night. It's hard not to.

"Oh my God, you're like the female version of Cam," Kota laughs, shaking her head.

"That all depends. When's your birthday, Perry? If I'm older, he's a male version of me. I would be the original."

I smirk because she already knows my birthday and that I'm older. Besides, she was skipped a year. I have a full year and change on her, given that her birthday is in October.

"We were born in April," Cal answers before I can.

He's been trying to stay involved in the conversation all night. Although he's been distracted by Nicole, and Maribel's sarcasm has given him a challenge, I haven't missed Nicole helping him.

Nicky has fast turned into one of my favorite people. She's replacing me as one of the most important people on his team. I had thought I would be jealous if this day ever came.

However, now that it's here, I'm grateful. Not because she's taking my place but because she's giving my brother things I never could. There's no question that he loves her. He talks about her all the time when she's not around.

His biggest worry is that she's not falling for him the same. My brother can't read the looks like I can. The way Nicole looks at him tells me all I need to know.

She's in love with him all right. All my initial worries have been put to rest. Cal's heart is safe with her.

Joelle returns and Kay excuses herself to head to the bathroom this time. My thoughts shift to how unwelcoming she's been all night. I get it. Most of the time, we've all been talking about classes and who's graduating at the end of the semester, but that's no reason for her behavior.

Amina stands to head into the kitchen for another beer. I can't help myself. I end up following her. I've kept my distance all night, but I can't any longer.

"Hey," I say quietly as I grab a bag of chips from the cabinet then lean against the counter.

"Hey," she says back, turning to look around at everyone.

"This is interesting."

"Yeah, who knew one of my best friends would end up falling for your brother?"

"You see it too?"

"Oh, she's a goner. He's crazy about her too. Nice guys are bred in your family. Your brother is sweet. I like him."

"Thanks. I think he likes you too."

"Oh please, he would have to look away from Nicole for more than two seconds to get to know the rest of us. Don't get me wrong, I don't mind. I would have loved having a guy obsessed with me like that."

"It's not too late for that."

She scoffs. "You know better. I have the obsession part. It's just from a psycho I don't want."

I pop a handful of chips into my mouth to keep from saying things I shouldn't. I'm becoming more bitter toward this topic the closer I get to losing my friend forever. I know that asshole is going to make her cut me out of her life.

"She's nice," Amina says, changing the subject.

I look her in the eyes and purse my lips. She's full of shit, Kay has been a bitch to everyone except Nicole, but she's been a super bitch to Amina. Amina bursts into laughter.

"Okay, okay. A bit on the self-centered side, but she's gorgeous?" her voice raises at the end making her statement come out more like a question.

"I'm sorry about how she's been treating you. I don't know what's gotten into her. It's like we're back in high school."

"It's my fault. I may have said something I shouldn't have. Seeing her in the flesh, her saying she was your girlfriend, I got nervous and blurted out the first thing that popped into my head," she says and begins to chew on her lip.

"Well, what did you say?"

"And I quote, 'Oh, so nice to meet you. I'm Maribel, Cameron's future wife.'"

She says the words with such a straight face I know that's exactly how she delivered them. I don't know if I want to groan or laugh. I end up laughing.

"You're a fucking troublemaker," I say through my laughter.

"A menace indeed. But, seriously, I'm sorry for any trouble I've caused. I wasn't trying to be a bitch. I just freaked out."

"That was nothing. You did more damage with the bracelet you left in my car."

"Huh?"

"I've been meaning to give it back. I had it fixed for you. I think you popped it, and it fell off in my car."

She reaches for her wrist with a gasp. "The bracelet my grandmother gave me. I thought I lost it forever. You've had it all this time?"

The look of relief in her eyes makes me happy I've had the piece of jewelry fixed for her. I know from our conversations how important her grandmother was to her.

"Yeah, sorry. She was driving me crazy about it and I forgot to give it back when I got it out of the shop. We argued for about a week or two over her finding it," I say in a low tone.

"Wow, I'm so sorry. Does she know it was mine?"

"No." I shake my head. "Only that it belongs to a friend. Nothing to be sorry about. The whole thing was weird but not your fault."

"I have that class during the Tuesday sessions. I'll get you my notes and you can see if that helps. Can't have one of our stars flunking out," Amina says, causing me to look at her like she's crazy.

Just then, Kay walks up and wraps her arms around my waist. I get this odd feeling in my chest. Not guilt for talking to Amina behind Kay's back, but as if I'm cheating on Amina or something.

Which is crazy because we're nothing more than friends. Kay is my girlfriend and from the way my mama has been hounding me, she might be my wife someday. Yet there's something in Amina's eyes.

Hurt, shame, longing … I can't place it all, but I know I don't like this feeling I have. I'm starting to feel incomplete. Kay snuggles into my chest, and I wrap my arms around her.

"Nice talking to you, Perry. I'll see you around campus," Amina says and turns to walk away.

My heart sinks when she begins to say her goodbyes to the group as she gathers her things. I'm not ready for her to go. I don't want any of them to leave, but it's clear the party is over.

"Let's get ready for bed," Kay purrs up at me.

"You go ahead. I'm going to help Cal clean up. You know he's not going to go to bed until this place is spotless and put back to the exact way it was before they all came over."

"You're right about that. I'll help out too. I think Nicole is spending the night." She wiggles her brows at me.

"Then he needs the help. I'm sure his brain is already overstimulated."

"I have something I want to overstimulate," she purrs and cups my junk.

"You're staying over?" I lift a brow.

She hasn't been staying over as much lately, so I'm taken by surprise. She bites her lip and gives me a seductive smile as she bobs her head. Running her hands up my chest she lifts to her toes to kiss me.

I go with it, but something feels off. It's never been like this before. I can't help wondering what has changed.

Not just tonight. Something has been different for a while. I've just been overlooking it and focused on other things in my life.

Why doesn't this feel natural?

CHAPTER TWENTY-SIX

Thanks for Coming

Kayleen

Two months later ...

"Thanks for being here, Kay," JR murmurs into my neck as we lay in bed. It means a lot to me to have your support during this."

"Are you nervous?"

"Not really. I wasn't going to declare for this draft. My dad wants me to play football. I was going to declare for basketball only.

"We agreed that if I'm still on the board after the first and second rounds, then I'd play basketball. Whatever happens in the next few days, I'll be fine with it."

"Do you think you have a shot at the first or second round?"

"Nope."

I laugh and turn in his arms to face him. "No wonder you're happy with whatever happens."

He pecks me on the lips as he runs his hand down my naked body under the covers. I smile at him as his eyes light up while he looks at me.

"I'm happy because you're here. Everything else will be a cherry on top."

"You promised we wouldn't talk about any of that."

"Any of what? I'm just letting you know I'm happy you're here."

"Okay, fine. What are we going to do for the rest of the night?"

He gives me a wicked smile and rolls me onto my back. I cry out as he thrusts into me. Clinging to his back, I stare up at the ceiling, wondering what I'm doing.

"Oh my God," I cry out as he picks up the pace.

I wrap my legs tightly around him and try not to think about anything else. I want to be here. I want to figure out what's right for me.

"Fuck, Kay. I love you so much, baby."

"I love you too," I whimper.

I'm so fucked. This isn't going to end how I want it to. I know it's not.

CHAPTER TWENTY-SEVEN

Happy Birthday

Maribel

I don't know why I'm so nervous. It's probably because I texted Cam in the middle of the night to come meet me on this rooftop. It's his birthday.

I wanted to give him his birthday gift in person on the day. He once told me he was born at 2:18 a.m. His brother was born at 2:34 a.m. So I texted him an hour ago and asked him to meet me up here at 2:18 a.m.

I know he and his brother have a big party tomorrow at his parents' house. I figured this would be my shot to give him my gift and still be a part of his day. This might be his last birthday I get to be a part of.

"Hey," his deep voice rumbles from behind me.

I turn to find him watching me closely. He has a smile on his face, but his eyes aren't lit up like I'm used to. Concern fills me right away. Maybe I shouldn't have texted him this late.

"Is everything okay? Did I interrupt you and Kay?"

He snorts. "I spent the day with Cal and Nicole. I haven't seen Kay in the last two days. Nope. You didn't interrupt anything. I was in my room alone, thinking. You saved me from my thoughts. What's up?"

"Happy birthday," I sing and hold my arms out to hug him.

He scoops me into his arms and holds me tighter than I'm expecting. I'm taken aback when he buries his face in my neck and starts to rock me from side to side.

"Thank you," he chokes out.

"Hey, Cam? Is everything all right?"

He pulls away and nods his head. "Yeah, I'm good. We lighting up? You have some birthday hash or something?"

"No, but I do have a gift for you. Here," I say, pulling the box from my pocket and handing it over to him.

He takes the box with a boyish smile on his face. Then he tears into the paper like a little kid. I watch his face as he pulls the box open and pulls out the chain from inside.

He lifts the necklace in the air and studies it. A smile comes to his face and his eyes lock with mine. This time, the smile reaches his eyes.

"A Jodeci chain? Do you know how much I wanted to get one of these? Kay and Kota said it would be corny, so I never did." He chuckles as he puts down the box and goes to clasp the chain around his neck.

If I didn't know him and how much he loves the group, I would have thought it corny too. However, knowing the fan he is, it's perfect for him. I had it iced out and everything.

"You like it?" I ask, hoping he doesn't think it's corny now.

"I love it. I'm never taking it off. It will have to turn my neck green first."

"That's not going to happen. That thing wasn't cheap to have made."

"I bet, but where'd you get the money? Shouldn't you be saving for whatever the plan ends up being?"

I wave him off. "Don't worry about it. My dad gave me some money for some shit I wasn't going to use it for, so I put it to better use."

I don't tell him he's wearing part of my wedding gown budget. I'm not spending a quarter of a million on a gown for someone I want to marry. My father is tripping, thinking I plan to spend that much of anyone's money to marry Dez.

After getting Cam the necklace, I did squirrel the rest away. I thought about buying a new car, but I don't know where I'll land after graduation.

I thought it best not to purchase anything that could track me or hold me down. I've been getting around fine without my car since no one was able to bring it back to life. Ubers and rides from friends have done the job just fine.

"Come here," he says and holds his arms open once he gets the necklace on. I step into his embrace, and he hugs me tight.

He breathes me in. "You have been one of the best things about the last four years. I thought I couldn't trust you, but you turned out to be one of the few people I could count on. Thanks, Mina. This means a lot to me."

"I'll always be here, Cam. If I can, I will always be here when you need me."

"That's my line, darlin'. I don't care what happens. You need me; you call me, and I'll come running. No one can stop me from having your back or protecting you. No one."

Tears burn the backs of my eyes and my nose burns from my unshed tears. I believe him. Cam has done nothing but show up for me. It's a part of who he is.

I pull away before I burst into tears. Looking away from Cam, I busy myself with pulling out my next surprise. I'm able to take a deep breath to hold back my tears before turning back to him.

"Let's eat this brownie I got you. They didn't have any cupcakes left, so I went with the brownie."

We sit on the crates Cam brought up here two years ago and he takes the brownie and unwraps it. I stifle a laugh as he sees it's a normal brownie. One from the bakery we both like in our neighborhood.

"Shit, you got me excited. I thought you got me a weed brownie instead of some pot."

I pull a face and look at him. "You're starting to sound like a pothead. Just eat the damn brownie, Anna Mae."

He snorts out a laugh as he breaks the brownie in half to share it with me. I take my half and we bite in at the same time. Cam groans and bobs his head.

"I should be bouncing off the walls right now. Nicole baked us cookies and cupcakes. I'm probably going to be sick in the morning. I ate a whole plate of cookies by myself."

"That's what you get for being greedy."

He grabs my hand, holding my half of the brownie up to my lips and pulls it toward him. He then bites most of my half. I sit with my mouth open as I look back at him. He laughs as he chews and watches me.

"Now who's greedy?"

"I hope you shit yourself," I mutter.

He laughs harder and holds his half of the brownie up to my lips. I narrow my eyes at him but take as big a bite of his as he took of mine. He winks at me and pops the last piece into his mouth.

"You made my night, sweetheart. Thank you, Mina."

Cameron

I think I'm crashing from all the sugar as I stumble back into my apartment. When Amina texted me, I was happy to get out of here. Cal and Nicole were getting carried away.

Wanting my brother to enjoy his girl and whatever they were doing in his room, I took off. I was already in my feelings because Kay had been acting weird again.

I'm still not sure if she's going to show up for the birthday party at my parents'. I'm twenty-one now. This is the year that will change my life forever. I don't know; I thought my girlfriend would want to be more of a part of that.

Like Nicole is doing for Caleb. Watching my brother's relationship has shone a light on the delusion I've had in my own. I chose to continue with my relationship with Kay because she was safe and knew my situation.

I trusted her. Now, things are so different. I can't help wondering if things would be different between myself and Amina if she hadn't lied when we met and she didn't have a psycho fiancé.

I pull out my phone to see if I have a call or text from Kay. Instead, I find a text from Amina letting me know she's home safe.

"Go to bed, Cam. Get some rest and deal with your feelings tomorrow," I mumble to myself as I flop onto my bed.

CHAPTER TWENTY-EIGHT

Not What I Want

Cameron

"What the hell is wrong with you?" Kay growls at me as we leave the bar and head for our car.

Kota left with Cal and Nicole. Thomas and Hamilton haven't ended their night just yet, so they're heading to another bar. That fight wasn't enough to take much out of any of us.

If you ask me, it was over before it started. I wish I could say I was shocked when Caleb slugged that dude, but I wasn't. That shit had been building up.

"What are you talking about?" I snap back at Kay.

Once again, she's been starting fights over anything. It's not the same as when we would just fight over bullshit because we clash naturally. This shit has been her nitpicking.

It's been like this since my birthday. She showed up the morning of and had this attitude with me like I was the one who disappeared on her. To be honest, I'm over it.

"What was that? Are you kidding me?"

"Are you kidding me?" I shout back incredulously. "My brother was in the middle of a fight. What the fuck do you think I was supposed to do?"

"Not join in. You both could have ruined your careers. What if he broke his pitching hand, or you got yourself hurt?" she yells back at me.

"Why do you think I jumped in? Fuck my career. I wasn't about to allow my brother to get jumped or lose his shot at pitching in the major leagues."

We climb into the car and Kay slams the door shut so hard I'm surprised the window doesn't break. I glare at her as she folds her arms over her chest.

She turns to me and narrows her eyes. "What do you mean fuck your career?"

"Fuck baseball. I'm not going to get drafted to the same team as Cal. He doesn't need me anymore. I'm done."

"Wait, when did you decide this?"

"I've been leaning toward this for months now. If you talked to me instead of poking and nagging at me, you would know this."

"So you plan to work for your daddy?"

"I don't know what I plan to do."

"What does that mean?"

"It means I'm going to take some time to think about what I want for once. I'm going to figure my own shit out. I'm not a boy who wants to please his mama to keep her off his brother's back.

"I'm a man who wants to experience life. I want to know what it's like to live a life I've chosen, not one chosen for me. I'm tired of being manipulated.

"I'm sick of this toxic shit we have going on. You stop by, we fuck, and then you're off to do whatever it is you do. Shit, Kay. You're not happy with me. Why are we together?"

"Are you breaking up with me?" she sobs.

"We've been together since I was fourteen. I've never been with another girl. You were my first. I've been in college for going on four years and I've never lived out the full experience.

"I think it would be better to break up now. I don't want to get married and become someone I'm not because I didn't do the shit I should have when I was eighteen, nineteen, or twentysomething. Don't you want to know if someone else is better for you?"

She blanches. I would swear the look on her face was one of guilt. However, she has nothing to be guilty of. Neither of us do.

Our mamas forced us into this. We should be able to take a step back and see if we're what we want. I do feel a little bad as she begins to cry harder.

However, I'm not going back on this. I need to do this for myself. Seeing Cal find happiness, hearing Nicole tell him she loves him, knowing the joy they have, I want to find that for myself.

I'll never get to do that as long as I'm with Kay. There could be some girl out there for me, but I'm missing out on that because I'm trying to force this.

Enough.

Kay sucks in a breath and nods. "Can you drop me home?"

"Yeah, no problem."

The rest of the ride is made in silence. I feel like a weight has been lifted off my shoulders. It's time I find what I want, where I belong.

Kayleen

I thought I'd be happy when Cam broke up with me. However, I feel devastated and shocked. He has never been with anyone else. I was sure Cam had slept with other girls on campus or at away games.

"What have I done?" I sob quietly.

I feel like I fucked up something good because I wanted to have my cake and eat it too. This isn't right, but it's what I wanted to happen. My mama already has my wedding gown hanging in her closet.

I don't know how I'm going to tell her this. I take a deep breath and sit on my bed. Tears are still streaming down my face.

My hands are shaking as I go to dial JR. I just need to feel better. It's like I've lost more than my boyfriend. Cam is one of my best friends.

Even though I don't think I've been much of a friend in a really long time. Sometimes I feel like we don't know each other anymore.

"Hello," JR says sleepily on the other end of the phone, pulling me from my thoughts. I can hear him moving around and then he whispers. "Kay, are you all right?"

"We broke up," I sob.

"Wait, what? Take a deep breath. I can't understand you."

"Cam broke up with me. He wants to start seeing other people."

"That's a good thing, right? You can come to graduation with my parents now."

"I guess so. JR, why are you whispering?"

"It's late. I'm trying to keep my voice down."

"For who? Where are you?"

There is a loud thud on the other end. "Fuck," he growls. "Son of a bitch."

"Are you okay?"

"I just ran into something and stubbed my toe. Listen, I'll call you in the morning. We can talk then."

"Okay, I'll call you in the morning."

"Ja, baby, you—" The line goes dead before I can hear the rest of what's said, but that wasn't the voice of any of his friends I know of.

That was a female. I sit feeling stupid and confused. We never said we were exclusive because he has always known about Cam, but I never thought about the other girls he could have been with while we were apart.

I drop my phone to the floor and place my head in my hands. I've imploded my life and for what? JR has been funding my lifestyle for the last three years.

With the way he spoiled me, even as I stayed with Cam, I never thought he would mess around with anyone else. I've been so naïve. I can't believe I lost Cam and now I have nothing.

Moving into the center of the bed, I curl up into a ball and begin to sob. I fucked this all up so bad. I have to figure out a way to get Cam back.

I'll give him some time to cool off and then we'll get back together. That's it. All he needs is time. I can give him that.

Jareil

"Ja, baby, you all right?" my mom calls as she turns on the lights and comes out of the bedroom of the hotel suite we're staying in.

I joined her last minute on her vacation. I've been sleeping on the pullout couch in the common area as when I arrived the resort was fully booked for a convention or something. We head out in the morning, so we went to bed early.

"I'm fine, mom. I just banged my toe in the dark."

"Well, what were you doing walking about in the dark?"

"Kay called crying, I didn't want to disturb you so I was trying to move out to the balcony or something so you wouldn't hear me."

"Hmm, I still don't know what you see in that girl. Why not find yourself a nice girl who's not rumored to be dating you and another prominent athlete?"

My mother holds my gaze and gives me a pointed look. I knew this was coming soon. My mother has never warmed up to Kay.

"It's not that simple, mom. I care about Kay and I'm willing to give her time to figure things out."

"You are too trusting, Ja. I have always feared you would give your heart to someone who doesn't deserve you."

"I'll be fine, mom. I think you would like Kayleen if you gave her a chance."

"Hmm, son, I've seen a fool, been a fool, and known a fool in this life. I'm not about to watch my child be a fool for no one when I can point out the signs and prevent it."

Seeing that I'm not going to win this argument or convince her to believe otherwise, I hobble over to the couch bed and take a seat. I lift my foot and grab my still-stinging toe in my hand.

"You want some ice for that?"

"No, I'm just going to go to bed. Thanks, Mom. See you in the morning."

"Night, baby. See you in the morning."

She turns out the lights and heads back to bed. I lie down and think back to what Kay was trying to tell me. They broke up.

I can finally have what I've always wanted. I'm not going to play professional football, but things are looking great for the basketball draft. Kayleen and I can have a great life together.

I'm going to marry my high school crush. My patience paid off. We were always meant to be.

CHAPTER TWENTY-NINE

What I Needed

Cameron

I turn from the conversation I'm having and head for the door to leave. I'm over this party. I've done nothing but party since breaking up with Kay.

I don't know what I was expecting, but I haven't found what I'm looking for. I feel hollow and alone. No different from how I felt in my relationship with Kay.

As I walk out onto the street, my thoughts go to the one person who makes me feel alive. Amina hasn't been at a single one of these parties. It dawns on me that that's what I've been waiting for.

I've been looking for her to walk through the door and light up the place with her presence. None of the girls who have approached me have brought that light with them. I'm longing for the one person who makes me feel.

I hop into my car and drive aimlessly. I don't know how I end up at Amina's front door with two cases of beer in my hands. However, as she opens the door and I see her sad eyes, I know there's no other place I need to be.

"Cam?" she says with her brows knit.

"What's wrong?" I ask before she can speak another word.

"Come inside. You have to see this one for yourself," she says and takes a step back to allow me inside.

I breathe a sigh of relief. Part of me thought she was going to turn me away. I walk into the apartment and take a look around.

It's nice. I've never been inside before. I've only ever walked her to the door and that has only been a few times.

Most times, I've only made it to the front door of the building. Now that I'm in her space, I feel like our relationship has just reached a new level.

"You can put those in the fridge if you plan to hang out for a while." She gestures with her head for the kitchen. "What brings you here?"

"I can't come check in on a friend?"

I walk over to the kitchen and place the beers inside the fridge. I grab two and walk back to the living room, where she's now sitting with her head in her hands. It's as I take in the scene fully that I notice the half empty bottle of tequila on the coffee table.

Next to it is a gift bag and tissue paper that looks like it was once inside the bag. I sit down beside her and place the beers on the table. I then place a hand on her back and begin to rub it.

"Talk to me, Mina. What's going on?"

She looks up at me with tears in her eyes. When she opens her mouth, no words come out. She shrugs and points to the gift bag as her lips tremble.

I reach for the bag and look inside to see what has her like this. I take out what looks to be a card and read it first. It's handwritten and signed by that asshole.

My Maribel,

Time is up. I thought it time you started to wear this. I will see you soon.

Your husband,

Dez

I have to fight not to crumble the card in my hand. I toss it down on the table and dig into the bag to pull out the box. When I open the box, I can't help the low whistle that leaves my lips.

The guy didn't cut any corners, although the princess-cut ring doesn't say Amina. I would have gone for something totally different for her long, slender finger.

"Put it back in the bag. I don't want to look at it," she breathes beside me.

I close the box and toss it back into the bag. Once the bag is back on the coffee table, I pull her into my arms and hold her tight. I hate this for her.

"It just became real. I'm going to be married to some guy I don't love and barely know beyond a few dates that I didn't even know were dates in the first place. How is this happening?"

"Shh. I've got you. We're going to get shit-faced and forget that thing ever arrived. Tonight, you get to be and do whatever you want without having to worry about that asshole," I murmur into the top of her hair.

"What made you come here?" she sniffles.

"It felt like the right place to be. I was at a party, but something felt off. The girls there were ..." I purse my lips and shake my head.

"Girls?" she snorts. "What were you doing worrying about girls?"

"Kay and I broke up a few weeks ago. I'm single. How do you not know this? Girls have been chasing me down since the night we broke up. I still don't know how everyone found out."

"Do you know how many times girls have tried to spread rumors about you being single or breaking up with your girlfriend? If I listened to half the rumors I've heard about you, we probably wouldn't be friends."

"I don't think Kay is it for me. I want to see what's out there before I commit myself to something I was told I should want."

"Look at us. We're a mess. You want some tequila? I might have started the party without you."

I peck her cute little nose. I can tell she's been drinking for a bit. Not only is the bottle half empty, but her nose is no longer brown.

"I can see that. Your nose looks like a little cherry. I didn't think that was possible."

"I guess you don't think I can blush either." Her words dropping with sarcasm.

"I know you can blush. I've seen it plenty of times. I'm the cause of it most of the time."

She rolls her eyes and goes to stand. I reach for her hand to stop her. She looks back at me and lifts a brow.

"Where are you going?"

"We're going to need another bottle of tequila. I have a stash. Make yourself comfortable."

I release her hand and allow her to go. My eyes drop to her round ass as she walks away. She has on a pair of gray short shorts that are made of sweatpants material. The tiny shorts are just barely covering the bottoms of her butt cheeks.

I bite my lip and pull a hand down my face. Those legs are sexy on their own. Add to them her nice plump ass—fuck—I'm hard just looking at her.

"Keep it together, Cam. That's never going to happen," I mutter to myself.

Maribel

I race into my bedroom and close the door behind me. I do have another bottle of tequila in here, but I also needed a second to pull myself together.

"Come on, girl. Pull it together. Please," I whimper as I lean with my back against my bedroom door.

I was devastated when the carrier arrived with that package for me. Never in a million years did I think it was an engagement ring from Dez. I started drinking as the panic set in.

"Suck it up, Maribel. This is your life. You're getting married whether you like it or not," I scold myself.

I swipe at the tears that begin to spill. I hadn't expected Cam to show up at my door. However, I was happy to see him.

I feel so cold and alone inside. The best idea I've come up with to get out of all of this has been to fake my death and hope to God Dez never finds me. I would never get to see my family or my mom again.

"I can't do that to her. She tried to save me from this, I can't break her heart now," I murmur to myself.

My thoughts go to Cam and his idea to run to Paris. I wonder if he'd still consider that option. Hearing that he and Kay have broken up would have made me excited if I didn't have to return home to marry someone else.

I would have finally been able to tell him how I feel. However, now, tonight, the knowledge of their breakup feels suffocating.

Pushing off the door, I move to the mirror and groan. I look like a mess. My nose is red at the tip, and I have on an old, faded T-shirt with sweat shorts.

At least my legs are shaved and look silky from my bath and the cream I slathered all over them. I palm my forehead as I notice I'm not wearing a bra either. In my defense, I had no idea Cam was on the other side of my front door when I answered.

I hurry to put a bra on and grab the bottle of tequila to get back out there. I don't change my clothes because I don't want to look as desperate as I feel to have him look at me as more than a friend.

I take one more glance in the mirror as I clench the bottle of alcohol to my chest, then I huff. Reaching up, I release my hair from the ponytail and comb my hand through it.

A groan leaves my lips as I've only managed to make it frizzy. My curls have recoiled from washing my hair this morning. I haven't had a chance to blow it out.

Giving up on trying to look presentable, I head back out to the living room where Cam is waiting. I find him with his shoes and socks kicked off. He's in his jeans, but his button-down is thrown on the back of my couch and he's in a sleeveless T-shirt sitting on the floor in front of the sofa.

I stand admiring the view. A grin comes to my lips as I see he has emptied the tequila bottle I left behind. He holds it up and gives me a smile when he sees me.

"I thought I'd catch up. Come on. I figured your TV out. Let's find something to watch. Food is on the way."

I laugh and go to sit on the couch beside where he's sitting on the floor. He leans his head against my leg and wraps his arm around my calf. I think we both release a contented sigh at the same time.

"This is what I needed," he murmurs softly.

I bite my lip and keep silent. He's talking about the tequila, not me. Even if his words were meant for me, nothing can come of these feelings.

As I have the thought, I look to the coffee table, but the bag is no longer there. My heart swells. This is why I love him.

He always takes care of me and never asks for anything in return. It would have been so amazing if I would have had a chance to explore things between the two of us. I hate Dez.

CHAPTER THIRTY

What About Us?

Cameron

I'm smiling so hard my face hurts. We've finished two more bottles of tequila and scoffed down a ton of Chinese food. Two movies and a jam session later and we're laying side by side on the floor, laughing our asses off about everything but nothing at all.

She's happy. That's all that matters to me. The playlist turns to one of mine and "Love U 4 Life" by Jodeci starts to play. I grin and begin to sober up. Turning to look at the side of her face, I lift and prop up on my forearm.

She's so fucking gorgeous. Not a stitch of makeup on her face and her wild curls are all over the place. They look silky as the large ringlets sprawl around her head and face.

I want to reach for a lock and rub it between my fingertips. I bet she would look sexy beneath me with her hair like that as I thrust into her while she cried out my name.

I clear my throat and shift my thoughts as I feel myself hardening. I've been semi-hard all night. I don't need her to know how much she's been turning me on.

"Can I ask you something?" I murmur.

She turns to me and blinks a few times. That tequila has hit us both hard. Finishing both cases of beer didn't help.

"Yeah. Go ahead."

"Do you have any regrets? Have you done all you wanted in the last four years?"

"Yeah, I have a few."

"Like what?"

"Lying to you and messing things up in the beginning. Never losing my virginity. Now I'll have to give it to someone I never wanted to have it. Not telling someone I care about how much I care about him—"

I cut her off as her words sink in. My lips are crushed to hers as she moans into my mouth. I kiss her hungrily, wanting desperately to take her V-card away from that asshole.

I tug her body closer until she's beneath me. I've taken someone's virginity before, but this time I have skills. I want to do this for her and make it something she'll never forget.

I break the kiss and look into her eyes to see if she's okay with this. Panting, she nods her head frantically. I reconnect our lips and kiss her deeper this time.

Amina reaches for the hem of my T-shirt and tugs it from my jeans and then over my head. I help her to pull it off and toss it aside. Reaching to cup the back of her neck, I lift her to connect our lips again.

"Cam," she moans as I kiss my way down her neck.

"I want you. If this isn't what you want, tell me. I'll stop," I say into her ear.

She shivers and tugs her own shirt over her head. "Please don't stop. I want you too," she moans.

I look down at her full breasts in the purple lace bra she has on. I glide my hand across her skin until I reach around her back to the clasp of her bra. I release it effortlessly and it falls away from her body, revealing her perfect brown mounds with their perfect chocolate tips.

I palm one and dip my head to pull the peak into my mouth. She bucks and cries out my name as I suck harder. I shift to sit on my backside with my back against the couch as I pull her to straddle my lap.

Both of her breasts are now in my face as she grinds against my lap. I'm ready to come through my jeans to thrust into her right now. However, I remind myself to slow down.

This is her first time and it's going to hurt like a motherfucker if she's not ready for me. I'm no small guy. She's going to feel me either way, but I would rather it be in pleasure and not pain.

I alternate between breasts as I suck and lick her nipples. Their weight in my palms is perfect. Burying my face between the two, I suck on the patch of skin there.

"Cam," she breathes.

I lift my head and look into her eyes. "Yeah, baby?"

"Maybe we should go into my room. My cousin pops in unexpectedly sometimes."

I nod and wrap my arms around her back. She kisses me and dives her fingers into my hair. I kiss her back eagerly as I climb to my feet with her in my arms.

"Follow the music. The sound system is connected to another set of speakers in my room," she says against my lips.

I follow the music as I move up the hallway. Getting to the end of the hall, I make a right into the room the music is flowing from as the song changes and "Freek'n You" comes on. I realize which one of my playlists this is and smile. There are only four songs on this one. The two that have played as well as Jodeci's "What About Us" and "Alone."

It's perfect for this. Placing her down on the bed, I grin down at her as I pull out my phone that she linked to the sound system earlier and place this list on repeat. Tossing my phone down, I go to unzip and unbutton my jeans.

Amina hurries to stop me so she can do it for me. I brush her hair out of her face as I watch her. Her eyes go wide when she starts to push my jeans and underwear down my hips.

I spring free and she licks her lips as if in approval. My cock twitches, wanting to be what she's licking. It doesn't have to ask twice.

Amina takes me deep into her mouth and hums. She runs her hands up my abs before she pulls back, gasping for air. I'm covered in her saliva and hard as fuck.

"Fuck," I growl.

"I'm a virgin, but I've given head before," she says as she smiles up at me.

I don't know how I feel about that. A part of me is jealous and wants to erase all thoughts of anyone else. However, as she dives back in and makes my toes curl and my eyes roll into the back of my head, I forget all about anyone before me.

She's mine now. That gorgeous mouth is full of me and only me. She looks so fucking pretty with her lips wrapped around me.

I bite my lip and groan as I watch her bob her head and soak my shaft. I cup the sides of her face and pump my hips, pushing into her mouth. She relaxes her throat and allows me to slide in with ease.

When she drops from the bed to her knees and lifts my length to stroke it while she sucks on my balls, I think I fall in love. She's giving me the best blow job I've ever had. I mean, she's doing shit I didn't know I liked and then some.

It's no wonder I come with a loud roar in no time. The way she licks me clean while looking into my eyes tugs at something in my chest. It feels like she's telling me she loves me too.

I shake my head clear and reach under her arms to lift her up from the floor and place her back on the bed. She still has on her shorts and panties. I need them off.

Grasping the waistband, I tug the shorts down her long legs and find a purple pair of lace panties that match the bra I discarded earlier. I stare down at her hot-looking body and bite my lip. I can't believe this is real.

"You're so beautiful, baby. So fucking gorgeous."

"I could say the same about you."

I grin and drop to my knees. Reaching for her panties, I then begin to peel them off slowly. Her pussy is glistening at me as it comes into full view.

Holding her legs open, I run my hands from her knees down her inner thighs to the apex between her legs, raising goosebumps as I go. Looking into her eyes, I press my thumb against her clit and rub it gently.

Her chest begins to heave as she wiggles beneath my touch. Her moans fill the air, turning me on more. The lust in her eyes almost matches what I feel inside.

I say almost because I want her so bad it hurts. I dip my head to get my mouth into the party without looking away from her eyes. The *O* her mouth drops into as I take my first lick is so sexy. She tastes better than I imagined she would.

I hum and groan as I start to feast on her fat pussy. She's already so wet for me and I'm just getting started. As I rub her nub, I fuck her pussy with my tongue.

"Cam. Oh my God, yes. *Fuuuck,*" she whimpers.

I keep feasting on her until her legs begin to shake. That's when I begin to finger her. I start with one finger and keep adding another until I have three insider her as she comes hard for me.

I'm instantly obsessed with the way she looks when she falls apart for me. I keep going down on her, wanting her to come again. I'm hard again and ready to go as I stroke myself while eating her out.

"Cam, please. I need more," she cries out as she comes once more.

I kick my jeans and drawers the rest of the way off. Then I climb onto the bed. Scooping her body up, I move her farther onto the mattress. I take her mouth and devour her sweet moans.

Amina runs her hands all over my body as I drink from her mouth and squeeze one of her breasts in my palm. When she reaches between us to stroke my length, I groan and break the kiss.

Reaching for one of her pillows, I lift her hips and place it beneath her. "Freek'n You" is playing again, bringing a smile to my lips. I settle between her legs and peck her lips hard.

Then I place my forehead to hers and breathe her in as I reach to line up with her entrance. At first, I tease her slit, allowing her juices to coat my shaft.

She moans and wiggles her hips, almost causing me to slide in. I clench my teeth with need. The last thing I want is to come too soon, so I give myself a few beats to compose myself before I start to push in.

"Pull your legs back into your body," I command.

She pulls them in and pins them to my sides. I reach for her hands and lace our fingers together, lifting her arms over her head. Then I begin to slide into her tight heat as we stare into each other's eyes.

I don't realize I'm holding my breath until she whimpers as I push past her barrier. I still and allow the breath to swoosh past my lips. She tightens her hold on my hands while she adjusts to me stretching her tight little pussy.

"Cam, I need you to move," she moans.

I kiss the side of her mouth and groan as I begin with slow strokes. The feel of her walls rippling and sucking against me is the most amazing thing I've ever felt.

"Are you okay?" I ask against her lips.

"Yes, you feel so good. I'm not going to break, Cam. I want you. Don't hold back."

I growl at her words and start to roll my hips and thrust down into her. She begins to scream my name, causing me to nearly lose my mind. Sweat is dripping from my forehead and down my back.

"I knew we'd fit amazing together. You feel so good, baby. I never want to stop. You feel how hard you have me?" My Southern drawl is thick as the liquor and the sex high weigh in.

"Yes, Cam. Please don't stop. You feel so good inside me."

Fuck yeah. She's talking back to me. I love dirty talk. When I do it and when they talk back.

"I'm coming, I'm coming. Give me that fat dick. I'm going to come all over it," she cries.

"Fuck, I'm going to pound this good pussy out until I can't stay hard a second more. You ready for me?"

"Yes, Cam. I've been ready for you."

I crush my lips to hers and kiss her as deeply as I can. When she begins to throw it back at me, I think I might come right then on the spot. Not ready for it to end so fast, I pull out and roll her onto all fours.

The way she sings my name when I thrust back in from behind makes my toes curl. I stick my tongue out to catch the sweat on the tip of my nose.

I grind into her to the rhythm of the song playing as I hold her hips tightly. Not only does she feel good, but she also smells delicious. The sight of her ass bouncing back on me has me ready to blow again.

I pull out and squeeze my cock as I try to calm the fuck down. Using my forearm, I wipe the sweat from my forehead and take a deep breath. Amina turns and gets onto her knees in front of me.

I wrap my arms around her and hold her to me as we kiss. Pushing a hand into her curls, I hold her in place as I devour her mouth. The kiss turns passionate, and I need to be back inside of her.

Reaching for her ass, I then lift her. She wraps her legs around me and I lower her onto my waiting erection. I groan as her pussy pulses around me.

"You belong to me now. You will always belong to me, no matter what," I say through my teeth as I move her body up and down while pulsing inside her as she ripples around me.

"Yes, yes," she cries as she throws her head back.

She's so wet and I'm hard enough to cut through a boulder. It's perfect. My climax is coiling through me once again.

I don't think I'm going to be able to stop it this time. It rushes me so fast as she rocks and rolls her hips, finding this insane rhythm that's blowing my mind. I cup the back of her head and bury her face in my neck as I growl out my release.

I have to blink a few times to clear my vision. I kiss her shoulder as I hold her tightly. That was the best sex of my life.

When I feel I'm still hard, I lay her down and begin to slowly rock into her. We look into each other's eyes, and something silently passes between us. Knowing if I say what I'm feeling, it could change everything, I kiss her and pour it all into the searing kiss.

I note that "What About Us" is playing. Jodeci once again speaks my feelings for me. I want to love her. I want to answer all her needs and show her she can be happy.

CHAPTER THIRTY-ONE

In Our Bubble

Maribel

"You know, I haven't been skating since the last time we went. I almost forgot how fun this is," I say as I look up into Cam's eyes.

He has his arms wrapped around my waist as he holds me close. What should have been a one-night stand has turned into us spending more time together. That night was amazing. Cam is hung and he knows what he's doing with that thing.

I couldn't have asked for a better way to lose my virginity or a better person to lose it to. He spent hours bringing me pleasure and then held me in his arms like I was the most precious thing in the world to him.

Our heads were pounding the next morning, but I will never say that I regret a second of that night. Nor will I complain about the nights he has spent at my place since. Sex with Cam is amazing.

"I promise you it's the company. Being with you is making this awesome," he replies before dipping his head to kiss me on the lips.

I look around nervously when he pulls away. He cups the side of my face and brings my lips back to his for another searing kiss. I look up at him, cheeks burning as he breaks it.

"I brought you several cities away from campus to be able to kiss you without looking over our shoulders. Relax. No one knows us here."

I suck in a sharp breath. "I don't know. I always have this feeling like I'm being watched. I just want to be careful."

He cups the back of my neck as he searches my gaze. I bite my lip as I stare back. Once again, I wish I could call him my own.

It feels like we're on borrowed time. Any minute now, this bubble is going to explode and I'm going to lose the only man I've ever loved. Gently, he tugs me forward and places his forehead to mine.

"I would take the world on to protect you. Stop worrying."

I want to believe his words, but Dez isn't some guy in a street fight or some dude on campus. I would never forgive myself if something happened to Cam because of me.

"Let's get back to skating. We can do all the rest of that stuff once we get back to my place."

"Just one more kiss," he croons.

I dip under his arm and take off before he wraps me back in his embrace. He growls and takes off after me as I move into the flow of the other skaters.

With his powerful legs, he catches up to me easily and wraps his arms around me from behind. I lean into him as we begin to skate in unison to the music playing.

His arms are so comforting around me. The smile on my face is so wide my cheeks hurt. If you told me a month ago that this would be my life I would have called you a liar.

Now, this seems like the way my life has always been meant to be. He leans into my ear and kisses just beneath it. I shiver as I feel his warm breath against my skin.

"Want to head out soon."

"Are we still going to the batting cage?"

"We can, or we can skip all of that. Save it for another day. Your choice."

I sigh and snuggle deeper into his hold as we continue to glide. I really never want this to end. Cam spins me and looks into my eyes.

He has this sexy grin on his lips that I commit to memory. I save it to think of when the bubble is gone and I have to return to my reality.

To my surprise, he lifts my hands in the air as we continue to skate. "Don't Wanna Be A Player" by Joe and Big Pun is playing. I grin at Cam as he winks back at me while bobbing his head.

For the next thirty minutes, we continue to skate, dance, and laugh. Cam gets hungry so we grab a bite to eat before we head to the batting cage.

Cameron

I thought skating was fun, but I'm having a blast here at the batting cage. Our banter has kept me on my toes. Not to mention I get to show off a bit while here.

I smack a ball and set up for the next. I can feel Amina's eyes on me. She has fallen silent, causing me to glance at her after I hit the next ball. She's biting her lips while watching me.

I have on a T-shirt that's hugging my muscles as it stretches around my arms. I look down at my arms and then back at her. I step over to her and peck her lips.

"You look hungry," I tease then peck her lips again.

"Then I think it's time you feed me."

"What are you in the mood for?"

"Sausage. The nine-inch kind."

I chuckle. "It's closer to ten, baby. It's definitely time for us to go. I don't want you to starve."

She bites her lip and bats her lashes at me. God, does she know how perfect she is? Everything about her draws me in.

Once again, I think about sharing every detail of my life with her. With Caleb wanting to share his truth more, I can't help but wonder if Amina would be safe to share the truth with.

"Hey, where did you just go?" she asks, placing a hand on my chest.

"Nowhere, I was just thinking about something."

"Come on, let's get out of here. You're showing off and others are beginning to stare. We should go before I have to beat these chicks off and the guys surround you for autographs."

I snort. "I'm not interested in any of them. Not a single one of them can hold a candle to you."

"You do know I'm getting naked for you already. You don't have to sweet talk me."

I wrap my arms around her waist and pull her to me as I bury my face in her neck. I growl against her skin and palm her ass. Not able to help myself, I take her lips.

"I can't wait to get you back to your place," I groan.

CHAPTER THIRTY-TWO

Feenin'

Maribel

I sit with my back against the headboard of my bed while Cam is standing shirtless over by the window. He's been standing there for a minute, rolling two *L*s while he seems to be lost in thought.

"What are you thinking about?" I ask as I sit with my knee bent, rocking it from side to side.

Cam looks over his shoulder at me and knits his brows. Then he shakes his head without saying a word. My curiosity is piqued as he turns back to the window and returns to his task.

"You know that says a lot. I know you better than to think you're not thinking."

"I didn't say I wasn't thinking, baby," he murmurs.

I smile. It still makes me giddy to hear him use the endearment toward me. My stomach drops and does all types of weird things.

This thing between us has been going on for two weeks now. He's at my place anytime he's not in class, at a game, or at practice. It's so hard not acknowledging him when he's with his brother picking Nicole up from class.

However, I always know once his brother and Nicole get to wherever they're going, Cam is going to double back to me. I get that, for some reason, Cam needs to be with his brother all the time. If he's not with him, Dakota is.

I haven't asked because I figured that's Cam's one secret he keeps from me. Knowing how protective he is, I don't want to pry. I trust that if he wants me to know, he will tell me.

"You want to order from that new Italian place later?" he asks, changing the subject.

"Sounds good. I'm all egg rolled out. I could avoid Chinese for a month."

He scoffs. "Now, I didn't say that. I'll probably stop by there on my way home."

"Seriously?" I allow my gaze to travel over his muscular back down to his tight ass in his jeans.

As much as he eats, I don't know where it all goes. His body is the picture of perfection. All that silky smooth skin over those tight muscles makes my mouth water.

"I'm a big boy. Besides, I plan to burn off plenty of calories before I leave here." He turns to me and winks.

"What party are you supposed to be at this time?"

I know from Nicole that he's been telling his brother that he's been out partying all the time, but he's not partying. Not unless you consider beating the brakes off my pussy a party.

"Hamilton was going on and on about some party. Cal assumed I was going with the guys. I didn't correct him."

"Who knew you were going to become an anatomy major at the last second of your collegiate career?"

Cam laughs as he leans his butt against my desk and looks me over like he wants to devour me. I smile as I notice the growing bulge in his jeans.

This man has become an addiction for me. It's not just sex though. We have so much fun hanging out together.

He keeps my mind off the bullshit. I know we both enjoy it when Dez calls while Cam is eating me out. It's like Cam does it on purpose.

He knows when it's time for my calls from Dez and right before, he gets me worked up and ends up with his blond head between my thighs. Each time I answer Dez and act as if nothing is going on. However, after the last time, I don't think we should do that again.

I almost screamed into the phone at one point. Cam had his face buried so deep in my honeypot and he was doing that thing with his fingers and tongue. I was ready to come out of my body and just barely managed to get off the phone before I gave myself away.

"Have you thought any more about what I said about running away together?" Cam asks, pulling me from my thoughts.

I lock gazes with him. Looking into his eyes, I know this is what he was really thinking about. My heart begins to race a little.

I focus on anything but his eyes as he stares through me. His playlist is once again playing in the background. I've given up on trying to school him on other groups. His obsession is real.

I actually don't mind it anymore. It is what it is. I've accepted it as a part of Cam.

"Huh?" I reply.

"At the beginning of the semester, I said I would take off with you. Have you thought any more about what I said? Would you consider it now?"

"I thought you were joking. You have your family and everything here. You can't just run off with me."

"Why not?" He lights up, then pulls the joint from his lips and frowns at me.

"For one, you have your brother. You've never said anything, but I get that he needs you somehow. He's important to you.

"I'm not asking why or what that's all about, but I get that you're supporting him in some way. Caleb means the world to you. I would never come between you two."

Several emotions come to his face as he stands there silently. The air fills with a thick tension and I'm not sure which way this conversation is going to go. He could grab his things and storm out, or maybe, just maybe, he'll open up to me.

Still not saying a word, he takes a pull from the L in his hand, then tips his head back and blows the smoke out. I do notice he's bouncing one of his legs. Then as if a string has snapped, he drops his head back down and picks up his phone from the desk.

He taps at it a few times before dropping the phone back on the desk. The song changes and "Feenin'" comes on. Slowly, he begins to stalk toward the bed with the blunt hanging out the side of his mouth.

I watch as he climbs up the bed like he's stalking his prey. When he gets to my legs, he lifts my bent one and wraps it around his waist. Pulling the blunt from his lips, he leans over me and hovers his mouth over mine.

I open for him to share the shotgun, and he breathes the smoke into my mouth. I moan when he slips his hand under my shirt and palms my breast, flicking my nipple with his thumb. Cam takes my lips and kisses me passionately, but something feels different about this kiss.

"I've wanted to tell you something for a long time," he starts, but my phone rings.

I groan and roll my eyes. People have the worst timing. Sometimes I feel like someone is watching and letting everyone know when Cam is here, so my phone will start to ring and interrupt.

Knowing most times it's Dez calling to annoy me, I don't want to reach for my phone. However, I do and I bare my teeth as I see his name on the screen.

Cam huffs and flops onto his back beside me. The moment between us completely shattered. I glance at him as he pulls from the blunt he placed back in his mouth. Good thing there's another one.

I don't miss the frustrated and pensive look on his face. Suddenly, he stands and leaves the room. A deep, bereft feeling settles in the pit of my stomach. Shaking my thoughts off, I answer the call.

"Hello."

"What are you doing?" Dez snaps into the phone.

I jerk my head back and look down at the device. He has some nerve calling me with an attitude as if I'm the one interrupting him. I don't know why he's been calling at random times lately in the first place.

"I'm getting some studying done," I say as I roll my eyes.

He gives a weird laugh. Almost a scoff of disbelief. "You wouldn't lie to me, would you?"

"What? What are you talking about?"

"Nothing, Maribel. Nothing. You don't know me well enough to know my limits and expectations." He sighs like a lunatic.

Then he continues. "This is why I'll be lenient. I'm sending you a list of honeymoon locations. Pick one. I want an answer within the next twenty minutes. Not a minute more."

With that, he hangs up. I stare at my phone. I'm not even going to try to figure out what his problem is.

My phone chimes with an email, and I see it's from Dez. I open the email and find a bunch of links to honeymoon destinations. I'm not about to sit here and waste my time going through them. I want to go on a honeymoon with him as much as I want to marry him.

I count through the top of the list. "One, two, three, four, you're it."

Copying the link for the fifth one, I send it back to Dez in a replying email. There, less than twenty minutes. Wanting to forget about Dez and needing to get high, I get up and go looking for Cam.

Hopefully he can fuck my frustration away. I already have a slight high, so I'm struggling to pinpoint what it was about that call that was off to me. A smile comes to my lips as I hear the music playing at the front of the apartment.

However, when I find Cam sitting on the couch with a scowl on his face, I come to a dead stop. I forget all about my nagging thoughts and Dez. I stop in front of Cam and step between his legs as he sits slumped down on the couch.

He sits up slightly and leans in to press his face into my belly. My stomach fills with warmth from the feel of his cheek pressed against me.

I run my hand through his blond locks and close my eyes. For a moment, I allow myself to absorb his presence and the feel of him in my arms. *I love you, Cam,* I think the thoughts I can never say.

Cameron

I almost told Mina about Cal. Hearing her say she knows there's something I haven't told her and that she's okay with that made me want to spill my guts. Amina is everything I've always wanted.

I need to figure things out and find a way we can be together. I don't want to let her go. She shouldn't have to marry some old mobster because her father wants her to.

She's mine. I love her. I think I always have.

This shit is killing me, and I haven't had to let her go yet. I hate when that asshole calls. I can always tell it's him.

It's in her body language and how the mood shifts. I've never loathed anyone more in my life. He's trying to take my world from me, and I hate it.

"Hey, talk to me," Amina says as I keep my face buried against her belly.

I had to leave the room before I snatched her phone to tell that asshole I was fucking his fiancée. She never wanted him to begin with. She's mine and he needs to back the fuck off.

However, I'd never do that to her. I see how nervous he makes her. She fears what he'll do to me more than anything.

For her, I'd take whatever comes my way. I'm not scared of that asshole. He's a piece of shit in my book.

Not able to say anything I'm thinking, I sit back and pull her to straddle my lap. I palm the back of her neck and bring her lips to mine.

I kiss her with all the passion I feel for her. Placing my hands on her hips, I then push her top up until her breasts are exposed. Breaking the kiss, I look down at her tits and lick my lips.

She tugs her shirt off and tosses it on the floor. I palm both globes and dip my head in to suck each nipple in turn. Amina moans and throws her head back.

"You know I'm never going to be able to let you go," I breathe against her soaked right nipple.

"Cam, I—"

I don't give her a chance to deny me what I want. I take her lips and kiss her until she begins to quake against me as I roll her nipples between my fingertips. She's been grinding in my lap as I devour her mouth.

She reaches for my jeans and releases me as I continue to kiss her. Breaking the kiss, she stands and steps out of her leggings. I push my jeans from my hips and kick them from my legs.

I groan and drop my head back as she gets to her knees and starts to blow me. My heart is hammering. She's the only one who can do this to me.

"Fuck, baby. Your mouth is amazing. Suck that shit, I want to come in your mouth," I hiss.

She grins around my cock as she looks up through her lashes at me. I grow harder as she pumps her hands over me and soaks every inch of me. My eyes widen as she grips the base around my shaft and holds it tight as she slurps and bobs over me.

I rock my legs back and forth as if that's going to help me not to come. It's all I can do to keep from grabbing her head and holding her in place as I pump my hips into her face. Not that she would object; I think she loves that shit.

I just want this to last. I lose my shit every time she looks like she's enjoying the fuck out of sucking me off. She lifts her head to take in a breath and spit bubbles form in her mouth as salvia connects from her lower lip to the tip of my length.

"Fuck, baby. Fuck. Come here. I need you to ride me."

As she stands, I reach for my pants and grab a condom from the pocket. I put it on quickly before she settles over me. I hold myself up with one hand and place the other on her waist as she lowers onto my pulsing, waiting erection.

"Cam," she cries out as she rolls her head back.

I guide her hips up and down as she begins to ride me. Her tits are bouncing in my face as she rocks her way to pleasure. Leaning to the side, I look down at her ass as I spread her cheeks and start to pump into her from beneath.

"Fuck, you're so hot. You enjoying that dick, baby? You want that hard cock in your mouth again? Does my baby want to taste her tight pussy on me?"

"Yes, Cam. You're driving me crazy. I want to suck your dick until you come down my throat. I want to taste your cum inside my mouth.

"Fuck me like I'm yours and only yours," she screams.

My heart swells. I want her to be mine and only mine. The thought of having just that makes me tighten my grip on her ass as she rocks and gyrates her hips. As she bounces on me with more enthusiasm, I palm her breasts and squeeze them.

I begin to swell inside her. I reach for her ponytail to tug her head back as I thrust up into her. I feel her tightening around me while she comes all over me.

I bury my face in her neck and breathe her in as my own release hits me. I'm breathless as I kiss all over her neck and shoulder.

"We can do it. We can run together. Promise me you'll at least think about it."

"Okay, I'll think about it."

I breathe a sigh of relief. She cups the sides of my face and kisses me deeply. I love this girl so fucking much.

She definitely has me feenin'.

Dez

"Fucking whore," I roar as I slam the laptop on my desk shut and swipe my arms across the desk surface, knocking everything to the floor.

My chest is heaving as I stand staring at the mess. She fucking lied to me. She's been fucking that motherfucker for two weeks now. I had those cameras snuck into her cousin's place over three years ago when I learned she wasn't staying in her dorm.

My little virgin has become a whore for that white boy. He's been in my pussy every chance he gets. He's stretching that shit out and she's allowing it.

I don't want a whore in my bed as my wife. The women I've been bedding here in Cuba are the only whores I want to fuck. Maribel was supposed to come to me pure.

I pull my phone from my pocket. I'm not going to allow this to continue without any repercussions. She has caused everything that's about to happen.

"Have the jet fueled. I'm heading to New Jersey," I say into the phone.

I will start with the one who failed me first. It's time I leave Cuba. My vacation is over.

CHAPTER THIRTY-THREE

You're a Madman

Dez

Two weeks later ...

"No, please. No more. Make it stop."

"Silence," I demand as I grin down at my victim.

"Please, I don't deserve this."

"You deserve this and so much more for what you have cost me. Making promises you can't keep is a character flaw," I croon.

I'm growing tired of this. I've been here for hours now after murdering his staff and security. Reaching into my suit jacket, I pull out the silencer and screw it on the end of my gun as he begins to sob harder.

"Wh ... why are you doing this?" he sobs.

I grin down at him. "You want to know why? I will tell you why.

"Four years ago, I had been in a rush to rise to power. My older brother was in the way, so I removed him. He was going to destroy our family.

"I knew from the moment he began to talk about joining that fucking Alliance that he had no backbone and he would ruin everything. So I killed him."

This prick begins to whimper at my confession. I ignore his cowardly response and continue with my explanation.

"I was to be his second-in-command. The throwaway son. The just in case. Well, I made just in case happen.

"The problem is, I didn't know my grandfather would place all these stipulations on my rise to the position my brother was just going to be handed. If you ask me, he's only doing this because he believes in what those fucks are trying to do.

"I won't allow it. Not in my family. That's why I wanted to complete this union back when the Alliance started to gain traction."

I pause to think of all they have done and how at one point I thought they would be successful. Oh, how things can change in the blink of an eye. Just like our arrangement has.

Seething, I continue with my words to this asshole. "However, Amina was bought some time. The plans LaSalle Locatelli and Logan O'Brien have been making have hit a few walls and from what my connections have shared, this is only the beginning. Not everyone is on board the way they thought they would be.

"It will take them years to get the support needed for their plan. Years I plan to take advantage of. Not rushing things has earned me more trust from my grandfather as I play his little lamb.

"He has no idea of the wolf I've been hiding right in front of his face. I gave my little dove the time she needed to mature into the *Princesa* I need her to be. Maribel is a beautiful young woman.

"She's feisty too. I like that about her. Sure, I could have declined the arranged marriage that was made while I was a mere boy. However, you have reaped your reward, so why shouldn't you deliver my bride?" I snarl.

I look at this sniveling piece of shit before me as he's tied to his bed, whimpering for his life. His blood stains the sheets from the torture I've already put him through. Not because I need information out of him, but because I'm pissed.

"You act as if I haven't spent a fortune on the engagement party for you two instead of throwing her a graduation party. She will be home soon. You will have your bride. I still don't get why you're doing this," he cries.

"Didn't I tell you to shut the fuck up? You could have prevented this had you delivered my sweet girl to me before she spread her fucking legs for some country-ass white boy. Now she's nothing more than a whore.

"Do I look like I want to take a whore as my wife? Do I?" I bellow.

"My daughter is not a whore. How would you know this anyway? She's been in Texas working on her degree.

"She's always busy with school. She hasn't dated the entire time she's been away. I have asked. Her cousin has confirmed this," he shouts back defensively.

"Well, that's the difference between the two of us. I don't trust my information to come from unreliable sources. I never trusted my young fiancée away from me where she could run free and do anything she pleased.

"From the time I agree to allow her the four years away, I had eyes on her. The white boy has been around the entire time, but I never thought she would spread her legs for him. I should have killed him a long time ago.

"I thought of doing so multiple times." I shrug. "I'm still considering it. The only reason he's still alive is because I believe he will be my leverage to get your daughter to do as I say."

"What?"

"Oh, you didn't think I was counting on you to keep her in line, did you?"

I release a deep laugh. This is humorous. If delusional was a person, it would be him.

"Your daughter hates you for this. You missed out on her entire life and then when she got to know and trust you, you handed her over to me. You are as useful to me as an ass with no hole."

"What have I done to my little girl? You're a madman."

"You know, I hate when people call me that. You weren't worried about your little girl when my family had something you wanted. You didn't think of what kind of man I would be when you promised your daughter's hand so you could run a multimillion-dollar empire.

"Where was your concern for your daughter when you accepted my grandfather's offer to get you out of the ghetto and make you the man who lives in this mansion? Were you thinking of her then? Were you?" I bark.

"No and I've regretted it ever since. I should have walked away like her mother told me to."

I lift my gun and point at his head. "Yes, you should have."

Cameron

My bat cracks against the pitch Cal just threw. The sound echoes through the night, bringing a smile to my face. I've been smiling a lot since Amina and I have been together.

Sex with her is amazing. That first night, we fucked for hours. It's been the same every night I've spent at her place since. Just thinking about her is enough for me to still feel the tight grip of her pussy around me.

"Good shit, Perry. That's the tenth home run in a row. You do that in the next few games, and we'll be unstoppable," Ricki, another senior, says.

"I hope so, bro," I croon.

"You're on fire. You have to tell me your secret," Josh, another of my teammates, says.

Cal and I have been out here on the field with a few of our teammates, tossing balls and hitting. I feel invincible. This is a high like none other. I could hit like this all night.

However, the guys are starting to grumble about needing to eat and wanting to call it quits. I start to unfasten my gloves as I walk over to my bag. I have a grin on my face as I roll my shoulders and crack my neck.

I pull my phone from my bag and go through my messages. I have a few from my mama, which I ignore. It's the messages from Amina that I open right away.

My smile grows as I read the texts she has sent. Man, if we had started things three years ago, I would have been obsessed with her. I'm already finding it hard keeping our secret arrangement.

I saw her on campus earlier and almost walked right up to her to take her lips in front of everyone. Instead, I kept my distance and winked at her.

I reply to her texts and let her know I'll be there after I stop to get a bite to eat with the guys. A part of me wants to bail on them and head to her place now. However, if I do, I know there will be questions I can't answer.

Feeling like someone's watching me, I lift my head and look around. I pause and squint my eyes as a guy outside the fence catches my attention. He's looking right at me.

He doesn't look familiar. I'm sure I don't know him from anywhere and yet his attention seems locked on me. I glance around quickly for Cal to make sure he's all right.

When I turn my focus back in the direction of the guy, he's gone. I shake my head and shrug it off. People come out to watch us practice or when we're just fucking around all the time.

"You good, man?" Ricki asks.

"Yeah, I'm fine."

"You mind if I ride with you and Caleb?" Hamilton asks as he comes and claps me on the back.

"No problem. Let's go," I say to him and nod to Cal as he grabs his bag.

CHAPTER THIRTY-FOUR

Painful Loss

Maribel

"Hello, may I speak with Maribel Jones," the man on the other end of the phone says as I answer.

"This is she. How can I help you?"

"This is Harris Buckley. I was your father's attorney. I have an important matter to discuss with you."

"Excuse me? Was. What do you mean by was?"

"I'm sorry to inform you that there has been an unfortunate incident in your father's home. He and several employees were fatally injured during a home invasion. There were no survivors."

I gasp and clench my T-shirt over my stomach. I stumble forward and flop down on the couch. Knitting my brows, I blink in confusion for a moment as I sit in silence.

"Hello, Miss Jones? Are you still there?"

"Yes, I'm here."

"I'm so sorry to be the bearer of bad news. I know this has to be difficult and devastating to say the least."

"Do they have any suspects in custody?"

"No, as of now, they don't have any suspects and the investigation is ongoing."

"What makes you think it was a home invasion?"

My heart is pounding. Dez comes to mind, and I can't help wondering if he had something to do with this. I should be returning home next week, but I managed to sign up for summer session to make up for some credits I purposely failed and need to graduate.

"The safe in the bedroom was empty and sitting open when the authorities arrived." Mr. Buckley pauses and clears his throat. "It looks like the code for the safe was tortured out of him before he was executed."

I swallow down a sob, only feeling slightly relieved. I'm trying to process what he's saying to me. I'm thankful this wasn't Dez, but it's setting in that someone has murdered my dad.

He's gone.

I break down sobbing and can't register anything else being said. I've been so angry with my dad for the last four years, but I didn't want to lose him like this. My heart hurts.

"I will try you again in the morning or you can call me back on this number when you're ready. I'm so sorry for your loss."

I vaguely register the words before the line goes dead. This hollow feeling fills me and my stomach rolls. I jump up and rush to the bathroom to empty my stomach.

Cameron

As we sit in Amina's living room on the couch, I rub her hair as she lies sobbing on my lap. She's been this way since I arrived. I was shocked to hear her father was murdered in a home invasion.

Shit like that seems like the stuff that happens in the movies. I've never known anyone who's been murdered in their own home. People are crazy.

"I'm so sorry, baby. I'm going to be right here with you through this."

She stiffens in my hold. I wrinkle my brows. Sitting up, she looks at me with her tear-soaked face.

"Cam, the thing is, I don't think this was just some robbery. I don't believe this was something random."

"What are you talking about, baby?"

"I should have booked my flight to return home. Instead, I signed up for summer classes. I flunked a few classes I need for my degree so I wouldn't have to go back yet."

"Yeah, I know that, but what does that have to do with anything?"

"Cam, can't you see what's going on? This was Dez. He's behind this. I know he is. I can feel it in my gut."

"If that's the case, we'll take off. Right after the tournament and the draft, we can go. I just want to make sure my brother gets on a team and is set. Then we can go."

"I don't think I have that kind of time, Cam. That's another two months. If he's done this to my dad, what do you think he would do to us?"

"So what are you saying, Mina?"

"I'm saying for your safety, I think we should stop seeing each other. We always knew it would come to this and we would have to end things. I care about you, Cam. I can't allow you to get hurt because of my mess."

I shake my head. This can't be happening. I'm not ready for things to end. I'm willing to face what comes.

"We don't have to end things—"

"Cam, you're an identical twin. Think about your brother. What if something happened to him because they were looking for you?

"I couldn't live with that or if something were to happen to you. We have to end things. I'm going to have to go home at some point."

Her words hit their mark. Cal wouldn't even know to watch his back. He knows nothing about Mina or what I've gotten myself into. Thinking about how he would likely miss the social cues to know he's in danger sends panic through me.

My heart is breaking because I know she's right. She's slipping right through my fingers. I love her so much and would do anything for her, but Caleb can't be a casualty of my shit.

"Mina, you just learned your father was murdered. Let's not rush things. He allowed you four years. Maybe he'll be fine with another semester for you to finish.

"Promise me you'll just take some time to think about this and don't run back to him just yet," I plead.

"I'll have to speak to the lawyer and find out what he wanted. I'll probably have to return for the arrangements and all that. I don't know about after that.

"What I do know is that this wasn't smart to start up with each other. To keep you safe, I really think we should cool things off. I'll text you to keep you updated," she whispers.

"Baby, I—"

"Please, Cam. Don't make this harder than it already is. The man is going to be promoted to a mob boss after we're married. I won't allow you to be hurt."

I clamp my lips shut. It's not fair to her to tell her I love her now. Not while she's grieving her father. Maybe after a few days she'll see how wrong this is.

We belong together. I'm not afraid to fight for her. There has to be a way to protect my brother and her at the same time.

I press my lips to hers in a kiss that feels too much like goodbye. Rage fills me. I need to get out of here.

CHAPTER THIRTY-FIVE

Ruined

Kayleen

A month later ...

I pace my room as my hands sweat and moisture dews on my upper lip. I haven't spoken to JR since I called him that night. I blocked his number.

Two weeks later, I learned that I was pregnant. The problem is, I don't know if it's JR's or Cam's. I'm now two months pregnant and I'm not with either of the potential fathers.

I haven't told my mom because she would kill me. I quickly swipe at my tears. Mrs. Jemma is here having lunch with my mama, but I'm avoiding them both.

"Kayleen Douglas, you stop being rude and get your tail on down here right now," my mama calls through the house.

I blow out a breath and wipe at the tears that are still falling. I have no idea what I'm going to do. If this is JR's baby, I can't pass it off on Cam. If this baby belongs to JR, Cam will never speak to me again.

"You really fucked up this time," I murmur before I go to leave out of my room.

I jog downstairs and into the kitchen where Mama was setting up lunch before Mrs. Jemma arrived. To my chagrin, Mrs. Jemma is the only one there. She beams at me as I come into view.

"Kay, it's been so long since I've seen your pretty face. Come sit. Talk to me.

"How are you doing? Why haven't I seen you at the house? Kyle has insisted on grounding me here in Texas until after the boys' season and the draft are over. I thought you'd be by the house by now," she prattles on.

"Uhm, Cam and I sort of broke up. I didn't want to run into him and cause trouble."

"Trouble," she scoffs. "You're no trouble. If I would have known you two broke up, I would have dealt with that son of mine."

She makes a sour face and grabs two glasses to pour champagne and orange juice in them. She pushes a glass in front of me.

"Have a drink with me. We'll put our heads together to figure this all out."

I shake my head. "Can't."

A gasp leaves her lips and her eyes widen. When her gaze drops to my belly, my cheeks begin to burn. This is exactly what I was trying to avoid.

I don't know how to explain this situation to her. It looks bad no matter how I put it. I'm going to disappoint her and my mama.

"This is such wonderful news," she exclaims. "Wait until you tell Cam. That little bundle of joy is going to fix everything."

"Mrs. Jemma, wait. It's not that simple."

"Why, yes, it is, sugar. You're gonna go see Cam and tell him he's gonna be a daddy. You two are gonna work things out and we'll have ourselves a wedding."

"Did Cam propose?" My mama gushes as she rushes back into the kitchen.

"No, but our Kay is pregnant. He's sure to put that ring on her finger now."

Everything spirals out of control so fast. I can't get a word in to tell them what's really going on. Before I know what's happening, Mrs. Jemma has called Cam over for us to talk.

My baby needs a daddy and a future. I'll just have to pray this baby comes out white. I'm so fucked if this isn't Cam's baby.

How do I get myself into these things? Single, no job, and I don't know who the father is. I used condoms with them both.

Fuck my life.

Cameron

I look at Kay in complete disbelief. I have to be hearing things. In the six years we've been having sex, not once have we gone without a condom or ever had a slipup.

Why is this happening now? I had been working on a plan to get Amina away. Her trip to New Jersey to bury her father wasn't the greatest.

She texted me that she was sick to her stomach the entire time. As much as she cried, I could understand why. With everything I am, I wanted to be there with her.

I didn't ask about that asshole. I don't want to know if he was around. All I wanted was to take her away and keep her safe from him. Now Kay has dropped a fucking bomb in my lap.

"Maybe we can work things out for the baby. You know, get married like we planned. We've always dreamed of starting a family together," she whispers.

My head is ready to explode. I had broken away from this. I found exactly what I wanted in Amina.

However, I'm being thrown back into what everyone else wants for me. I can see my mama and Kay's eavesdropping from here. Now I understand the look in their eyes when I arrived.

They're all planning my life for me. I can't walk out and ignore what has been said. I have a baby on the way. I did this.

I fucked up. I stare down at my palms as if watching all my dreams spill through my fingers and out of my hands. My life has fallen out of my grasp and so has my control of my destiny.

I had looked into hiring security for Cal. Special ops guys who could handle a situation like this. I found a home for Amina to live in for the next few weeks while I got things situated with my brother.

Then, we were going to be free to live wherever in the world we wanted. I didn't care where we went as long as we could be together. I even bought her a car. I had planned to give it to her when I told her the plan.

Caleb wants to marry Nicole. He's about to be drafted. He'll most likely be one of the first pitchers off the board. We did it. We made his dream come true.

All I had left to do was take care of my girl. I wanted to be a father to children with her. We didn't have to get married right away, but I would have married her as soon as she was ready.

I checked out a few rings while Cal was shopping for one for Nicky. I admire his determination to make this happen. He deserves it.

I pull a hand down my face. There's no turning back now. I'm going to be a daddy.

"Yeah, I guess we should try to work things out. How have you been feeling? Have you been to a doctor yet? Do you need anything?"

"I'm fine. I just miss you. I need some time together. I think that will make me feel a lot better."

I nod. "We should spend some time together to talk. We have a lot to talk about."

Kay gives me a bright smile, but I can't find one to return. We were once best friends. There has to be a way to make this work.

CHAPTER THIRTY-SIX

Can't Be Real

Maribel

I flush the toilet and straighten to go wash my hands. My head is spinning. I had been so sure this was all because of my grief over my dad.

It dawned on me this morning as I was awakened out of my sleep to puke my brains out that I'm late. A trip to the store and four positive tests later, I'm positive I'm pregnant.

I don't have any tears left to cry. I've lost the man I love and now I'm pregnant with his baby. I've been crying every day and night since I broke things off.

I've sent him a text or two because I miss him so much and I knew he would worry about me while I was gone. Each time he replies, my heart breaks more.

"What do I do now?" I sob as I look into the mirror.

I gasp for air and cover my mouth as I sob harder. Turning, I slide down the counter to the floor and bury my head in my knees. I know exactly when this happened.

It was that first night. We were so drunk Cam didn't use not one condom. We were fucking for hours. I lost count of how many times he came.

I'm sure all it took was once, but there was more than enough opportunity that night for this to happen. I want to scream and throw a tantrum. Dez is sure to kill us both now.

The possessive way that man looked at me creeped me out. For a moment, I didn't think he was going to allow me to return to Texas. I was so relieved when he said he had to leave on business.

However, the way he kissed my forehead before he left sent cold chills through me. I couldn't get away from him fast enough. However, it was his parting words that left me raw and filled with fear.

"Don't make me do anything else I don't want to. I'll forgive you this once. I think you've learned your lesson."

Dez left me with no doubts about who killed my father. The cold look in his eyes told the truth and dared me to speak on it. I think Cam should know about the baby, but I don't want to place a target on his back.

Maybe if I tell him, we can run together. I don't know what Dez will do when he finds out I'm pregnant. At this point, running might be my only option.

CHAPTER THIRTY-SEVEN

Shocked

Maribel

It's official. I didn't win the trip to Paris. Although I don't think that would have worked out. Dez would have found a way to track me through those tickets.

When I disappear, it needs to be without a trace. I sit in my rental car, staring at the baseball team facility. If Cam is serious about helping me, I need him and his help.

I chew on my lip. I'm nervous about telling him about the baby. I don't want him to think I'm trapping him into anything.

Our baby needs to be safe. If Dez finds out I'm pregnant, I don't think any of us will be safe. I suck in a breath and build up my courage.

"It's now or never. You're running out of time. You can feel it," I murmur to myself.

I watch as the team jogs off the field, heading into the facility. Caleb comes into view first and not that far behind him is Cam. I rush out of the car to catch Cam before he disappears into the building.

"Cam," I call out to stop him.

He turns and a smile comes to his face. I swallow hard as I almost change my mind and turn to run. Instead, I force my feet to keep moving forward.

"Can we go somewhere and talk?" I say softly.

Concern fills his eyes. "Yeah, of course. Come inside. There's a meeting room we can sit in."

I nod and follow him into the building. Once inside, Cam places his hand on the small of my back and leads me to sit down in one of two chairs that are facing each other. I sit and fidget in the seat nervously.

"What's up? I was going to call you to talk before flying out for the draft. Is everything okay?"

"I was wondering if you still want to help me," I push out before I chicken out.

"Of course I do. That's why I was going to call. I leave for the draft with my family in the morning."

"Wait, you entered?"

"Yeah, long story. I figured I'd see what happens."

"Oh," I say, looking down into my hands.

"Mina, what's wrong, baby? You're making me nervous. Did something happen with that asshole?"

"No and yes."

"Listen, I have a plan for you. I can't go, but I can get you somewhere safe if you need it."

He can't go with me. I start to panic. Why can't he go with me?

This was a bad idea. I'm totally screwed. How am I going to raise a baby on the run by myself?

"Mina, tell me what's wrong."

"I'm pregnant," I blurt out in my panic.

I watch as his face turns white as a sheet. I've never seen him look this white. His skin is always tanned from all the time he spends outdoors.

I stand and begin to back away. This was dumb. He doesn't owe me anything.

This was my stupid mistake. He doesn't need to put his life on the line for me. I will figure things out on my own.

"I'm sorry. I shouldn't have come here. This was a mistake. Forget I said anything."

I turn and race back to my car. I can hear him calling after me, but I don't stop until I'm behind the steering wheel of the car, speeding back toward my apartment.

I need to pack my things and make a plan. Tears are streaming down my face, making it hard to see the road before me. My phone begins to ring, but I ignore it.

I fell in love with Cam. Never once has he told me he loves me as more than a friend. I had gotten my hopes up for nothing. He doesn't want me or this baby.

I feel so stupid. As I stop at a light, I place my hand over my belly and take a breath. I have to figure this out for him or her.

"I'm going to keep you safe. If it's the last thing I do ... I would give my life to keep you safe. We'll be fine," I sob to the tiny being growing inside me.

I manage to get to my place in a daze. A plan slowly begins to form. I'm going to need Ximena's help. Hopefully she can get me on a flight without me using my real name or being tracked.

Somehow, I get out of my rental and make it to the apartment. I'm startled from my thoughts as Taylor calls my name. I look up to find her waiting in front of the door for me.

I almost forgot. She's here to borrow some outfit or something. I really couldn't tell you what it is at this point.

"Maribel, what's the matter? Why are you crying?"

I shake my head. I hadn't told the girls why I had to rush off to New Jersey or anything about what happened between me and Cam. I don't have the time to get into all of that now.

"I'm not going to finish my last semester. I'm dropping out," I say, not wanting to give too much information.

My friends shouldn't know much about where I'm going or why. I don't want it to come back to bite them. Taylor has been nothing but a friend and I love her for it.

"Let's get inside and we can talk about it," she says.

I shake my head. "There's nothing to talk about, I need to pack."

"Then I'll help you pack, and you can help me understand what's going on."

I run my arm under my nose. My head is starting to hurt, so I'm not going to argue with her. I'm relieved when we step into the apartment and Ximena is home.

Because Taylor is watching me like a hawk, I pull out my phone and text my cousin to set my plan in motion. I'll be gone before the end of the night.

My child comes first. As long as my baby is safe, I'll figure out the rest. This is my sign—I can do this by myself.

Cameron

I had entered the draft to see where I would land. Now that I know I have not one but two babies on the way, I need to be in the draft.

I didn't mean to upset Amina. I was just shocked. For the second time in the past month, I've been told I've gotten someone pregnant. First, I was hit with shock, then I was filled with overwhelming excitement.

By the time the excitement kicked in, Amina was running away from me. I tried to chase her down, but there was a crowd in the way when I got outside the building, and I didn't see which way she went.

I tried to call her phone, but she didn't answer. I've been trying all day. It keeps going to voicemail.

"You look like you have a lot on your mind," my father says as we're cleaning up in the back of the coffee shop after Caleb proposed to Nicole.

"I do."

"Want to talk about it?"

"What if marrying Kay isn't the right thing to do? I know about the baby and all, but something isn't sitting right with me."

"You mean your little friend is still in the picture," he replies.

"Yeah, something like that."

"I'd say take care of your responsibilities. Don't forget you and Kay took some time apart. If I were you, I'd make sure to sweep under the rug before lying down your hat."

"You don't think the baby is mine?"

"I think you need to make sure you have an ironclad prenup and a clause to walk out of the marriage on your terms. That little girl wants to live a comfortable life. If that's my grandson or granddaughter, fine.

"I'll be happy to spoil the whole lot of you. But if not, your happiness is all I'm worried about. I want you to have what your brother has. Someone you're crazy about.

"Life is hard enough as it is. I've learned money doesn't fix everything, but love will make it tolerable. You want to have peace in your home," he says.

I nod as I think his words over. He pats me on the shoulder and gives it a squeeze. I look into his eyes and read his concern for me.

"Don't allow your mama to rush you into anything. Kay is what *she* wants. I want you to have what *you* want."

"I hear you, Daddy. I need to go make a call."

I leave out the back of the coffee shop where I parked. I drove the SUV I bought for Amina. I was hoping she would answer so I could take it to her and explain my plan.

This vehicle seemed like the best choice. It's brand new and reliable, it's spacious for her things and her height, and now that she's carrying my child, he or she will have plenty of room for a car seat. It will also be hard to run off the road.

As I sit in the driver's seat, I stare down at Bernie's phone. I asked him to borrow it to see if Amina would answer a call from his line.

Blowing out a breath, I dial her number and wait as it rings. My heart is hammering as I place it on speaker, and it continues to ring. I start the engine, ready to race to her place.

Caleb doesn't need me anymore tonight. I've done my part here. Now it's my turn to get my girl.

"Hello?" she finally picks up.

"Baby, don't hang up. You misunderstood. I'm so excited we're having a baby.

"I want to take care of you. I want to be there for you and our baby. I was just shocked," I begin to explain before she can disconnect.

"But you said you can't come with me. Don't worry about it. I'll be okay, Cam," she whispers.

"Mina, please. There's so much more you don't know. Kay and I were going to try to work things out. I didn't know you were carrying my baby."

She scoffs on the other end of the phone. "Stay with the one you want. I'm only going to bring you drama."

Anger fills me. She's not listening. I need her to hear me out.

"Maribel," I bark. "Listen to me. You are the one I want. You never bring me any drama I don't want.

"You told me we should break up, but I've been making plans for us. I was planning to run with you. You mean everything to me, baby. I'd do anything for you."

The line falls silent. As I pick the phone up from the cup holder, I see it's still connected. When I zero in, I can still hear her breathing.

"Then why did you say you couldn't come with me?" she finally says.

"I fucked up. Everything is so fucked up. Kay's pregnant and she says it's mine. My mama called me to Kay's place for her to drop the bomb on me.

"You and I ... you told me we were done. I was going to go through with the engagement and work things out. It felt like the right thing to do for the baby."

"Maybe it is. Listen, Cam, he practically admitted to murdering my father at the funeral. I can't go back.

"He'd kill me and this baby and then you. Let me go. Marry Kay. That's what's best. I'll take care of our baby."

"What's best for who?" I growl into the phone. "If he wants us, let him come. I'm going to protect what's mine.

"I'm coming over, baby. We need to talk. I'm going to get you two somewhere safe. I leave for the draft with my family in the morning.

"I'll go to support Cal, but I won't accept my offer. I have somewhere for you to go that's safe. When I get back, we can disappear."

"I'm already gone, Cam. I had to run."

"Then I'll come to you. Where are you?"

"We can't."

"Why not? Please don't do this. Don't take my family from me. I want you. I want you both. Please."

The line falls silent again. However, this time, I think I hear her trying to muffle her cries. It's then that I realize my face is soaked with my own tears.

I lean my head back and look up at the roof of the truck. My mind is racing. I don't want to lose them. I'd die to protect them.

"Please, baby. I'd do anything for you. Please."

"We need to be smart. You coming to me isn't smart. I think he knows about us. He didn't just kill him because I wouldn't come back; he knows about us."

"What makes you say that?"

"I found cameras in the apartment," she says.

All the blood drains from my face. This guy is a fucking lunatic. Who cams up their fiancée's place? It's not even her place. That's so fucked up.

"Okay, I was going to hire these special ops guys for Cal. I'll hire two extras to be with you until I can meet up with you."

"I said we have to be smart. That's not smart. Not smart enough."

"Okay, what are you thinking?"

I pick the phone up and take it off speaker. I breathe a little easier now that I feel some hope of getting to my family. My heart is still racing.

"Go to the draft and get drafted. I'm sure he knows all about you. If you don't go, he'll know you ran with me.

"We need you to look like you moved on with your life. Go through with things with Kay—"

"What are you talking about? You want me to marry her? No, Maribel. No."

"Cam, please. This man killed his own brother to get to the top. You and I are nothing to him. This baby is even less.

"If you marry Kay, that'll be even more convincing that you've moved on and I mean nothing to you. He's not going to watch you as closely or try to harm you to find me.

"You said I mean everything to you. If you care about me, trust me," she says.

"I don't just care about you, Mina. I love you. I need you to know I love you.

"I'm not marrying someone else out of love. Because it's you who will always have my heart. I do this; I need you to know I did it out of love for you. I would do anything to protect you," I say as my heart breaks.

"Cam?"

"Yeah?"

"I love you too. I'm so sorry. I didn't mean for this to happen."

"I'm not sorry. I got you away from him, didn't I?"

"Yeah, you may have. I wish I could go all *Colombiana* on his ass. He killed my dad. That can't go unanswered."

"One thing at a time. We need you and our baby safe. Maribel?"

"Yes, Cam?"

"He's never going to take you from me. I'm coming for my family as soon as we figure out how to get rid of him."

"You're getting married and getting drafted tomorrow, Cam. Stop sounding like your world is over," she teases.

"I'm getting married to the wrong woman and I'd rather be with my family than be at a draft."

"You will be with your family. Your brother needs you. You need to do that thing you do for him. Whatever it is you do."

I pause for a moment in thought. She's trusting me with her life. I can trust her with my secret.

"Caleb has autism. We've been hiding it so he can get drafted to the majors. My mama has wanted to hide it from the world all his life, but my daddy and I agreed to hide it during college to give him a shot at normal."

I scoff to myself. All we have ever wanted is normal. Not just Cal, but I've been longing for some sense of normalcy. Now, the concept doesn't make sense to me.

What's normal? Right now, my brother's life is more normal than mine will ever be. Yet I know if it means Amina is in my life, I wouldn't change a thing.

"Wow, Cam. I had no idea. I mean, now that you mention it ... you're an amazing brother."

"There's nothing I wouldn't do for him. All his dreams are coming true. He doesn't need me anymore. You do."

"Are you sure you want to do this?"

I sit, trying to find the words to tell her all I'm feeling. I wish there was more I could do. I wish I was there with her.

I want to be on one knee proposing to her for our family to be together. I want to rewind time and pull her into my arms after she spoke those words to me to let me know I'm going to be a father to our child.

Suddenly, I know just how to let her know how I feel. I connect my phone to the Bluetooth as I hold Bernie's. Then, I scroll for what I'm looking for.

The song begins to play. I close my eyes. When I hang up and go home, I'm going to be destroyed.

"Do you remember what I said about when I play one of these songs for someone?"

"If you play one of their songs, you mean the words from your heart," she breathes.

"Yeah, Mina. I mean this. I mean every word. I want to do this. I love you."

Tears stream down my face as we both remain silent as the song plays. I feel like someone is cutting my insides up. I double over, leaning against the steering wheel as I cry like a little boy lost.

This is tearing me apart.

CHAPTER THIRTY-EIGHT

Cry for You

Maribel

I have the phone on speaker as I sit curled into myself on this hotel bed. I'm sobbing so hard my ribs hurt. I knew I shouldn't have answered the call.

I was nervous and my emotions were all over the place as my phone started to ring. I had just finished dying my hair and was in tears because I hated it. I'm not a redhead.

Ximena thought it was a good idea to change the color of my hair. I didn't go with blonde because I thought it would be too attention-grabbing with my deep-brown skin. The cinnamon or auburn color, if you will, doesn't look bad. It's just a reminder of why I had to dye it in the first place.

I didn't expect Cameron to plead with me to stay with him. Hearing this big, strong man sound so broken as he pleaded for his family nearly broke me.

However, I know what's right for all of us. I can't go back, and he can't rush here to me. I won't even be here long. I'll be gone before morning.

Finding those cameras scared the shit out of me and Ximena. She immediately understood how important it was for me to disappear. She snapped right into action.

It was a good thing we had started texting our plans. We don't know if there was audio to go along with the visuals on the other end of those videos. I still can't believe he was recording my life.

Ximena suggested we place the cameras back where we found them. I only packed the essentials, making sure to do so out of sight of the cameras. Placing my things in garbage bags, we then took out the trash and I left out of the apartment as if it was any other night where I was going to meet up with friends.

The song ends and I swipe at my tears. "Cam, I should go. I'm going to have to dump this phone. You won't be able to reach me on it again. I'll call you from a burner once I'm settled."

"What about the security guys?" he chokes out and I can tell he's been crying on the other end.

"You can hold off on that for now. I don't want to draw any attention to myself. I should be fine where I'm going."

I don't tell him where I'm going or who I'm going to stay with. The less he knows, the better. I don't really know the people I'll be with.

"Are you sure?"

"Yeah. Will you promise me something?"

"Anything."

"Promise me you'll be safe. Protect yourself, Cam. Learn how to use a gun if you have to. Don't let him take you from us."

"I already know how to use a firearm, darlin'. You know about these hands."

I can't help the chuckle that comes from my lips as he tries to deliver the last part like a New Yorker through his Texas drawl. My heart aches as I realize how much I'm going to miss him.

"Keep Cal safe too. Nothing can happen to him."

"Fuck," he hisses, making my heart race.

"What? What just happened?"

"You'll see when you watch the draft," he says.

"Cam, I'll be traveling. I don't know if I'll get to watch."

"Cal shaved to propose to Nicole. We look exactly alike right now."

"Shit."

"Don't worry about it. I'll figure it out. You just try to watch if you can. I want you to know where our new home will be when this is all over."

I smile as I cover my stomach and dare to dream of us as a family. Then my smile falls as I begin to feel like a home-wrecker. Kay didn't ask for this.

"Cam, maybe we shouldn't. This isn't fair to Kay," I whisper.

"Don't you worry about that. You let me deal with her. I love you, baby. I'll be with you two soon."

"Love you."

I close my eyes as tears continue to spill. The call cuts off, leaving a hole in my soul. I find "Cry For You" on my phone and place it on repeat as I cry myself to sleep.

This hurts so bad.

Cameron

I climb out of the car to head back inside and hand Bernie back his phone. My daddy is on his way out the door as I go to step inside. He freezes and cups the sides of my face.

"Cameron, what's going on?"

I shake my head. This has turned far more dangerous than I anticipated before. I don't know if I can keep my family safe all on my own.

"Speak to me, Cam. I'm your daddy. If I can, I'll make it right. What is it?"

"Not here. I need to get a haircut and make some calls in a private place. Not my place."

I think of the cameras in Amina's and don't feel safe making arrangements there anymore. I'm also going to cut my hair off. Cal and I look too much alike with the long hair.

His is longer, but if you're not paying attention to the details, you won't make the distinction right away. I need there to be no doubt that I'm Cameron and he's Caleb. I need to protect him as much as I need to protect Amina and my unborn child.

"Come on, I have a place. I'll have my barber come to us. You can explain everything to me on the way there," Daddy says.

I rush inside to give Bernie the phone. When I return outside, my daddy is waiting for me. I relax a little, knowing I'll have help with all of this.

"I sent Jerry home. I'll ride with you."

I nod and head to Amina's new truck. I'll give it to her someday, I'm just hoping it's someday soon.

***

"Well, damn. I knew there was something special about that little lady," Daddy says as he sits with his forearms draped over his thighs.

We're sitting in two leather accent chairs facing each other. My father brought me to one of the bars he owns, and we came down to the basement to have this chat. Most of his places have these private rooms for VIP customers.

The room is soundproof, and you have to have a key card that comes with a private membership to gain access. I've just spent an hour filling him in on all that has been happening. Hearing my own words out loud has left me with a plethora of feelings.

"She is special. She's worth everything I'm about to do," I reply.

"Now that there is my grandbaby and its mama. There ain't no way you're handling this on your own. My only problem is how this will affect Kay.

"I may not want you to rush into things with her and I want you to end up with the one you love, but it ain't right to lead the girl on, knowing you don't plan to stay with her."

"I've been thinking about that, but I'm not about to place Amina and the baby in danger by telling her the truth."

My daddy sighs. "This could get ugly, Cameron."

"I know, Daddy. I know."

I've been spinning things in my mind, trying to figure out how to handle this. I don't want to hurt Kay, but I don't want to place Amina in danger either.

It already seems like Kay has a problem with Amina. I'm not asking her to be Amina's best friend, but I need to know I can trust her when it comes to my family. I need to know our friendship truly means something to her.

"You're definitely going to need that prenup," Daddy says, pulling me from my thoughts. "Let me think things over and I'll talk to my attorney to make sure you're covered."

"I don't want to leave my baby with nothing. Maybe I can offer something, knowing I'm going to divorce their mama."

"Slow down. My gut says you need to take caution."

Frustration fills me. I don't understand why he's so against my relationship with Kay. I wish I could say this is new, but it's not. Daddy has been side-eyeing Kay since my junior year in high school.

"Why are you so sure about Amina but you have questions about Kay? You've known Kayleen all her life."

"I have, but you yourself said you were the first man Amina has been with. I could be wrong, but I believe that girl would do just about anything for you."

He shrugs. "Kayleen comes from different stock. Them girls have a system on how to nab a man like you. I know her mama. I know yours. I know what they are willing to do to secure the luxury a man like you promises."

"You really think she'd try to pass off someone else's baby on me?"

"Are you about to marry her to save and hide the woman you love? People will do anything when they're desperate."

I run my hand through my hair. I'm about to cut all my locks off to protect my baby brother. Daddy has a point. I blow out a breath and lift my gaze to the ceiling.

"Here's our guy. Larry, my boy here needs a cut, and I could use a cleanup. We're headed to the draft in the morning. Make us look good," my father croons.

CHAPTER THIRTY-NINE

The Draft

Maribel

"I'll get that order for those wings and fries in right away," the bartender calls to me as he pours some guy a few seats down a drink.

"Thanks," I whisper and nod even though I know he can't hear me.

I'm sitting in the bar at the airport. I wish I had something stronger than this glass of water in my hands. My nerves are shot.

I'm exhausted. I didn't come straight to my final destination. We didn't know if Dez was having me followed. After going to the hotel and dying my hair, I then hopped on a bus and rode a few states over.

Ximena met me there as she was able to swap flights with another flight attendant. There, she was able to get the help of some friends who got me onto my flight to my final destination. So here I sit in a bar in the airport in Boston.

Ximena told me to wait here for a friend of hers who would keep me safe. "They will find you." Her words are ringing in my ears as I sit here with knots in my stomach.

My eyes are glued to the TV screen. The draft is about to start. The bartender was more than happy to turn to it when I asked.

I clench the glass between my hands as the program starts. The announcers are going through all the baseball hopefuls. My chest swells with pride as Caleb is mentioned and they begin to show his highlights.

I'm in complete awe as I realize this guy has been autistic all this time. I smirk. This is some Cam shit for real. Way to stick it to those who say what can't be done.

They begin to talk about his twin brother next. My eyes start to tear up as I watch the highlights of the father of my child. Then, they cut to a frame of the brothers sitting together. Nicole looks amazing sitting next to Cal.

Then there's Cam. My mouth falls open as they zoom in on him. Cameron has always been fine. But Cam, with a low-fade crew cut, is fire.

David Beckham has nothing on my baby daddy. Cam is clean-shaven as usual, so when he looks up into the camera and smiles, those cute-ass, sexy dimples pop and my heart stops. Butterflies take flight in my belly and my eyes burn with tears.

The twins still have the same face, but now you can't mistake the two for each other. I'm super nervous now. I have to remind myself to breathe as I continue to watch. Caleb is the first of the twins to be drafted. I'm so happy for him.

I watch as Cam hugs his brother tightly before he heads for the stage. However, when he releases him, they both look nervous. For a moment, I think Cam is going to follow him up on stage.

His face says he wants to. However, instead, he moves back to his seat as Cal strolls up on stage. The bartender comes and places a hot plate of wings and fries in front of me, causing my mouth to water.

"I sure do hope those twins go to the same team. I've seen a few of their collegiate games. They're dynamic together. I was hoping my guys would get them, but I'm happy for them either way," the bartender says.

He then raps his knuckles on the bar top and goes to pour a drink for another customer. I'm too nervous to touch my food. The next team is on the clock.

Like the guy said, I hope the brothers get to stay together. Especially now that I know about Cal. I hold my breath as they go to announce the next player to be drafted to Atlanta.

"Cameron Perry."

It's like his name echoes through the bar. I don't know how to feel. It's not New York or Texas, but that's as much a problem as it is a good thing. Cam will be so far from his family and his brother.

I still don't know how this is supposed to work out. Cam smiles for the camera and puts the cap on his head like this is the greatest day of his life. I'm proud of him.

"This is the father, no?" I turn to find a woman standing right on top of me.

I mean, she's all in my personal space. She's around my height and has pretty brown eyes. Although she's not making eye contact with me, her eyes stand out. They are large and bright, and her lashes are amazing.

Everything about her face is pretty, her nose, her mouth, those eyes. Sis has some of the nicest locs I've ever seen. They are neatly styled and look freshly done.

I blink a few times as I look up at her. I'm at a loss for words. She looks around us then lifts her hand for the bartender.

"We should get moving. He can box your food, or you can wait for them to prepare you something at the house. My chef is world-renowned. You will enjoy her cooking," she says in a robotic way.

"We can leave it," I say, having lost my appetite.

"I am Symphony. Ximena has sent me here for you. First rule, never do what you just did. If you don't know someone, do not engage."

"But ... wait, how do I know you're the one who I'm supposed to be waiting for?"

"Do you have the Rubik's Cube?"

I nod and go to grab the cube from my bag.

"Go ahead and mix it up," she says then holds her hand out.

I twist it and mix the colors up. Then I hand it over to her. She solves it right before my face. I don't even think she takes a minute to complete it, just as Ximena said.

She hands it back to me. Then pulls her phone from her pocket and starts tapping away at it. My burner phone chimes and I look down at it.

I open the text and find a picture of Symphony holding up a phone. I zoom in and see Ximena giving me a thumbs-up on the phone screen.

"I and anyone connected to me will always verify themselves with two forms of verification like this."

I nod and stand to grab my things so we can leave. She settles my bill, and we go. We're both silent until we get to the parking garage.

There is a driver waiting for us with a sleek black car. We slide into the back as the driver takes my things to place them in the trunk. I have so many questions, but I don't know where to start.

"Ximena is a good friend of mine. You are safe here with me. Not only am I protected and looked after, but I also have the skills of someone your ex never wants to meet. If he finds you here, he will die," she says matter-of-factly.

"How do you know my cousin?"

"I once saved her life, and we became friends. I don't make friends easily. She was kind to me."

I nod my head. That was one of my questions. I still have a million more.

"You are allowed free rein of my estate. However, if my family comes to visit, I will restrict some areas."

"I will need to find a doctor."

"Yes, for the pregnancy. I will help you with that. I have a client who owes me a favor. You will be taken care of."

"A client? What do you do, if you don't mind me asking?"

"I'm an assassin for hire, but if you meet my husband, you are not to tell him what I'm up to. As far as he is concerned, I am a principal dancer and an accomplished pianist."

After those words, I have nothing else to say. I think I'm pretty damn safe with this woman.

CHAPTER FORTY

Revealing Prenup

Kayleen

Mrs. Jemma has been tearing up my nerves. She insisted I travel to the draft with her ahead of Cam and the others. The tension in the air when Cam and Cal arrived with their daddy and Nicole was suffocating.

Once she saw Nicole's engagement ring, she started in on me to apply pressure to Cam about proposing to me. I don't want to do that. I'm still not sure who the father of my child is.

Cam has been putting on a smile for everyone, but I can see he's not happy. I'll be honest. I'm not happy either.

I don't understand what happened between me and JR. If this baby ends up being his, I will have lost the man I fell in love with, and I'll lose one of my oldest friends. Cam will never forgive me.

I won't forgive myself if I go through with this and say nothing. Cam should at least know there's a chance this baby isn't his. I just need his mama to get off my back.

"Kay," Cam calls through the villa we've been staying in.

Draft night was so exciting. I know nothing about Atlanta, but Cam was drafted pretty high. This baby isn't going to want for anything. Between Cam's trust and contract, we'll be sitting pretty for the rest of our lives.

However, if this baby is a little girl, I'm going to make sure she goes to school and finds her own thing. I've depended on a man my entire life. My mama made it seem like it was the only way.

Now, I find myself wishing I did something more with my life. If I had, I wouldn't be in this situation. I could have taken my time to figure things out and then make my own decisions.

"Kay, did you hear me?" Cam says as he appears in the bedroom we've been sharing.

Cam had tried to take one of the empty rooms for himself, but Mrs. Jemma insisted we share a room together. Cam hasn't had sex with me since we've been back together. Not that I haven't tried.

He's kind to me and we haven't been fighting. Not even the tiny squabbles that we've been having for forever. If it looks like we're heading in that direction, Cam concedes or changes the topic.

"I'm sorry. I was in my thoughts. What's up?"

"Daddy just took Mama back home. I thought we could hang back and figure some things out. I have a few things I want to talk to you about," he says.

Thank the Lord. I'll have to give Mr. Perry a big old hug next time I see him. I literally feel the weight being lifted off my shoulders. That woman was going to drive me crazy.

"Oh, okay. What's up?"

"Come on downstairs. We can talk and you can eat something. How are you feeling?"

"Okay, I guess. I haven't been having morning sickness or anything like that. I'm just tired here and there."

"Everyone is different," he murmurs almost to himself.

I get up from the vanity I've been sitting at and follow him out of the room. My mind begins to wander. Maybe now that Mrs. Jemma is gone, I should come clean.

My stomach twists in knots. What if I come clean and he breaks up with me for good? I can't tell him about the baby without telling him I was cheating.

I can't do that to my baby. I can't ruin its future. I bite my lip as we enter the living area. The first thing I notice is the charcuterie board and what looks like sparkling cider.

There are candles lit as well. It looks like a romantic date. I look up at Cam and smile. Guilt laces my belly, and I think I might puke.

"Come on. Sit down," he says, giving me a smile that doesn't quite meet his eyes.

"What's all this about?" I say, trying to sound cheery.

"I thought we could talk about our future. We're working on things and that means getting engaged will be our next step with the baby coming and all."

My smile falters. His words leave me feeling like shit. If he only wants to get married for the baby, I need to say something. Cam has always been my friend first. It's how we always end up making up.

"Are you all right?" he asks as I stare down into my lap.

"Yeah, I'm fine. I think I just need to eat something."

I scoot forward in my seat to place some cheese and crackers on a napkin to stuff my face and keep myself from spilling the truth. Cam pours us both a glass of cider and hands me one.

I down the cider, then start to stuff the food into my mouth. My stomach sours as I think about all the wrongs I've done to my friend. Can I even be considered a friend at this point?

Cam has been nothing but good to me, but I've been a bitch since we graduated high school. Maybe even before then.

I whined about being left behind when all of that was my fault. I placed his brother's health in danger more than once. Then I cheated on him for almost four years with someone he once considered a friend.

Yeah, I'm not a friend at all. If I do this to Cam, I'll just be driving that fact home.

Cam continues. "If we get married, I'd like for you to sign a prenup. I have a copy here for you to look over. You can take your time."

I swallow hard and place my now empty napkin down so I can reach for the papers he's holding.

I begin to read them over and my head begins to pulse. My vision blurs as tears fill my eyes. The entitled spoiled brat I had been deserves this. The woman sitting here now, in her newfound maturity, understands this.

However, when I get to the clause about the paternity of the baby, my tears spill over, and I know I can't go through with this. He must know I'm hiding something, and this clause will leave me with nothing if this baby isn't his.

"What's wrong? Why are you crying?" he asks, looking at me with concern.

"Cam, I need to tell you something."

"Okay, I'm listening. Go on."

I take a deep, fortifying breath and begin to gather my words. I need to say it all. He needs to know the whole truth.

"I'm so sorry. I love you, but I've been in love with someone else. I … we hooked up during that break we took your freshman year. I was so confused and conflicted about what I had done.

"Then we got back together. You know the pressure our mamas have been placing us under. I didn't want to disappoint them.

"But I liked the way he made me feel. It was different from us. I thought for sure you were hooking up with girls all along. I figured it wouldn't hurt to keep things with him going.

"Christmas break turned into a year. Then a year turned into three and then I had fallen in love with him, but I love you too. I'm just not in love with you. Not like I thought I was.

"Truth is, we broke up right after you and I did, and I'm not sure whose baby I'm carrying. It could be yours. It could be his, but I can't keep lying to you. It makes me sick. I'm so sorry, Cam."

His face is full of shock, making me feel even worse. The tears won't stop falling from my eyes. I'm losing everything, but at least I can stop feeling disgusting.

"I promise I wasn't going to go through with this. Your mama just figured out I was pregnant and assumed it was your baby. You know how she gets.

"Before I knew it, I was telling you it was yours. I completely understand if you never want to have anything to do with me. If it is your baby, we can co-parent if that's what you want. If not, I understand," I sob.

Cam is so silent I don't know what to do. I blink away my tears and try to calm myself. When I look into his eyes, he's giving me that smile I know him so well for.

It's warm and inviting. It's the smile of my friend I've known all my life. I'm so confused as he slides closer and tugs me into his embrace.

Cameron

I should be mad as fuck that she was cheating on me for four years. I should also be pissed she was going to pass someone else's baby off on me, but I'm not. I'm relieved more than anything.

I could laugh my ass off right now. I came into this villa feeling like a total asshole for what I planned to do. My father had the paternity clause added to the prenup.

If the baby is mine, I planned to give her twenty million in the divorce. That should have been more than enough for her and the baby to live comfortably. Not that I don't plan to be around to help raise my child.

I don't want to spend the rest of my life with Kay. The baby has nothing to do with that. However, if it was not my child, she wouldn't have walked away without a dime. That was my daddy's stipulation.

Now, knowing what I know, I can breathe. I don't care about this guy she was fucking or about being angry. I need her help, and it seems like she might need mine.

"I will have the prenup changed. I'll marry you. If the baby is mine, you'll still get the twenty million. If not, after a year, we'll divorce, and I'll give you five. Is that fair?"

She pulls out of my hold and looks me in the eyes. "What? Why?"

"It sounds like this guy isn't in the picture anymore. Will he be there for the baby if it's his?"

"No, I don't think that will ever be an option," she says sadly.

"Then I'm helping a friend. You have a baby who needs a stable financial future and I need to get married."

"You need to get married? Since when?"

This is where I think fast and begin to lie. I don't know if I can trust Kay with the real reason I need to take her as my wife. I need to protect my woman and child at all costs.

"There's another clause on my trust. Another portion of the trust is released after I'm married. I have something I want to invest in, and I need more money to do so," I say and shrug.

It's not a complete lie. There is a marriage clause on the trust that unlocks a greater sum, but I have years to fulfill that clause. However, if she were to ask my mama about it, she would confirm the clause is real.

"So I get the money for me and the baby either way?" she asks cautiously.

"Yup, but we only need to stay married for a year. In a year, we'll get divorced."

"Okay, I'm in."

CHAPTER FORTY-ONE

Got It Wrong

Kayleen

Three months later ...

I sigh as I sit down in the restaurant to wait for my friend Emma Jean. My feet hurt and my belly is itching. At five months, my belly is beginning to pop.

I went for my first ultrasound today. Cam couldn't be there. He's in Atlanta with his team. I hated Atlanta from the moment we moved there, so I moved back home. Cam didn't protest.

We've actually grown closer. Our friendship has slowly been rebuilding. Although I'm not sure we'll ever get back the trust we once had.

Cam comes to Texas often to spend time with me and check on the baby. We look like a happy couple. However, we do put on our little squabbles for his mama.

Cam didn't think it was smart to become a perfect couple out of the blue. I can't say I'm not happy. I just really miss sex. Cam added to the revised prenup that there would be no sex.

I was taken aback by that, but I wasn't going to blow everything because he didn't want to sleep with me.

I can't blame him. I did cheat on him for years. At this point, I'm happy with my little vibrator.

"Hello, Kayleen."

I look up into the face of the man who just purred my name. I reach for my belly and cradle it as my heart begins to race. I got what I deserved with JR.

I can't be in my feelings when I did the same thing to him and Cam. I blink back tears as I think of how much I miss him. I had so many hopes for us.

"Hi, JR. What are you doing here?"

He points to the seat across from me. "May I?"

I lick my lips and nod. He drops into the seat smoothly. He looks great.

"Why are you here?" I ask again.

"I might have called in a few favors. Simone asked Emma Jean to set this lunch up."

"But why?"

"I need some closure. I don't understand what happened. You cut me off. Blocked me. Then I found out you married Cam.

"What did I do? Is it the baby? You know I would have raised it as mine, right?"

He looks down at my swollen stomach. Anger fills me. I know I'm wrong for it, but I can't convince myself otherwise. He cheated on me.

"I found out about the baby after. It had nothing to do with her," I snap.

"After what, Kayleen? What went wrong?"

"That night I called you crying. I heard her. You didn't hang up before I heard her."

The pain of that night stabs me in the chest all over again. I swipe at my tears and take a deep breath. I don't want to upset the baby.

JR's expression goes from confused to sad. He reaches across the table to tuck a strand of hair behind my ear. I draw away from him and the sadness deepens.

"That was my mom. I had joined her on her trip and had to stay in her room because the resort was booked. I didn't want to wake her so I was trying to whisper and make it out of the room. I banged my toe in the process.

"What you heard was my mom checking on me. Not another woman. I love you, Kay. It's always been you," he explains.

I sit there feeling stupid, with tears flowing down my face. How did I once again fuck everything up? I place my head in my hands and start to ball.

I hear the sound of a chair scraping the floor. Next thing I know, JR is holding me, cooing in my ear.

I don't know how long I sit there crying. When my tears dry up, he drags his chair beside mine and returns to his seat.

"At least now I know. I'm sorry things didn't work out. Congratulations on your marriage and the baby. She's a lucky girl. The Perrys will spoil her for sure." He chuckles sadly.

He goes to stand and leave, kissing my forehead before turning. I reach for his hand to stop him before he takes a full step.

"Wait, would you like to see a picture of our daughter?"

Cameron

"Better luck next time, Perry. We all go through it," one of my teammates calls as I step out of the shower and head for my locker.

I've been playing like shit. There's too much on my mind. All I want is to be with my girl and our baby.

It hasn't been safe for me to go to her yet. I'm not willing to take the risk. I think I need to wait a little longer until we're sure that motherfucker isn't still watching us.

My blood boils every time I think of him. I swear I want to be the one who takes his life. However, I'm sticking to the plan.

My father has some friends investigating that asshole Dez. The bastard is smart, and they haven't found anything that will put him away for any amount of time yet, but we're hopeful.

"You coming out for a bite, Perry?" another one of my teammates asks.

"Nah, I'm headed home. Need to get back at it and find my swing again."

"Suit yourself."

I grunt and grab my phone from my locker. I smile down at the ultrasound picture Kay sent me. She's having a little girl. I've known for about a month and a half now that I'm not the father.

Kay had the paternity test done not too long after we got married. I was willing to wait, but it was weighing on her. I could see she was stressing herself out.

That's also why I didn't argue when she wanted to return home. She wasn't happy here. I covered for her with my mama. We told everyone she wasn't happy and moved back on her own.

My daddy is the only one who knows that to be a lie. We knew telling them anything else would have seemed out of character for Kay. It was my daddy who footed the bill for the house in Texas

Kay now lives in. He still feels bad for her, knowing I'm going to leave her for my family.

There is nothing tying me to Kay other than our friendship. Amina still doesn't know what we're having. She's about a month, almost two, behind Kay. I'm hoping to be there when she finds out.

I'm moving heaven and earth to get to her soon. I miss her so fucking much. The burner phone I keep for her calls dings. The people she's staying with suggested we not use my personal line or any others connected to me to communicate.

I answer the phone quickly, wanting to hear her voice so bad. Forgetting about getting dressed to get out of here, I sit to take the call. My heart races until I hear her voice on the other end.

"Hello," I say.

"Hey, babe. I'm sorry about the loss."

I shrug as if she can see me. "My head just wasn't in the game."

"Ugh, you were thinking about chocolate chip cookies too?"

I chuckle. I can always count on her to make me laugh. I've come to look forward to her calls after a bad game.

"Yeah, something like that. How's my baby?"

"Little Perry is fine. Just a little exhausted from cheering daddy on."

"Shit, I bet. The way I sucked tonight that had to zap you both."

"We're happily zapped now that we can hear your voice. Don't be so hard on yourself. You're not even the worst player on the team. The rest of those guys could start pulling their weight too."

"Spoken like a woman who loves me. It's so good to hear your voice, darlin'."

"It's good to hear yours too."

"I think we have a solid plan. I'm going to attempt to come see you soon. Daddy's working on covering the flight logs and anything that could reveal where I've been.

"I can't wait to see you. As soon as I know details I'll fill you in. I can't wait to see your face and hold you in my arms."

"Me either. So what's Kay having. Today was the day, right?"

"A girl. Uncle Cam will still teach her how to swing a bat. She can use it for other things."

"You're a great guy, Cam. If we have a little girl, I know she's going to adore you."

I snort. "That baby is a boy. He knows it, I know it, and you know it. He better not come out flashing nothing but a pair of balls."

Maribel bursts into laughter on the other end of the line. It's good to hear her laugh. I wish I had the visual to go with the sound. I could watch her gorgeous face for hours.

I love that her skin always seems to glow with a bronze hue. It's like that light is beaming from within. I close my eyes and try to picture it now.

"Cam?" she yawns.

"Yeah, baby?"

"It's a struggle to keep my eyes open. I should probably go to sleep. I'll call you tomorrow, okay?"

"Get some sleep. I love you."

"I love you too. Brush this one off, babe. There's always the next one."

"Sleep tight, gorgeous."

I don't tell her that if I keep going like this, there might not be a next one. I'm either going down to the triple-A or they're going to place my ass on waivers. Either way, I can't find it in me to care. I want to be with my family and I'm not going to be happy until I am.

"Goodnight, Cam."

"Night, baby."

CHAPTER FORTY-TWO

Twins

Maribel

Two months later …

"We will need to leave now to make the appointment. It is a thirty-minute ride with traffic. There is a fifty-one-percent chance of rain which could increase our travel time and cause a delay in our arrival," Sim says as she enters the kitchen where I'm finishing a bowl of fruit.

I'm going in for an ultrasound today. Dr. Livingston wants me to come into his office instead of the home visits because of my size. I look like I swallowed a whale.

I'm six months pregnant but look more like twelve. I should have known this would happen. I mean, look at this kid's father, nearly six-seven and built like a tractor. This kid is bound to rip my little kitty up.

"I'm ready," I say as I place a hand over my huge belly.

"Let me carry your bag."

She comes forward to take my oversized purse. I give her a smile, but she doesn't return it. I'm not offended.

I've come to learn this is who Sim is. She's extremely smart and if you ask her something, she's going to give the most detailed response she can, often sounding like an encyclopedia.

I begin to waddle behind her as we head for the garage where the cars are parked. I'm a little nervous about this visit. Dr. Livingston has been getting this look on his face that worries me.

I missed the ultrasound scheduled at his office last month because Cam wanted to be there, but his plans didn't work out. He felt like he was being followed and turned back.

I was so disappointed. Dr. Livingston was going to bring in a portable machine but one of the other doctors in his practice broke the only one they had and we ended up not doing it at all. Sim was ready to order one just for me, but I wouldn't allow it.

She has already spoiled me like a big sister. I get that she makes good money in her line of work and her husband—whoever he is—keeps her pampered with anything she wants. However, I'm not here to take her money.

"I would like to start a nursery for you and the baby. We don't know how much longer you will be with me, but I don't want to be caught unprepared. If you leave before the baby is born, I can have it all shipped to you."

"*Sim*," I drag out.

"It is not a problem. You have become a friend. I want to do this for you. My family doesn't mind if I spend the money. Allow me to do this for you."

"Can I ask you something?"

"Yes."

"What's the deal with your husband?"

I feel bad for asking as soon as the words are out of my mouth. Symphony begins to pop the band she keeps on her right wrist. It's something I picked up on within my first week here.

When she's uncomfortable or upset, she begins to pop the band. My mind races with things to change the subject to.

"We are not married in the traditional sense. My husband married me as a favor to my grandfather. It was to keep me safe.

"There is more I cannot tell you. Not if I want to leave you alive. I like you and I don't wish to kill you."

I look at her like she's crazy, waiting for her to laugh. She never does. She's totally serious.

"I think we understand each other more than you know. My story isn't exactly the same, but I get it," I say, trying to cut through some of the tension.

"Back to my husband. I am married but I have never lain with my husband. I believe he avoids me because of my disorder and our age gap.

"I was a child bride. He was no more than a boy himself. He remained with me until I turned sixteen and then, for some reason, he disappeared.

"I see my brother- and sister-in-law more than I see my husband. I haven't seen him in a very long time," she says with a note of sadness in her voice.

"Well then, it's his loss. You're one of the dopest people I've ever met. If he doesn't want to see that, that's on him."

"I wish I were more like you. I have wanted him to want me. I loved him. I've tried to become just like him in hopes he will love me when he returns to me."

"What do you mean?"

"Again, I would have to kill you."

"I'm going to stop talking to you," I say as I give her side-eye.

"Please don't. I have never had a friend to talk to about my husband. I don't know what I should do to get him to come to me."

"How old are you, Sim?"

"I am twenty-eight."

"How old is your husband?"

"He would be thirty-three now."

"Well, how long has it been since you've seen him?"

She twists her lips up and begins popping her band again. Her eyes are unfocused for a beat. Then she clears her throat.

"I was sixteen. It was just before I went to school for music. I was a prodigy and played classical piano. While there I fell in love with dance and ballet.

"You play beautifully and you're an amazing dancer. You're amazing, Sim."

"I wish he could see me dance. He was the one who placed me in front of a piano. I have loved him ever since."

"Then tell him. Call him up and tell him you miss him."

"It can't be that easy," she says in disbelief.

"But it can. Trust me. Call him and tell him you want to see him. If that doesn't work, go to him and tell him you want a divorce," I tease.

This look comes to her face and I'm not sure I should have said that. I don't know how she has taken my words, but I don't get to ask as we pull up to the doctor's office.

"Thank you for the talk, let's get you inside. We still have ten minutes before we are late."

Cameron

I just landed in New York. I'm tired as fuck and frustrated. I've been trying to get to Amina, but I know I'm being followed. Daddy and I have someone watching Dez, so I know for a fact he's watching me.

I pull my phone to call my girl to find out how her doctor's appointment went. She got to see our little one today. I know she wants to know what we're having, but she's been waiting on me.

I hate that for us both. I need to make Dez disappear. I don't want to miss the birth of our baby.

"Hello," Amina answers the phone excitedly, bringing a smile to my face.

"Hey, baby. How did it go?"

"Are you sitting down?"

"No, should I be? What's going on? Is the baby okay?"

I stop in my tracks, ready to jump on a flight as close to Boston as I can get and then air-drop in or some shit. My mind races with a million different things that could be wrong. I need to get to them now.

"Cam, babe, breathe. You can relax. The babies are fine.

"Dr. Livingston suspected that I was carrying twins, and it turns out I am. I'm not huge for nothing. I'm carrying two baby Perrys."

I release a swooshing breath, only to stumble back as her words hit me. I bite into my fist to keep from yelling out and fist-pumping. I swallow hard, trying to find my words.

"Hello, babe, are you there?"

"Yeah, baby," I choke out. "I love you so fucking much. We're going to be together soon. I promise we're going to make this right real soon."

"I can't wait. I miss you so much."

"Mina?"

"Yeah?"

"I'm taking you away to marry you as soon as we're together again."

"You might need to get a divorce first," she laughs.

"I'm going to make that happen. What do you think about moving to New York?"

"Huh?"

"Cal's team wants to sign me. He's not doing well without me. To be honest, I miss his ass too. When that asshole is gone, it will be safe here for you again. We can call this home."

"I would like that. My mother is going to be so excited to have two grandbabies to spoil. Oh my God, Cam. This is going to be perfect."

My other phone begins to ring. I pull the phone from my pocket to see it's Cal. My smile broadens.

"Hey, baby. Let me call you later. That's my brother."

"I love you. Talk soon."

"Love you too, baby."

I hang up and pick up the call on the other phone. Cal and the team aren't here, but I'm in town to speak with some of the bigwigs. Cal knows I'm here to talk to them.

I was shocked to hear he told his coach the truth. The coach is one hundred percent behind him and doing what it takes to get him back to playing the way only he can.

"Hello," I say.

"Thank God. Cam, are you in New York yet?"

"Yeah, bro. What's up?"

"It's Nicole. She's not feeling well. I can't focus. I need you to go to our place and check on her. Just text me and let me know if she's okay. I need you to see her with your eyes and let me know she's all right."

"I'm on it, bro. Don't worry about her. Go out there and do your job. If something is wrong, I'll take care of it."

"Thanks, Cam."

"No problem, bro. That's what I'm here for. I've got you."

***

I can't stop smiling as I lie here on Cal and Nicole's couch. I'm having twins and my baby brother is going to be a father. He's freaking out tonight, but he'll be fine in the morning.

My mind goes to Amina. We've been apart for too long. I wish there was a way to speed things up. We know he's going to fuck up sooner or later.

I need it to be sooner. I open my phone to stare at the ultrasound picture Amina sent me. I'm amazed as I look at the two tiny humans growing within the woman I love.

"Daddy's coming," I say and kiss two of my fingers before I touch them to the screen.

CHAPTER FORTY-TWO

From the Shadows

Jareil

A month later …

"Why are you doing this? What do you want?" I ask, trying to figure out what's going on.

I was jumped on my way into my home after I left the arena tonight. I stepped out of the car and a bag was thrown over my head, then I was thrown into another vehicle. I don't know where I've been taken.

I have a little girl on the way and Kayleen and I have been talking about getting married after she divorces Cam. This can't be happening. I've been waiting so long for my life to be everything I want.

The cars, the money, they can take all of that. It all can be replaced, but my life with my little girl and future wife ... those things are irreplaceable.

"Please. Tell me what you want. Is it money? Tell me how much, it's yours."

The air has become cool wherever they have taken me. I can feel it ripping through my T-shirt and biting into my skin. I don't dare to think of where we are. I'm trying to stay focused on getting back home to my girls.

I was in such shock when Kayleen told me she is having my baby. It hurt to see her pregnant and to think she had moved on and forgotten about me—but then she said it was mine. I wish I would have known what she thought happened.

Between graduation and getting ready to be drafted to play basketball, I hadn't had the time to track her down and find out what was really going on. Then came the news that she and Cam had gotten married. I was devastated.

Suddenly, the fabric covering my head is ripped off. I find myself standing on the edge of a rooftop. I go to step back, but someone tugs at me to keep me where I am.

I turn my head as my eyes begin to focus. Staring back at me is a guy with cold brown eyes. He almost looks like a demon.

He stares at me and I duck back. My hands are tied so I can't defend myself and if I move too much, I'm going over the edge. I don't know what this bastard wants, but he's got my back up against the wall.

"You have been fucking the little white girl, haven't you?"

"What?" I ask in confusion.

I haven't been fucking anyone. Kay and I plan to wait until after her divorce. Before she was married, I didn't have a problem with what we were doing.

Now she's someone's wife. I'm going to give their marriage some respect. I have no idea what this guy is talking about.

"My friend, my problem is not with you. I don't care if you're fucking that motherfucker's wife. What I care about is my fiancée he's hiding from me.

"Now start talking. You are fucking his wife because their marriage is bullshit, aren't you?"

I knit my brows in confusion. This guy is giving off crazy vibes. My first thought it to protect Kayleen and our baby.

I don't know what Cam has gotten into, but it has nothing to do with me or Kayleen. I need this guy to understand that and stay away from us both.

I go to make that happen, but he barks in my face instead. "When I find her, I'm going to kill her, then I'm going to come back for him and his *puta* wife."

I freeze. I need to cover for Cam and Kayleen. This guy is unhinged. I can't allow him to think I know about this woman he's talking about.

"Bro, I have no idea what you're talking about."

"*Sí*, you do. You know this Cameron Perry, baseball player with the little wife with green eyes. I plan to pluck those eyes right from her head.

"She knows he's fucking my Maribel and she's helping him hide her. That's why she's fucking you. He's not around to see her hopping in and out of your cars, but I am.

"What kind of man fucks another man's pregnant wife? I should push you over for that alone. No, that's not what I will do.

"I want you to admit that you know their marriage is fake and that's why you've been fucking her on the side. Why else does she live here while he's in Atlanta?"

"All her friends and family are here. I'm a baller, I get it. He's not even in Atlanta most of the time.

"He travels for away games. She's left home alone. She's pregnant, her support system is here.

"Bro, I'm not fucking her. We all went to high school together. We're friends, I'm looking out for her while he's away."

He cracks me upside the head with the butt of his gun. I drop to my knees, thankfully away from the edge, but not far.

This guy begins to talk to himself. Blood is gushing from the wound on the side of my head. I have to think fast to get out of this alive.

I need to warn Cam and get Kayleen away to safety. As I think his words over, he might be onto something. Kay said she needed to stay with Cam for a year before they could divorce. I found it odd at the time, but I didn't push for more.

Whatever the case may be, this has to end here. I can't allow him to hurt my woman or my child. Glancing to the side, I note two other guys are by a van. It seems we're on a rooftop garage.

The other two aren't focused on us so I begin to work my restraints off as he argues with himself in Spanish. I manage to get a hand free right as he turns back for me. It's now or never, I have to act now.

I get to my feet and rush him. I knock the gun from his hand before he can aim it at me. This dude is strong and doesn't go down as easily as I want.

I keep fighting. I get the upper hand and start fucking his ass up. I'm making it home to my family. As I hover over him, raining punches down on him, a loud bang fills the air.

In the next instant, a sharp pain runs through me. I drop to the side and roll onto my back. So much pain fills my body. I'm being kicked in the side, but I don't have the strength to fight back.

"I'm going to kill you, you motherfucker," he growls through his thick accent.

I open my eyes and see him standing over me with his gun aimed at me. All I can think about is how my little girl is going to grow up without me. I'm never going to get to see her little face.

My life ends here. I don't get to win a chip, I don't get to earn MVP. I'm going to be just another black man gunned down before his prime.

They'll probably make it gang-related or some bullshit when I'm a biological science magna cum laude graduate who's never seen a gun outside of a gun range until tonight.

The sound of sirens in the background gives me little hope, I'm bleeding out and this guy seems like he finishes whatever he starts. I black out before he pulls the trigger. At least my girls are safe.

Your girl is safe too, Cam. Take care of mine. It was nothing personal. I've just always been in love with Kay.

Kayleen

"That feels so nice, thanks," I moan as Cam rubs my aching feet.

"No problem. Is Bug okay in there?"

I beam at him. "She's fine."

He's in town for a few days. He came in with gifts for my little girl's nursery, looking like a proud uncle. He's been spoiling Bug, as he so affectionately calls her.

Seeing him with all those gifts and steaks to throw on the grill warmed my heart. Dakota and Thomas came by, and we made a time of it.

While the guys were grilling, the game was on the outside TV and I got to see JR win his game tonight. Cal played a game tonight as well.

Overall, it's been a good day. Now, we're sitting in the living room as we watch TV. Cam seems to be lost in thought, but I'm too relaxed to interrupt him.

This is nice. I've come to cherish this friendship over the last few months we've been married. JR had been right, I love Cam as a friend, but that's it.

I'm going to miss hanging out and having my friend to support me when we get divorced. I can't help but wonder what he has planned once we part.

The news comes on after Cal's game we were watching goes off. I go to turn the channel when a breaking news report comes on and JR's photo is plastered on the screen. My breathing stops.

I tug my foot from Cams grasp and stand. I keep moving closer to the screen as the reporters speak. It all sounds like white noise. I grasp my pregnant belly protectively.

"No," I scream and drop to my knees. "No."

Cameron

At first, I have no fucking clue what is happening. I mean, I know Jareil and I recognize him from the picture. He was one of my friends in high school before he left for some academy to play basketball and football there.

We didn't keep in touch much after he was gone, but I do remember him being there at that party Mama threw freshman year when Cal had that seizure.

"This is the baby's father," I speak my thoughts out loud. Not asking, but already knowing.

Kay nods as I hold her in my arms. She's near hysterical at this point. Her reaction is more than one of that for a friend.

I nod to myself. I'm waiting to be angry, but it never happens. Jareil has always been a good guy.

I think I've always known he had a thing for Kay, so I'm not that surprised. What does shock the fuck out of me is when an image of Dez and two other men pops up on the screen. I grab the remote and turn the volume up.

"This just in. Authorities say they have these three men in custody at this hour. The man on the right is said to be the ringleader, Dez Demarco.

"It's still unclear as to why Dez and his accomplices kidnapped and assaulted basketball rookie Jareil Reese. Or JR, as his fans so lovingly call the young man. Sources say Reese was shot at least once and is in critical condition and undergoing surgery for the wounds he has sustained.

"He will be in our thoughts and prayers. We're pulling for you JR. Hang in there, man. Such a talent. We'll bring you guys more as this story continues to develop," the reporter says.

"I need to get to him. I need to be there," Kay cries.

"Go get dressed. I'll drive you."

She nods frantically as I help her to stand. I notice that there's blood on the seat of her shorts. I calmly grab her by the elbow, not wanting to freak her out.

"Kayleen," I say in a calm, soothing voice. "You're bleeding. I need you to go in the bathroom and check on Bug.

"I'm sure she's fine, but I need you to check and then get cleaned up. I'm going to call for an ambulance. Don't panic.

"I'm right here with you. I've got you both. Everything is going to be fine."

"I can't lose them," she sobs.

"Shh, darlin'. I'm here. You're not losing anyone. We're both about to get all we wanted.

"He's going to pull through and Bug's going to be a big, strong girl for her Uncle Cam. I ain't done spoiling her. She's going to be fine."

CHAPTER FORTY-THREE

My Hero

Cameron

I pull a hand down my face as I step out of the hospital. Kay and the baby are being monitored and Jareil's condition has been updated to stable. I was able to talk to him for a bit.

He risked his life to keep Kay and Amina safe. He could have given Amina up, but he didn't reveal what he suspected. JR earned my respect for that.

All the rest of the shit going on between us, we'll have a talk about when he gets out of this place. I honestly don't give a shit. I pull my phone from my pocket with a smile on my face as I dial the number of the only person I want to talk to.

"Hello," she yawns into the phone.

"It's over. You can come home," I breathe.

"What? Are you serious?"

"Yeah, baby. I am. Dez finally fucked up and my guys were on his ass. He's behind bars as we speak."

"Cam," she sobs. "We can come to you?"

"I'll be looking for a place for us first thing in the morning. If you can't come to me, I'm coming to you."

"This is finally over? I can't believe it."

"Believe it, baby. We finally get to be together."

"Where are you? What are those sirens in the background?"

I turn to look behind me. An ambulance has just pulled up. It reminds me that I need a ride back to the house since I came in an ambulance with Kay.

"I'm at the hospital. Kay had a scare with Bug and the father of her baby is here because of Dez. They're going to be able to hold him for attempted murder at the least," I reply.

"Oh my God, you're kidding, right?"

"No, I'm not. I'm going to talk to the detectives in the morning."

"Is the father okay?"

"Yeah, he's going to survive."

"What about the baby?"

"Kay and the baby are fine. They are holding her for observation."

"It's over. It's really over," she sobs.

"Yeah, baby. It's all taken care of. I'm filing for that divorce as soon as my lawyer draws up the papers."

She laughs through her sobs. "Really, Cam? Let the girl and her baby daddy get out of the hospital first."

"Yeah, whatever. Go back to sleep. You're going to need your rest. I love you."

"Love you too. Thanks, Cam. Thank you for everything."

Maribel

I hang up the phone and stare up at the ceiling as I hold my hand over my belly. The babies are moving as if they too woke to talk to their father. I can't put into words how relieved I feel.

I'm almost scared to believe it's true. This nightmare is finally over. I can be with the man I love and not have to look over my shoulder.

"You're going to love your daddy," I say to my children as they move around.

I dry my tears, and a huge smile comes to my face. With each second, it begins to sink in deeper. For the first time in about five years, I can breathe easy.

"I'm finally free. Your daddy is my hero."

CHAPTER FORTY-FOUR

Hey Baby

Cameron

"That's it?" I ask after Kay and I sign the divorce papers.

I look at my dad hopefully as I wait for his attorney to answer. I don't realize I've been holding my breath until he finally answers. It also dawns on me that Kay has a death grip on my hand.

"Yes, that will be all. I'll get these into the judge and have him finalize the divorce immediately. It's good to have friends in high places," the attorney chuckles as he looks at my dad and smiles.

"See you on the course, Eric?"

"Sure thing, Kyle. I'm glad I could get this all taken care of for you. Your check will be delivered as soon as the paperwork is final, little lady. Looks like it couldn't be soon enough," Mr. Birmingham says to Kay as he looks down at her huge belly.

Bug is due any day now. I get the feeling I won't be around for her birth, but her daddy is getting stronger, and he'll be around. As long as I'm there for my firstborn's, I'm okay with that.

I stand and shake Mr. Birmingham's hand. My daddy tugs me into a hug and holds me tight. I can't thank him enough for all he's done for me and Maribel.

"This part is over. You go get our family. Let me deal with your mama. Your happiness comes first," my dad whispers in my ear.

Our mamas ain't too happy about the divorce. I can tell my mama is going to be a problem. She's been calling every day since Kay was released from the hospital, asking why Kay thought I wanted a divorce.

She lost her shit when I told her it's because I do. We both do. Kay didn't object to moving the timeline up.

We sat and had a long talk. I finally told her everything and she took it surprisingly well. I actually think she was relieved to know I'm in love with someone else too.

She's ready to move on with her life as much as I am. Too bad my mama isn't listening when we tell her that. She's convinced the marriage can be saved.

"Thanks, I'll see you when I get back," I say and give my dad one more hug.

Kay touches my arm, and I turn to her. She has tears in her eyes, but she's smiling. I pull her into a hug and kiss the top of her head.

"I'm happy that you're happy, Cam. You're going to make such a good father and husband. I guess she wasn't joking that day. You were her future husband.

"I was so jealous of her because deep in my heart her words rang true. I knew it and knew I was going to lose you to her, but I hope I never lose your friendship.

"Maybe someday you'll come back to Texas and our little ones can grow up together. If you have boys, I promise not to force Bug on one of them," she chuckles.

I laugh and give her a squeeze. I have no doubt Kay will always be a part of my life. It may not be the part we were told all our lives she would be, but we'll still be friends.

"Uncle Cam will be around for his Ladybug. Her daddy ain't shit on a baseball field, she's going to need me for all her softball games," I tease.

"Go on, get out of here. It's time you finally get to live your life the way you want it. I'm so proud of you, Cameron Perry.

"Maribel is one lucky woman. One thing she should never question is how much you love her. I'm glad you didn't tell me why we were getting married.

"I would have been so jealous and probably wouldn't have done it. I'm glad I did though. Being married to you gave me my friend back. Thanks for taking such good care of us."

I look into Kay's eyes, feeling a little choked up. It was good to restore our friendship. She looks happier too.

I can see how much she and Jareil love each other. I'm happy for them. When he fully recovers, they're going to be able to start their lives together.

"Take care of my girl. I want to meet her as soon as I come home to Texas."

"We'll be waiting. Now go on and get. I'll help hold your mama off." She gives a teary smile.

I gave her hand one last squeeze before I turn for my duffel bag and leave. I have business to handle. There's somewhere I need to be.

Maribel

"I will be sad to see you go," Sim says as she sits with me in my room while I fold little baby clothes.

"I'm going to miss you too. We'll talk on the phone whenever you want. I'll have to bring the babies to see you too when they get big enough."

"I would like that. I want to see your baseball player play in a live game. I think I might enjoy that."

"I'll be sure to get you tickets. I can't wait to go to my first major league game to see him play."

"If you ever need my help again, you are to call me. You don't need to go through Ximena. You are my friend. You call me directly."

I smile. Symphony is a complex person, but she grows on you. I feel bad for her. I want her to be happy. This place is starting to feel like it might be her very own gilded prison.

"It's finally over," I breathe in disbelief.

I can't believe all of this has come to an end. Dez is rotting behind bars for attempted murder. The lawyer said he can get up to twenty years for what he did to Jareil.

The cops caught him red-handed because of the investigators who Cam and Mr. Kyle had following him. They called the cops when the kidnappers nabbed Jareil.

Then they followed them to the rooftop where he was shot. Thank God they did. They saved his life. Dez would have killed him if the cops hadn't arrived, or he would have bled out from the gunshot wound.

I've wanted to go home since they confirmed Dez wouldn't be getting out anytime soon. However, I'm too pregnant and Cam is playing for his new team.

I'll have to stay here just a bit longer. The one saving grace has been being able to be distracted with shopping for the babies. I was finally able to have a long conversation with my father's attorney.

My dad left everything in my name—his cars, his houses, his money. I don't have to worry about finances ever again. In fact, me and the babies are set for life.

"*Ay dios mío*, look at you."

I snap toward the familiar voice as a gasp leaves my lips. Sim's butler is ushering my mom into the room. My lips are trembling as I rush forward into her embrace.

"What are you doing here? How?"

"I received a call that I'm going to be a grandmother. Then this handsome young man showed up on my doorstep to introduce himself and ask if I was okay with him marrying my little girl. Look at you, you look so beautiful," she replies as she cups my face in her hands.

"Wait, you met Cam?"

"She sure did. I had to get her permission to take your hand before I came to get you."

I close my eyes as the Texan drawl washes over me. I nearly collapse as I open them and find Cam leaning in the doorway. My mom grabs my arm and holds me up. Cam is in motion before I can steady myself.

He tugs me into his big, strong arms and kisses me senseless as tears spill from my eyes. Stupid pregnancy hormones. I cling to him as if he might disappear.

"Hey, baby. It's good to see you too," he breathes against my lips.

I gasp as I feel two strong kicks in my womb. They must know their daddy is here. Cam places his hand on my belly and there's another kick.

He laughs and gives me the biggest smile. "That had to hurt. You okay?"

"Yeah, I'm perfect. I'm used to the abuse."

"They don't mean it. Consider them love taps."

"You carry these boxers and then say that." I pull a face at him right as they start kicking and moving again.

Cam reaches up and fingers a lock of my fading auburn hair. I can't wait to have someone fix it back to my natural color. I want to wash away all traces of what happened with Dez.

"You're gorgeous. I never want to be away from you this long ever again."

"The feeling is mutual."

He places his forehead to mine and begins to sway us to a rhythm of our own. We are completely lost in each other as we stand here.

"Hello, I am Symphony. Everyone calls me Sim. Come with me, I will show you to your room.

"I think Maribel and her baseball player are going to be occupied for a while. I can keep you company. It is almost my practice hour. If you like classical music, you can listen to me play. *¿Preferirías que hable español?*" I hear Sim say to my mom.

"I would love to listen to you play. English is just fine. It's very nice to meet you, Sim," my mother replies.

I can't pull my attention away from Cam. He takes my lips in another searing kiss. This time, he allows his big hands to roam my back and glide down to squeeze my ass.

"Cam," I moan into his mouth.

"I need you."

I whimper and nod. He lifts me effortlessly, huge belly and all, and walks me over to the bed. I push all the baby clothes I had been folding to the floor. I'll just have to rewash them later.

I can't get enough of his hungry kisses. He devours me like he'll never get to kiss me again. I arch my back and moan as he starts a trail of kisses down my neck.

Needing his touch more than ever, I reach for the hem of my shirt and tug it off. Cam groans deeply and cups my breasts as he kisses the tops of them.

I marvel at how my breasts have gotten huge with the pregnancy, but they seem so small in his massive palms. It's like his touch and kisses shoot sparks through me. My skin is humming from his attention.

Reaching behind me, he releases my bra and gently pulls it from my shoulders. He seems too far away when he moves to peel my leggings off my legs.

My face heats with embarrassment as my big-ass panties and unkept bush beneath them are exposed. I didn't know he was coming. I would have tried to do something.

"Cam, wait," I squeal when he drops to his knees, ready to bury his face between my thighs.

He looks at me in confusion. His eyes filled with so much lust. I prop up on my elbow to try to see down my body.

"I ... I haven't been able to see down there in months. I haven't shaved in I don't know how long. It's probably wild down there. Maybe we should switch.

"I can do you and we'll just wait until I figure things out for you to go down on me. Please," I plea and bite my lip.

Cam snorts at me and looks down as he licks his lips. Lifting his gaze back to mine, he gives me that sexy smile of his. His dimples pop and my heart skips a beat.

"I'm going to eat you up now and shave it for you later. I'm starving for you, baby. Nothing is going to stop me from feasting on your body. Nothing."

With that, he disappears behind my belly before I can speak another word. I cry out and fall back against the bed. All I can do not to scream is grasp a tight hold of the sheets and stare up at the ceiling.

"Oh my God, Cam. Fuck," I whimper when I can't hold it in any longer.

CHAPTER FORTY-FIVE

My Boys

Cameron

"I can't believe you dropped to one knee naked to propose," Amina laughs.

"I had planned to be more suave about it, but I went with my gut."

"You were in the middle of pounding it out from the back, Cam. I mean, come on, bro."

"The view was awe-inspiring. It took my breath away and I had to act. You said yes, didn't you?"

"Did I? My mouth was sort of full. I can't remember if I got the words out."

Her mouth was full, but she did say yes before it was. I cup her face and take her lips. Out of the corner of my eye, I can see her ring sparkling on her finger.

321

It looks right there. Like it's been meant to be there all along. I couldn't have been happier than when I slid it on her finger.

I'm grinning like a fool as I hold my woman in my arms. As always, the sex was amazing, even as I had to work around her full belly. The proposal was just the cherry on top.

It felt like I had to do it then. All the plans I had made seemed like they wouldn't happen soon enough.

"Holy shit, Cam. That wasn't your dick in my back. I think I'm in labor," Amina says, pulling me out of my bliss-filled thoughts.

"What?"

I sit up and look down at her. She's holding her stomach as her face is etched with pain. I try not to freak out.

Jumping up from the bed, I throw my clothes back on. Once I'm dressed, I'm moving in circles, trying to figure out what to do next. I don't know this place or where anything is.

"Cam," Amina grunts. "Grab my phone and call for Sim. She'll get the staff to help."

"Right, Sim. Where's your phone?"

"Over there." She points at the nightstand.

Fuck, I feel useless. I should have thought of all this on my own. I find Sim's number in Amina's phone and call her.

"Hello, is everything all right?"

"No, this is Cam. She's in labor. We need to get to the hospital."

"Thirty weeks. The survival rate is ninety percent. I will call Dr. Livingston and have him meet us at the hospital. How far apart are the contractions?"

"Hold on, I don't know."

I go over to the bed where Maribel is trying to put her clothes back on. I tuck the phone between my shoulder and ear and help her with her shirt.

I go to help with her leggings and another contraction hits. I look down at my watch and note the time. I don't even know if I'm doing this shit right.

Maribel grasps my wrists and holds on tight. I begin to rub her back until the pain passes. When it does, she releases my wrist and looks up at me.

Licking her lips, she nods her head. "Just help me get to the bathroom. I need to shower before we go."

"Really, baby?"

"Really, Cam. I'm not going to the hospital smelling like sex with cum dripping from the one place everyone is going to be looking up," she growls.

"Point made."

"Sim. I think they're about ten minutes apart. I'm going to get her into the shower, and we'll be ready to go in about twenty," I say into the phone.

"I will have the SUV brought around to the front of the estate. That will be the best vehicle for all passengers to accompany the patient and it will be best for her comfort. I have her bag.

"The hospital is a twenty-minute ride from the front door of the estate. There shouldn't be traffic at this hour and the weather is clear. I will get everyone in motion."

With that, she hangs up. I smile. She reminds me of Cal when he was younger before I helped him learn to filter down the information he shared.

I like her. Tossing the phone down on the bed, I rush to help Amina into the en suite. I strip back down to climb in with her in case she needs me.

I'm glad I do as another contraction hits. I rub her back through it and hold her hips as she rocks from side to side. I cut off the water once the contraction subsides and I have her cleaned up.

Suddenly, a gush of water hits my feet. I stare wide-eyed as I realize her water has broken. Shit, we need to get out of here.

"Cam, don't freak out on me. Relax. You're going to wrap me in a towel and help me dry off. Then you're going to help me to the bedroom to get dressed."

I nod and snap into action. I'm about to be a daddy. Shit, I got here just in time.

Maribel

I don't know if we're ever doing that again, but I can't say I regret having my two little boys. They are so adorable. They both came out with heads full of hair and the cutest little lips and tiny noses.

Identical twins, just like their father and uncle. Premature my ass, they were three pounds each. At thirty weeks, I was expecting them to be a pound and a couple ounces or something.

However, both my boys are healthy and have latched on with ease. The way they've been sucking down milk, they'll be big and strong in no time.

Chance and Cade Perry. The most precious babies I've ever seen. I'm in love with them already.

"They're so little. Look at how small his head is in my hand," Cam says in awe as he holds Cade.

"In his defense, your hands are kind of big. It's not hard for anything to look small in one."

Cam looks at me and narrows his eyes. "Say that when I have your ass in my hands," he whispers.

"Why are you whispering? They're going to know you have a potty mouth before they turn two months old. There's no keeping that a secret."

Cam chuckles. "That shit is true. I thought I'd at least try."

"Good try, babe. Good try."

He comes closer and dips his head to peck my lips. I smile sleepily at him. It's getting harder to keep my eyes open.

"I'll be here with them. Why don't you get some rest? I'll have something for you to eat waiting when you wake. My daddy is on his way," he says softly.

"I'll take you up on that." I yawn and settle into the bed.

It feels like I just closed my eyes when the energy in the room shifts. I pop my eyes back open and find Mr. Kyle and a blonde woman standing in the room. Mr. Kyle is smiling from ear to ear as he holds one of the babies in his arms.

Cam has the other baby as the woman stands with a sour look on her face while she glares at me. I look between the three and I can tell this is Cam's mom.

I knit my brows, wondering what her problem is. Sim took my mom back to the house to rest and get something to eat earlier. It looks like they haven't come back yet.

"Hey there, young lady. It's good to see you," Mr. Kyle says as he notices I'm awake.

"Hey, Mr. Kyle." I give him a warm smile.

The woman snaps her head to him and scowls. Both Cam and his father ignore her. I sigh because I know she's about to be some drama, and I'm not rested enough for this right now.

I suck it up and decide to be polite. "Hi, you must be Mrs. Perry," I say.

"I am. I'm sorry, but I'm still confused about who you are and why we are here."

"I'm here to meet my grandsons. You're here because you're nosey and hardheaded."

"I thought you were cheating on me. I wanted to meet her for myself," she snarls.

"I told you I was going to see our son and I would explain everything when I returned."

"Then hopped on our jet. While our son's *wife* was already in labor."

"I hopped on *my* jet and that's our son's *ex-wife*. Why can't you hear those words and allow them to sink in?"

I don't miss the shocked look on Cam's face as his father fusses at his mom. He shakes it off and comes to hand me the baby as he goes back to take the other from his dad to bring him to me as well.

I don't know if he's doing it to remove the babies from the tension or if he's doing it to keep me from leaping out of this bed. When I see Mr. Kyle place his hands on his hips as his face turns red, I think it might be a little of both.

"Because there's no way Kayleen divorced our son. I don't understand why we are here and not with our granddaughter."

"Because she's not mine," Cam growls. "Kay isn't my wife and her daughter isn't mine. If you're not here to meet my sons or introduce yourself properly to my fiancée, you can go."

"What's your name?" his mother asks with tears in her eyes.

"Maribel. Cam calls me by my middle name Amina."

"It's nice to meet you. These little ones are darling. I'm sorry. I'm just a bit in shock."

"I can understand."

Mr. Kyle snorts. "Ever gracious. You did well, Cam."

"Who are you?" Cam and his mom say in unison.

Cam seems amused, but his mother's face has turned red. She huffs and comes to take Cade from my arms. He whimpers, but she begins to sing to him in a pretty voice that calms him right down.

Well, my in-laws will be interesting.

CHAPTER FORTY-SIX

Missing Him

Maribel

Eight years and ten months later ...

"Cade, Chance, if you two don't clean this room I'm going to take the front wheels off your bikes and hide all your game controllers. Stop playing with me," I call through the house.

I'm four months pregnant and tired. I'm going to start whipping their little butts if they don't start listening to me. My mother stands in the doorway laughing at me.

She would think this is funny. I'm getting payback for being hardheaded. I've been lenient with the two of them because they've been through a lot.

My marriage to Cam hasn't been an easy one, not because of us but because of my crazy ass mother-in-law. That woman has done everything she could to be in our business.

We almost got a divorce because of her. It wasn't until Kay put her in her place that she got the damn point. She told her to leave her and her family alone. However, by then I had been fed up and moved to my father's house in Jersey.

I couldn't take that woman showing up in our home to start shit while telling me how great a mother Kay is to her daughter Chanel. Kay is a great mother and she's a loving wife to *her* husband. When his mother wasn't fucking with my head, she was fucking with Cam's.

I had had enough of her shit. Cam had to choose us. Raising two boys of my own is overwhelming enough when married to a baseball player who's never home and travels the country most of the year.

Cam no longer bats for his team. He stopped batting two years ago. However, the team wanted to keep him on because of Cal, so Cam took the batting coach job they offered him.

However, he was released after Cal's injury. Not to our surprise. I saw it coming before Cal fucked up his shoulder.

"They are taking advantage because their father is away," my mother laughs.

"Who are you telling? He needs to come home before I hurt one of them," I grumble as I shake my head.

My phone rings as my mother continues to laugh at me and the boys ignore me. I need a break from everything, so I pick it up happily. A smile comes to my face when I see it's Sim.

She's been here in New York for a few years now. She sounds happier these days. I've met her husband once.

He's handsome and interesting as well. The man is observant and gives off a dangerous vibe. Some of the things Symphony said about them and their relationship makes more sense to me after meeting him.

"Hello," I sing into the phone.

"Hey, Maribel. How are you doing?"

"Hey, Sim. I'm well. How are you?"

"I am well. I would like to share some news with you. You were on the top of my list to tell after my husband and family."

"Sounds important."

"Yes, it is. I have had the honor of being there for you and your twins and my brother's as well. Now I am expecting a child of my own," she says.

"*Aw*, I'm so happy for you. This is awesome, how do you feel?"

"I am very nervous and excited. Val has been helping me and allowing me to babysit. I am thirty-seven so I worry about the baby's health."

I smile as she rambles on the other end. I've heard so much about this Val woman. She seems to be important to Sim.

"My husband says I shouldn't be worried. We will love our child either way. Oh, wait. Those are not the things I want to talk to you about.

"I've called for your friendship and to make an appointment to spend time with you. Will the baseball player allow you to have lunch with me?"

I laugh to myself. I love Symphony. Hearing her think out loud is always amusing.

"Cam isn't here," I say sadly. "He's in the Dominican Republic. He's been working there for the last few months as a batting coach and trainer."

"This has you sad?"

"Yeah, this is the second pregnancy I've been through without him. It was a great opportunity. I couldn't allow him to not take it.

"Cam loves to work in the industry. I don't want to take that from him, but I miss him. Especially after the two years we were separated."

"I still don't like your mother-in-law. She made me feel very uncomfortable. You should have allowed me to make her disappear."

"Symphony." I bark out a laugh.

"Don't worry. Neither Uri nor Val would approve it. They don't believe she has done enough to earn it."

"I'm going to pretend you didn't say that."

"Good. I probably shouldn't have. Would it make you happy if Cam worked for a sports company here in New York?"

"That would be a dream come true, but that ain't happening. Cam comes with a price tag. None of the New York teams are interested or they were trying to low ball him."

"Nothing is impossible to my friends. He will be home for this baby. I have to go, Maribel. I will text about our lunch date. It was good to speak to you."

"Congratulations, hon. I look forward to our lunch. Later."

"Later. Be well."

Val

I smile and roll my eyes as Sim sits across from me, popping her band on her wrist. She wants to ask me for something, but she's going to sit like this until I ask her what she wants. I've grown used to her and her quirks.

Sometimes I forget that she's two years older than me. She's brilliant and has more knowledge than an encyclopedia but there are times when it's clearer than others that she struggles with social settings. The woman is a born killer, so I dare anyone to tell her to her face she's not normal.

"Spit it out, Sim. What is it you need?" I say as I look up from the reports I've been reading.

My business has grown exponentially since I started the bag and shoe company, and the Alliance has settled into place. So much has changed around us and continues to change.

"I have a request. It is important to me. I would ask Uri, but I find when you ask for things, he never says no."

I purse my lips to keep from laughing. I can imagine Uri's face if he heard this. I'm sure he would be amused.

Although there isn't a Donati man who would deny Sim. She has them all wrapped around her finger and doesn't know it. She's like a baby sister in the family and they would hush you in a heartbeat over her.

She makes a face and continues. "I would ask Nico, but he teases me all the time. This is something I want taken seriously. I cannot ask Michael because he will be upset with me for going against—"

She cuts off and waves her hand in front of her face in frustration. "I need your help. I feel most comfortable asking you. You understand women."

"Sim, just tell me what it is you need. I don't need you to explain yourself. If it's important to you, I will handle the request," I say before she can make herself any more flustered.

"I have a friend whose husband used to play baseball professionally. His name is Cameron Perry, number thirty-three. She is sad because he had to go away to the Dominican Republic for a coaching position.

"I believe he would be an asset to the sports agency. I would like Nico to offer him a job so he can be here in New York with her and the children and not miss this pregnancy as he did her other. He also has ties to Texas if they should need him there.

"He is originally from Texas. They have a home there. He would relate to Bradley. I would like if you could make this request on my behalf."

"Is that all you need?"

"He is very proud. I would like them to make the offer without mentioning me or his wife."

"That it?" I ask with a smile.

"Yes, that is all I needed to ask," she says and nods, her eyes landing everywhere but on mine.

"I will take care of this for you."

She falls back in her seat, looking relieved. I'm curious. Sim doesn't have many friends outside our circle and even within the circle, she's not super close to many. Not that she doesn't want to be.

I think she gets overwhelmed by all the different personalities. Everyone loves her, but we give her her space to be her. I want to meet this friend.

CHAPTER FORTY-EIGHT

He Needs You

Cameron

I was on a flight as soon as my father called me. It was good to hear his voice sounding so strong. He called to tell me Caleb is fucking up his life and he needs an intervention before our mama causes him to lose it all.

I'm so livid with her. The way she tried to wear me and Amina down almost cost me everything. Now she's working on Cal and Nicole.

Why can't that woman allow us to be men? We chose the women we love. She needs to go have a seat somewhere. The only good thing that came out of her bullshit was the opportunity to see my family.

I came to New York first to pick up my little crew before we all go to Texas, so I can knock some sense into my brother. Nicole is one of the best things that has ever happened to Cal. His babies adore him.

Having your family walk away from you isn't something I want to describe. It was worse than when Amina had to remain in hiding. I thought I was going to die.

I felt stupid for the seeds I allowed my mama to plant. None of it made sense in hindsight. I was just so focused on baseball and making something of my career so I could support Cal as a teammate and his brother, I allowed her to manipulate things that weren't there.

Thankfully, it all made us stronger. I hope the same can be said for Cal. He doesn't need this. He worked hard to build his life.

"Oh, my God. I was about to take your fucking head off," Amina breathes as she stands before me in the hallway of our home with one of my bats held up in the air.

I can't help but laugh. She looks adorable in her little pajamas with her little baby bump as she stands ready to protect our family. I saunter closer to close the distance between us.

"Damn, I've missed you," I say as I look down at her.

Reaching for the bat, I pull it from her grasp and use my other hand to palm the back of her neck and tug her to me. I crush her lips with mine and kiss her deeply. She moans into my mouth as I deepen the kiss.

I lift her onto my waist with one arm and drag the bat behind me with the other. Once in our bedroom, I close the door with the tip of the bat then drop it to the floor.

I cup her face with my now free hand as I continue to devour her sweet mouth. She pushes her hands into my hair and gives as good as she's getting.

I shove one hand into the back of her shorts and squeeze her ass. I'm so hard I could burst right through my pants. Instead, I shove my sweats down and carry my sexy wife over to our bed.

I've been away too long to fuss with any pretenses. I want my wife, and I want her now. Placing her on the bed, I then take a step back to pull off my shirt and kick my pants the rest of the way off.

"Cam, not that I'm not happy to see you, but what's going on? Why are you here? Is everything all right?" she says as she looks up at me with worry in her eyes.

"I'm needed in Texas. My mama is on her bullshit again. Caleb filed for a divorce and Nicole left him."

"No," Amina gasps. "What's wrong with that woman? Why can't she just be happy for y'all and enjoy being a grandmother? It's not that hard."

"Your answer is as good as mine. Mina, I haven't been home in months. I don't cheat on my wife, so would you mind shutting up so we can fuck? The last thing I want to talk about is my mama."

She laughs and starts to wiggle out of her sleep shorts. The silky fabric falls to the floor and my mouth begins to water. I chuckle softly when she only unbuttons the first few buttons of her top before tugging it over her head without bothering with the rest.

God, that baby bump is sexy on her. She's only four months, but she's starting to show a little. I was hoping for another set of twins, but that's not happening this time.

Hopefully, we'll try again. It only took this long to have another because of all the bullshit we've been through. I love being a father and I love making babies with this woman.

"You're so sexy. Do you know how much I love you?"

"I might, but it's always nice to hear."

"I love you so fucking much, baby. You are the love of my life," I say as I move back to her on the bed.

Before I can pounce on her, she has me in her mouth. I groan and drop my head back. She's only gotten better at this over the years.

Closing my eyes, I allow the sound of her sucking me off to fill my ears. It sounds almost as good as it feels. She tugs at my balls and makes this sharp hissing sound that causes me to look down at her in awe.

She's smiling back at me with a messy face. I can't wait any longer. I bend at the waist as I grasp her throat and kiss her wet mouth.

As I consume her face, I move her back on the bed and climb on with her. She holds onto my shoulders as our moans mix together. Reaching between her legs, I find her already wet for me.

I still finger her to rev her up some more. She throws her head back and whimpers as she rides my fingers. She's the perfect vision as I bring her to climax.

As she catches her release and convulses beneath me, I smile and lick my lips. Hard as granite, I push into her tight pussy. She cries out as she digs her fingers into my back.

I bite my lip as my eyes roll into the back of my head. I grasp her hips and pump mine at a steady rhythm that brings us both pleasure. She goes to wrap her legs around my waist, but I reach to hold them open as I thrust down into her.

I can feel her walls tightening as her juices gush with the action. Kissing her hard, I grind my hips and begin to alternate between deep strokes and shallow ones. From the way she's calling my name, I know I'm driving her crazy.

"I've missed you and this tight pussy. You keep this shit tight just for me, don't you?"

"Yes, Cam. It's yours. It's always been yours. Fuck me like you miss me, babe. Let me know how much you miss me."

"*Fuck*," I grunt.

I roll onto my back and bring her with me. Mina places her hands on my chest and sits up. Her dark hair has fallen out of the messy bun she had it in.

I allow my eyes to roam over her body and grow harder inside her. Running my hands up her sides, I then palm her breasts and knead them as she rides me. I plant my feet into the mattress and begin to thrust up into her.

Her thighs are shaking, her walls are clenching around me, and she's calling out my name like a prayer. I slip out and she squirts all over me.

"Fuck yeah, baby. You missed this dick, didn't you? You want to taste your sweet pussy on my cock?

"Come here, put it in your mouth. Show me how much you missed me. I want to feel the back of your throat," I grunt through my teeth.

My baby never disappoints. She hops off and lunges to take me into her mouth. I get lost in the feel of her wet mouth around me. I'm so tired of being without my wife.

I may have left camp to help my brother, but I've been thinking about coming home for good for a while. I love working with guys to bring out the best in them and get them batting at an all-star level, but I don't need the money.

There has to be a happy medium between working all the time and being lost in my wealth and privilege the way my mama is. I love the sport of baseball, I still have a lot of knowledge to share, but I love my family more. I hate leaving them without me.

However, there's so much more I can do in the sport if I stick it out. DR is a stepping stone. Amina gets that and I love her for supporting me through this.

She doesn't say much, but I know it's been hard on her. I do all I can to make it up to her. Sending gifts. Calling as much as I can, flying in when my schedule allows.

It's just the last two months haven't allowed for me to make any trips home. Trust me, I've tried. However, now as my wife sucks my cock like it's going to disappear, I can't help wondering if it's worth it to keep going like this.

"Fuck," I roar as I come down her throat.

Amina climbs back onto my body and kisses my lips. I hold the back of her head to keep her close. It doesn't take long for me to recover.

In no time, I have her back on my length, making up for lost time. It's going to be a long night. We can sleep on the plane.

CHAPTER FORTY-EIGHT

Boss to Boss

Val

"I have something you might want to know about," I say as I take a seat to have lunch with Tasha.

We're at one of the newer versions of Club Desire. Many of the club's owners, investors, and shareholders are now happily married men. Not wanting to ruin anyone else's fun or to lose the lucrative income, the decision was made to come up with another version of the club.

There are now multiple locations around the world just like this one. The private cigar and spa house features some of the world's most luxurious spa treatments and the best cigars and spirits known to man.

I'm talking facials, body wraps, and liquors that use twenty-four-karat gold. Cigars worth one point three million per stogie.

Even some of the foods are made with expensive rare spices and gold leaf.

The place caters to a specific type of client. Tasha and I have meetings here once a week. I mean, her husband is an owner, so why not?

"Oh boy, what now? I see that look in your eyes. Whatever it is, I hope it has a quick fix. We have hours of planning to do for this retreat in Texas."

"Funny you should mention Texas. I have a person of interest there," I say.

"A problem we need to handle?" She lifts a brow at me and becomes more serious.

Out of curiosity, I decided to do my own digging into this Cameron Perry and his wife. I still plan to do as Symphony has asked, but I needed to know who we're dealing with and who we're potentially bringing into the fold.

I learned a few things about Cameron and Maribel Perry. They are not a problem, but they know of one we once had and could have in the future.

"No, not at the moment. Actually, let me state that properly. Sim came to me with a request. She wants Nico and Uri to offer a job to a batter named Cameron Perry.

"I looked into him and his wife, the friend she's asking the favor on behalf of. On the surface, he's a family man, but he's very particular about allowing his family to be in the public eye.

"I found this to be interesting, so I did some more digging. I found the connection between our Sim and this wife. She was one of Symphony's clients.

"She lived in Boston with Sim for a bit at the estate. She was actually in hiding with her for about six or seven months. But you're not going to believe who she was hiding from."

"I'm listening," Tasha says as she narrows her eyes at me.

"Dez Demarco."

"As in Alejandro Demarco's younger brother?"

"One and the same."

"Do as Sim asks. This will be interesting," Tasha purrs.

"I thought you would say that."

"Now, about this retreat. It is a business trip, but I want everyone to have fun. I also want Brad's brother to feel like family.

"Bradley has asked for this favor because his brother Trevor needs a hand up. His soon-to-be ex-wife has made his life hell and he has four kids he's done everything for. That's our type of guy, LaSalle, and I want everything to work out for him."

"Did we decide on whether or not I should just kill that bitch?"

I've never liked Brad's sister-in-law. I wanted to take her head off years ago. The way she looked at my children and sized up my husband was enough for me to offer to kill her.

"No, there has not been a decision made as of yet," Tasha replies.

"Oh, you will decide in my favor. I know you will. Let's get this planning done. I'm ready to head to Texas," I say with a smile.

CHAPTER FORTY-SEVEN

Come Work for Us

Cameron

I'm sitting outside of my Texas home, watching my boys play in the front yard. Amina comes out of the house and sits on the porch swing. My family is picture-perfect.

My throat turns dry and it's not from the sun baking through the windshield. I swallow hard and look down at the offer that guy placed into my hand. He said his name was Uri.

I remember receiving the call from Nico a week ago. I looked up M.H.D. Group. They have a nice roster of agents. I heard some good things about them, but this offer.

I'd be able to stay at home with my family. They would be paying me more than my worth. The only problem is, one of the coaches I asked about them mentioned probable ties to the mob.

"I can't bring that back into her life," I breathe out as I drag my hand down my now sweaty face.

I've been sitting here trying to get my thoughts together so I can talk to my wife. I don't even know if I should bring this up. We both want me home in New York. Working with Justice Mack and Tim Essex would be career changing.

However, if taking this offer could make our lives anything like it was ten years ago, I'm going to have to pass. Our marriage can't take another hit.

It's bad enough I have to watch to make sure nothing changes with Dez's imprisonment. He's been trying to appeal for years. I had security secretly following Amina for the first three years just to be safe.

The second year, someone stabbed him up pretty bad and my sources said he was stripped of his power in his family. I waited a year before I became comfortable with letting the team go.

I close my eyes and lean my head back against the headrest. I don't know what to do. I don't want to go back to DR. I'm tired of missing out on things with my family.

This offer is for a significant salary and is a damn good position. J Mack and Essex are elite athletes. This is the sort of job I've been working toward.

"You've been out here for about twenty minutes. I wanted to give you time, but now I'm worried," Amina says as the sound of the door opening and closing behind her brings me out of my thoughts.

"I was about to come sit with you. You don't have anything to worry about."

"Bullshit. I know you, Cam. Remember? This is me. I can tell you exactly what you're going to do as soon as you walk into that house."

I snort. She reaches for my face and turns it to her. I look into her eyes and my heart warms to be able to be in the same space as her.

"You're going to walk in that house, kick off your shoes, walk straight to the kitchen and grab a beer. Then you're going to sneak into the pantry, looking through the boys' snacks to steal a few. Then you're going to go up to the bedroom to eat them before you come down for your second beer and ask me what's for dinner.

"You'll nod and head for the fridge to finish off the rest of the grapes before you go to work out in the gym. After your workout, you'll start calling for the boys to go in the backyard to play some catch before you tuck into the couch to watch some TV with them before dinner.

"So again, what's going on? What's wrong, baby? Is it Caleb?

"Is he doing that bad? Does he want me to call Nicole for him and talk to her?"

"No, it's not Cal, but I adore you for being willing to help him."

"Then what is it, babe? Talk to me."

I lean my forehead against hers and breathe her in. "I love you."

"I love you too."

I take in a deep breath. It's better I be honest with her now rather than her finding out later that I turned the offer down without talking to her. Nothing is ever simple in my life. Why would it be now?

"I was offered a batting coach job in New York. It's for a sports agency looking to add value to some of their players. Hiring me can make them top dollar and they're willing to pay the price."

"Baby, that's great. You can come home. Oh my God, why do you look like this is the end of the world?"

"I'm not done. I haven't said yes because I did some asking around about the firm and the owners. There are rumors that they have ties to a certain element.

"I don't want to invite anything crazy back into your life. I was going to pass. I've been so happy being home with you guys the last few weeks, but reliving the past isn't something I want to put any of you through."

"Okay, let's slow this down. What have they said about you returning? How much time are they giving you?"

I sigh. "I was told to take all the time I needed as of this morning. That didn't sound too good to me. I think I'm fucked if I don't get something before they let me go and word gets out."

"Yeah, I was thinking the same thing. We can afford the layoff, but you still have goals you want to accomplish. Are you sure this person gave you accurate information?"

"You know how competitive your industry can be. Was he trying to poach your offer?" she asks as the wheels turn.

"That's always a possibility, but I met two of the owners today when the boys and I picked up Cal. I got a dangerous vibe from the Uri guy. Not toward me, but I can tell he's not someone you want to fuck with," I reply.

"Uri? What was his last name?" she asks as her eyes go wide.

"Something with a *D*. Hold on. He and the Nico guy have the same last name."

I pull up my contacts and look through to find Nico's contact information from the initial call. "Donati. Uri and Nico Donati."

Amina bursts into laughter. I look at her like she's crazy. I have no idea what she thinks is funny.

"Take the job, babe. We'll be fine. Now come on inside and I'll get you a beer and some snacks. I got you some of your own, so you don't have to steal from our boys."

"They taste better when they're theirs," I tease.

She laughs and I tug her closer to me. I just want to sit here and absorb the moment. I'm not sure why she's so confident about this job, but I'm not ready to take that leap with her and my boys' safety.

I'm going to take some more time to think about this. Rushing into the fire is the last thing I want to do. Boy, would it be nice to be able to be like this all the time.

CHAPTER FORTY-EIGHT

Plotting Revenge

Dez

A year later ...

I stare down at the scars on my hands. I've worn these scars for six years. Had I not used my hands to block, I would have died in here that day.

When I woke in the infirmary, I vowed that someday I would get out of here and I'd make them all pay. The men my grandfather allowed to come in here and attack me. That bitch fiancée of mine and all her friends—especially that motherfucker who made sure I did time in here.

He sat right in court and pointed me out after running his fucking mouth. I'm going to kill his little white whore in front of him. I will save my Maribel for last.

I could have had her and her lover killed years ago, but I want them to die at my hands. That's why I've continued to push for my release. I plan to kill her just like I did her father.

Only, I plan to take what's mine before I do. Fucking cunt. My dick gets hard every time I think about it.

"Are you hearing me, Mr. Demarco? It is important you do everything just as I say in order for me to get you released," this suit across from me says.

I don't remember his name. I've been through so many of these guys, I've lost count and don't bother to learn their names. I only need to know the name of the one who gets me my freedom.

Freedom to finish what I started. I've allowed my grandfather to believe he has taken all my power from me. I still have ears and eyes on the outside.

My window has closed. The Alliance has formed. I will have to establish myself by force all around.

LaSalle might have forgotten about me because my brother is no longer one of his flunkies, but I haven't forgotten about him. I'm still on the board, whether he knows it or not. I've kept my eyes open in here, knowing they may try to end me while I'm trapped.

However, no one here wants to try me. I took all four out the last time they did. I have become my own man in here. I am feared and untouchable. No one would dare.

"Do your job. I will do mine," I say and stand dismissively from the table.

He stands to leave, shaking his head. I don't care what he thinks as long as he gets the job done. My family is falling to shit on the outside.

I need out of here to claim my rightful place. With my grandfather dead, I don't need a bride. I've had a long time to think about things and how to get what I want.

No one will see me coming. I grin to myself.

Cameron

"Come on, Justice. Focus. Keep your eyes on the ball, man. Not the girls," I growl.

This guy has been a handful over the last year. He and Tim live to drive me crazy. They remind me so much of myself but with way less discipline.

Some days, I wonder why I took this job. These two are giving me gray hair and I'm only thirty-two.

Don't get me wrong, M.H.D. Group has a family vibe, and they've treated me good over the last year. Amina is happy and I got to be there for the rest of her pregnancy once I came out of my head and took the job. LaSalle's son had a lot to do with that.

His words that day at the camp's football game rang with so much truth I thought I was being pranked. As I got to know everyone around here, I learned the kid is clairvoyant. I stop and listen to everything he says when he comes around.

I see him often with Uri. Uri. He's another interesting character. All the Donatis are. If anyone here is a part of the mob, I've never seen it for myself.

Brad Monroe and Ellerie Hathaway are former professional football players. Nico Donati is a former professional soccer player, and as far as I know, Uri Donati and LaSalle Locatelli are businessmen. I'd say I made the right choice.

Learning of Symphony's relation to the group explained to me why Amina was so sure I could accept this job without fear. I will forever be grateful to that woman. Sim and I have become friends because I get her.

We're able to have long talks because, for me, it's like talking to my brother. I know when she's tapped out and how to help her cope. However, there is something about her I've yet to put a finger on.

When she's around certain members of the circle they have around here, she gives off this dangerous vibe. I don't know if that's coming from her or if she's modeling after someone like Cal. There are plenty of others she could be modeling after.

"Justice," I bark when he almost takes a ball to the head because he's too busy staring at the girls who have just entered the facility with Brad and Uri.

I grin when I see little Sammy racing across the green, heading for me. He stops and places his hand in mine. He gives my fingers a squeeze as he looks up at me.

"Hi, Cameron."

"Hey, little buddy. What's up?"

His eyes go distant and then he focuses in again. This is one of those days. I hold my breath, waiting for what he will say.

"You didn't find us by accident. You were always meant to be here. Chance and Cade will be good friends of mine, but they are not meant to be like me.

"He will take their innocence if you don't take their offer. It's what they do. Let them.

"He's a bad man. He deserves this. Your family is only the first he will target. He's not meant to be my next; don't leave him for me because I will protect my family, Uncle Cameron."

The smile that comes to this kid's face strikes fear in me. My mind is racing as I try to think through his words. Who will try to take my sons' innocence? Who's offer?

"I'm only going to tell you once. She's off-limits. Don't play with me, Justice. Stay away from my niece," Brad barks, grabbing my attention.

I turn to find Brad standing between Justice and a pretty curly-haired blonde. I snort to myself. This guy is going to get his ass kicked one of these days.

Out of the corner of my eye, I catch a glimpse of Ellerie chuckling as his shoulders shake. He has a bouquet of flowers in his hand as he watches on in amusement. I can tell you one thing, there is never a dull moment around here.

"Hit the showers, J. You're done for the day," I command.

Rubbing my forehead, I try to clear my thoughts. Confused, I head to my office and flop down in my chair behind my desk as my thoughts race. What did any of that mean?

CHAPTER FORTY-NINE

Make Him Decide

Uri

I have Sammy with me today. He's been spending more time with me. I don't mind, I love the kid.

I chuckle each morning when his car arrives to drop him at my home. Usually before LaSalle and Tasha wake for him to get permission. His driver has been told it's fine as long as he reports to LaSalle where his son is.

Right now, Sammy is humming to himself, which wouldn't grab my attention if he were any other child. However, Sammy's humming is self-stimulation. Self-stimulation that he does around me when he wants to say something from his visions.

"Do you want to tell me what you see, mate?"

"Yes."

He stands from his place on the floor where he's been filling gun magazines and comes over to stand beside me by my desk. I place my palm on his head, and he stops squirming.

"I am listening. Go on."

"Dez Demarco is a problem not to be ignored. Cameron has allowed him to be unfinished business. Dez will die.

"The question is, will the hitters take care of him, or will I. If it's me, people we love will be hurt first. If it's your hitters, no one gets hurt.

"Cam will be conflicted, but it has to be his decision. There is karma we can't disrupt by taking this decision from him. You have to tell him.

"You have to give him the choice and it has to be now," he says.

I sit staring at this child. He shouldn't know anything about Dez Demarco. Alejandro Demarco was a friend of LaSalle's. He was to have a seat at the Alliance table.

His murder was a shock to us all. I personally felt like his brother was involved. No one could prove he was and it wasn't my business.

Alejandro's son has taken over in his father's absence. The Alliance seat belongs to him. He's young but ambitious and his uncle will have a challenge on his hands if he goes against him.

The only reason Dez is still alive is because he's no threat to us. Or so we thought. This changes everything. Sammy is rarely wrong.

"Bloody fucking hell."

"Chance and Cade aren't meant to be hitters, but they will be if Dez is ignored. Talk to Cam, please."

"Done. I will go talk to him now."

Cameron

"How do you know Dez Demarco?"

I look up to find Uri standing in the doorway of my office. I narrow my eyes at him, not knowing how he knows that name. Clearing my throat, I wave him in.

He steps into the office, closing the door behind him and takes a seat. I scrub a hand down my face. I think over what I want to tell him and decide on the whole truth.

"That asshole was planning to marry my wife against her will in an arranged marriage. He killed her father. We believe he did it because he watched us start an intimate relationship through cameras he had placed in her residence.

"Once he admitted to her that he killed her daddy, and she found out she was carrying my baby, she took off. Her cousin connected her with Symphony, and she stayed hidden with her until Dez tried to smoke her out and shot a friend of ours.

"My daddy and I were having him followed, waiting for him to do something we could use to put him behind bars to make things safe for my wife again. When he shot my ex-wife's now husband, that was what we needed. He's been in jail since," I explain.

"This must have been the year I didn't get to visit Sim," Uri says and nods his head in thought. "Cameron, I'm going to be candid with you.

"You have become one of us, so I'm trusting you with what I'm about to say. Your wife was most likely sent to Sim because she's an assassin—one of many around you.

"Dez was never going to get anywhere near your wife as long as she was with her. With a man like that, you don't trust your safety to the authorities. You handle him and make sure he doesn't lift his head in your direction ever again."

"What are you saying?"

"I'm saying that Sammy has given me a warning concerning you and Dez. I'm not allowed to make this decision for you. He says this has to be your choice.

"My hitters will take care of the problem. All you have to do is tell us to play ball," he says and stands to leave.

I fall back with my mind reeling. Now Sammy's words begin to make sense. I want to protect my family, but Dez is behind bars. Do I give the word to end a man's life based off the visions of a child?

When it means protecting my family, maybe I do.

CHAPTER FIFTY

Cameron

Present ...

Me: *Let's play ball.*

I frown down at my phone. My guilt for ordering the death of a man is not as heavy as I thought it would be. I feel relief more than anything.

My phone dings and I reach to read the text. My emotions don't change as I read the word. It feels more like a confirmation.

Uri: *Done.*

I nod and start to jog back toward the house. At least I gave it a few days to think about it. That says something for my moral compass.

Dez is a piece of shit and I'm not going to allow him to hurt my family. If anyone is to grieve or mourn, it will be his folks. Not mine.

Receiving a call last night that Dez has an attorney who could stand a shot at getting him released was my true deciding factor. There's no way Sammy could know the things he said to me.

Uri was right, Dez is not the type of man who you leave alive. I did things the way I knew how to back then. I'm trusting Uri's way now.

When I get back to the house, I know right away everyone's wide awake. I can hear Amina fussing at the boys as I step through the door and Cecilia is babbling as if repeating her mama's words.

"Chance, Cade, come eat breakfast. I don't want to hear you're hungry later at practice. You're not filling up on snacks either," Mina calls after the boys.

As I walk into the kitchen, she's spooning some type of baby food and cereal into Cecilia's little mouth, probably apricots. My baby girl's favorite. I lean down to kiss Cecilia's forehead and tickle her belly.

Her little eyes sparkle at me. She's the most adorable seven-month-old I've ever seen and I'm not saying that because she's mine. Mina and I make gorgeous babies.

Cecilia didn't get my blue eyes like Chance and Cade. She has her own colorless eyes that pick up whatever she's wearing. On top of that, her orbs are huge, making her look like a little baby doll.

She's a darker brown like her mama. My boys are more toffee colored. They look just like me, but my baby girl is a mix of us. She has her mama's dark hair, but my boys have more of a sandy-brown color to theirs.

Chuckling, I kiss Cecilia's chubby cheek as she coos at me and laughs from her high chair. Just looking at her makes me want to make another one.

I move to kiss Amina as I have the thought. It doesn't last long. The doorbell rings as the boys come running into the kitchen.

"I'll get it," Cade sings.

"No, you won't. Go sit and eat. I'll get it."

I turn and head for the front door. It's probably Mina's mother. She comes to help Amina out in the mornings.

"Good morning," she sings as I open the door.

"Good morning," I murmur and kiss her on the cheek as she enters the house.

"Where are my grandbabies? I have gifts for them."

I shake my head. This is why all three of my kids are spoiled. My mama don't help none either.

I thought my folks getting a place here in New York was going to be a bad idea, but the kids love it. Mama has gotten her shit together finally.

"I'm heading for a shower, baby," I call to Amina before jogging upstairs.

Maribel

I make my way upstairs after my mother takes over feeding Cecilia and the boys. When I woke this morning, Cam wasn't in bed next to me and Cecilia was in her crib.

My curiosity was piqued because my husband usually wakes me before he goes for a morning run. He seemed to have had something on his mind for the last few days. I haven't had a chance to pry as I've been busy with the baby and the boys and their sports.

Leave it to my sons to be multisport kids. I'm always at this game or that. If they don't eat me out of house and home, they're sure to put a hurting on my pocketbook with cleats for this and coaches for that.

I don't mind. I love my boys and seeing them happy as they play and find their way in sports. I'm glad they have decided to try other sports outside baseball. I don't want to feel like we forced them into their father's interests.

I walk into the bathroom, where the shower is running. I bite my lip as my husband's tight ass comes into view. This man is still fine as fuck.

I take a moment to admire his chiseled physique. His sculpted thighs and broad back, his arms are a work of art. It's no wonder he can hit home runs like nobody's business.

As if feeling my eyes on him, he turns to face me and pushes his wet hair from his face. He's been allowing the top to get longer in the last few months.

He never did grow it back out like Cal's. I think he knows how much I like it this way. It has also kept me from pinching his brother's butt and traumatizing him.

"You coming in?" he asks and gives me that sexy grin.

"Not with our kids. We won't get more than five minutes."

His Jodeci pendant catches the light, grabbing my attention. A smile comes to my lips. He truly never takes that necklace off.

Cam cuts the water off and steps out of the shower. I forget what I came up here to say to him. All that dick swinging has me mesmerized.

He keeps stalking toward me until I back up against the countertop. He then cages me in with his arms on either side of me, resting his palms flat on the countertop.

"Your mom is here that has to buy us another ten," he says against my lips before he captures them in a searing kiss.

It almost feels desperate as he drinks deeply from my mouth. I open to him and allow him to consume me. He palms one of my breasts and groans.

Our tongues dance together as he lifts me onto the vanity and steps between my legs. I palm his firm ass and tug him closer to me. Whimpers leave my lips as he kisses his way down my neck.

"Cam," I cry out.

"I need to feel you around me," he breathes in my ear.

He tugs my T-shirt over my head and tosses it to the floor. I lift my hips as he goes to pull my shorts off. The boys are definitely going to be late for practice.

Cam primes me for him with his long fingers. I bite my lip to keep from crying out. He takes my nipple into his mouth and sucks hard as he thrusts his digits in and out of me.

I'm a convulsing mess when he lets my peak pop free from his mouth. He looks into my eyes with heat oozing from his gaze. In the next motion, he has me in his arms.

"Oh shit," I whimper as he plunges into me.

With his arms locked under my thighs, he bounces me on his length. I throw my head back as my eyes roll in my head. He feels so amazing.

However, there's something primal about the way he's fucking me. I'm not complaining. I take each stroke happily as I drip all over him.

This only confirms my suspicions. He has something going on in his head. I'm here for him.

He can use my body for his pleasure as he works whatever it is out. This is no hardship at all. I take his thick dick happily.

"Yes, Cam. Fuck me harder," I coax.

He growls and kisses me hard as he turns and heads for our bedroom. Without pulling from my body, he climbs into the bed and starts to fuck me into the mattress.

I have to bury my face in his neck as it gets so good I want to scream. His freshly showered scent fills my nose and my mouth starts to water. I'm gushing all over the place.

"I love you so much. Everything I do is for you. I'll never allow anyone to hurt you.

"Not while I'm still breathing. No matter what I have to do," he breathes in my ear.

My heart bursts open. I know Cam has always loved me but there is something in his voice that makes his words hit different. My toes curl and my legs shake as my climax begins to approach.

"Mom, I can't find my cleats," Cade calls outside our bedroom door.

"Fuck," Cam grunts in my ear as he spills into me.

I can't help but laugh. I knew they weren't going to let us both finish.

CHAPTER FIFTY-ONE

He's Been Hushed

Symphony

I walk into the prison to handle my assignment. It was decided that Michael and I would handle Demarco. Val and Uri don't always use the same restraint and finesse we do.

This has to be clean. We don't belong here. LaSalle pulled some strings to get us in. This has to be an in-and-out mission.

"That was easy," I say as I find and cut the camera feed to the infirmary cameras and all in the surrounding areas.

Me: *Done.*

My text is to alert the inmate, who is also the brother of one of Demarco's victims, that he is in play now. It wasn't hard to find someone willing to assist us. All he has to do is get Demarco in place.

Once my tasks are done here, I report to my station in the infirmary dressed in my scrubs and white coat. I have placed a wig over my locs. It itches and feels unnatural. This needs to be quick so I can take this thing off.

I begin to pop my band on my wrist as the feeling starts to irritate me. Taking a deep breath as I walk, I settle myself and try to isolate the annoyance to block it out.

I nod at the guard who is standing in the exam room I enter. Not making eye contact, I move to sit on the stool by the bed.

"We have incoming," the guard says.

I nod but say nothing else. Hopefully this is the patient I am looking for. The inmate comes through the door and Michael steps in behind him, dressed as one of the correctional officers.

I keep my head down submissively. The guard who warned me of the newcomers steps out, leaving me and Michael alone with our patient.

Demarco ambles over with a gash on his head. He takes a seat and grumbles to himself. He glares at me as I remain silent, waiting for my signal.

"What are you waiting for, bitch? For me to bleed out? Let's go, you stupid cunt."

I snarl as he calls me names, but I don't lift my head. Not until Michael pulls out his pocket watch and flips it open.

"Cameron sends his regards," Michael says as the sound of "Für Elise" fills the room from his watch.

Before Dez can comment, I plunge a needle with poison into his neck. He is dead before he can register what I have done. Not as satisfying as pulling a trigger but the job is done. My friend and godchildren are safe once and for all.

"This problem has been hushed," I say as we go to head out.

EPILOGUE

Forever My Lady

Cameron

Two years later …

He did it. Cal sat before all those folks and spoke his truth. I've never been more proud of him.

Well, the day he stood before everyone to give Nicole the wedding of her dreams comes a close second. My little buddy, Tiger, did good as well. Everyone was afraid he was going to have a meltdown in front of all those people, but I had faith in him.

I haven't stopped smiling since we arrived home. Today was a great day for my family. Looking around at everyone, I realize I have no regrets.

I wouldn't be as happy as I am if I changed anything. Getting to see Ladybug and Kay reminded me that I have the life I chose. The one meant for me. I wouldn't change a single thing.

Kay wanted Chanel and the boys to hang out together, so she took them and Cecilia back to her hotel for a sleepover. I wasn't surprised to see Sammy appear with his sleepover bag to follow them. He's become friends with my boys and he's very protective over Cecilia.

I know they will all be safe around him. That kid is a scary twelve-year-old. I know grown men who don't have the presence he has.

The Reese family is in town because of Cal's conference and Jareil's game here tonight. It worked out for everyone. It's his last year playing.

He and Kay spoil my kids as much as Amina and I spoil Ladybug and Junior. Kay and Amina are actually friends. You can thank my mama for that. It's funny how life works out.

I stand in my bedroom, removing my suit as small hands glide up my chest from behind. I cover my wife's hands and smile. I can't remember the last time we had an empty house to ourselves.

I reach behind me to pull her in front of me. She's in only her panties and bra with the sexy heels she had on today. The smile in her eyes says a million words.

Images of our life together begin to play through my mind. I remember the first time I laid eyes on her. The time I ran into her in front of the Chinese spot, the moment I spotted her at that party, our first kiss, the day she gave birth to our sons, there have been so many great moments between us.

I think I love her more today than I ever thought possible. I pull my phone and connect it to the home system. This will forever be our thing.

"Forever My Lady" begins to play through our bedroom speakers. Amina looks back at me with sparkling eyes and a grin. I raise a questioning brow.

"What's going on in your head?"

"I find it funny you would pick this song. It's perfect."

"Oh yeah, why is that?"

"The first verse says it all," she says with a wide smile.

I think of the first verse and my heart swells. She can't be telling me what I think she is. I drop to my knees and palm her belly as she stands before me.

"You're pregnant?"

"Yup, we're having another one. I must be crazy. We already have two who think they're grown men and a two-and-a-half-year-old who acts like she's forty."

"But can you say you would change any of them? God, I love them and you."

I palm her breasts as I plant open-mouthed kisses across her belly. I had been hoping for another baby. I couldn't allow my little brother to outdo me. Hopefully, this will be another set of twins.

As the thought fills my mind, I stand and lift her onto my waist. It's time I make love to my wife. Knowing there will be no interruptions, I take my time.

Placing her on the bed, I kiss my way down her body and peel her panties off. In the next motion, I toss her legs over my shoulders and bury my face between her thighs. Kissing and licking her inner thigh, I then move to her core and begin to feast on her.

I'm going to be a father again. I can't help smiling into her sweet, wet center. I never thought this would be my life.

"Cam," she moans as she writhes beneath me.

Needing to get my slacks off to finish undressing, I work on my belt and push my pants off. Not once do I stop eating her delicious pussy. It's too intoxicating.

I reach up and lace one of my hands with hers as I use the other hand to knead her breast and fondle her nipple between my fingertips.

My mind drifts to all we've been through to get here. I've always wanted to fight for her. I have fought for her. Now, here we are.

When we fell apart, Amina said something simple to me that made everything click. I remember those words in this moment.

Decide what you want, Cam. You've spent your entire life helping Cal build his team. Now it's your turn. Either you want us, or you don't.

We're yours. You just have to show me you want us. Show me you want me.

This isn't anyone else's business. Leave your mama and all that other drama out there. It's me and your children. Either you're going to love me for life or let me go.

I'm glad I decided to get my shit together. This is where I always want to be. As I push into her body, I feel like I'm coming home. This is the only place I belong.

"I love you," I moan into her ear.

"I love you too, Cam. I always have."

ABOUT THE AUTHOR

Blue Saffire, award-winning, bestselling author of over seventy contemporary romance novels and novellas, writes with the intention to touch the heart and the mind. Blue hooks, weaves, and loops multiple series, keeping you engaged in her worlds. Blue writes for her own publishing company, Perceptive Illusions as Blue Saffire, as well as Royal Blue.

Blue and her husband live in a house filled with laughter and creativity in Long Island, NY. Both working hard to build the Blue brand and cultivate their love for the arts. Creative is their family affair.

Blue holds an MBA in Marketing and Project Management, as well as an MED in Instructional Technology and Curriculum Design. She is also an NLP Master Practitioner.

ACKNOWLEDGMENTS

Wow, this book has lived in my head for so long. I just never had time to get to it. I'm so glad I waited. There are so many things that have developed and that have me excited for the rest of this series and those connected to it. Cam has been one of my favorite characters.

Not everything is what you believe it to be at first sight. People make so many assumptions from optics. We can always have an opinion from the outside without knowing what's going on inside. I think Cam and Maribel teach us a lot about that. I hope you enjoyed getting to know their story as much as I did.

My dear reader friends, thank you so much for coming on another journey with me. This universe has grown so much and I'm working my way through as fast and as much as I can. Thank you for your patience and continued support. My brain doesn't work in straight lines, and I appreciate all who understand this is my creative process and I'm giving you my all with each creation as they allow me to. Thank you for the encouraging emails, videos, posts, shares, and DMs. Many hugs and much love.

To God be all the glory! I couldn't do this without you. The strength you provide is a blessing within itself. I'm so grateful. Thank you for giving me life and the wisdom to do what I love. Thank you for the working of my mind. Thank you for showing me the way continuously. As always, unapologetically blessed and highly favored.

Next! *Hush 3. We're spending the year in this universe. Let's go.*

Wait, there is more to come! You can stay updated with my latest releases, learn more about me, the author, and be a part of contests by subscribing to my newsletter at

www.BlueSaffire.com

If you enjoyed *Ballers 3*, I'd love to hear

your thoughts and please feel free to leave a

review on my website. And when you do, please let me

know by emailing me TheBlueSaffire@gmail.com

or leave a comment on Facebook https://www.facebook.com/BlueSaffireDiaries or Twitter @TheBlueSaffire

Other books by Blue Saffire

Placed in Best Reading Order

Also available….

Legally Bound

Legally Bound 2: Against the Law

Legally Bound 3: His Law

Perfect for Me

Hush 1: Family Secrets

Ballers: His Game

Brothers Black 1: Wyatt the Heartbreaker

Legally Bound 4: Allegations of Love

Hush 2: Slow Burn

Legally Bound 5.0: Sam

Yours 1: Losing My Innocence

Yours 2: Experience Gained

Yours 3: Life Mastered

Ballers 2: His Final Play

Legally Bound 5.1: Tasha Illegal Dealings

Brothers Black 2: Noah

Legally Bound 5.2: Camille

Legally Bound 5.3 & 5.4 Special Edition

Where the Pieces Fall

Legally Bound 5.5: Legally Unbound

Brothers Black 4: Braxton the Charmer

Broken Soldier

Brothers Black 5: Felix the Watcher

A Home for Christmas

Doctor Feel Good

Brothers Black 6: Ryan the Joker

Brothers Black 7: Johnathan the Fixer

Wild Hearts

Pieces of Trevor's Heart

Coming Soon...
King of Gods Book 4: Immortal Iron Brothers Series
King of Past Book 5: Immortal Iron Brothers Series

Hush Book 3: Hidden Family

Other Blue Saffire Series

Hold On To Me Series
My Funny Valentine
Be My Valentine

Hitter Squad Series
Remember Me

Work Husband Series
Unexpected Lovers
My Best Friend's Wish
The Ones Left Behind
The Last Ones Standing

The Lost Souls MC Series
Forever
Never
Always

The Moran Brothers Series
Love Notes
Stay With Me

The A**hole Club Series
Pit Book 1: The A**hole Club
Ox Book 5: The A**hole Club
Kelex Book 6: The A**hole Club

Immortal Iron Brothers Series
King of Knights Book 1
King of Inferno Book 2
King of Tides Book 3

Check out Blue Saffire exclusives on the
BlueSaffire.com website
The Fixer
His Miracle Baby
Razor
Dane

Trip
Professor Jones
Room 112

Other books from Evei Lattimore Collection Books by Blue Saffire
Black Bella 1

Destiny 1: Life Decisions
Destiny 2: Decisions of the Next Generation
Destiny 3 coming soon…

Star

**Other books from Royal Blue Gay Romance Collection written by Blue
Saffire**
Kyle's Reveal
Beau's Redemption